Jack O'Donnell is from Dalmuir, Scotland. Over the years he's tried his hand at just about everything, from washing dishes to mental health care, monitoring elections to joining floorboards, editing to surveying traffic, care work to lugging bricks.

And while accumulating all that life experience Jack has also been pursuing a love for the written word on ABCtales.com, where he's a generous contributor to the community, a competition-winner and a prized editor.

Lily Poole

Jack O'Donnell

unbound

unbound

6th Floor Mutual House 70 Conduit Street London W1S 2GF
www.unbound.co.uk

© Jack O'Donnell, 2016

Text Design by Ellipsis Digital Limited, Glasgow

A CIP record for this book is available from the British Library

ISBN 978-1-78352-235-4 (trade ppb)
ISBN 978-1-78352-267-5 (ebook)
ISBN 978-1-78352-300-9 (limited edition)

To those who buy into the dream

Dear Reader,

The book you are holding came about in a rather different way to most others. It was funded directly by readers through a new website:Unbound. Unbound is the creation of three writers. We started the company because we believed there had to be a better deal for both writers and readers. On the Unbound website, authors share the ideas for the books they want to write directly with readers. If enough of you support the book by pledging for it in advance, we produce a beautifully bound special subscribers' edition and distribute a regular edition and e-book wherever books are sold, in shops and online.

This new way of publishing is actually a very old idea (Samuel Johnson funded his dictionary this way). We're just using the internet to build each writer a network of patrons. Here, at the back of this book, you'll find the names of all the people who made it happen.

Publishing in this way means readers are no longer just passive consumers of the books they buy, and authors are free to write the books they really want. They get a much fairer return too – half the profits their books generate, rather than a tiny percentage of the cover price.

If you're not yet a subscriber, we hope that you'll want to join our publishing revolution and have your name listed in one of our books in the future. To get you started, here is a £5 discount on your first pledge. Just visit unbound.com, make your pledge and type **LILYPOOLE** in the promo code box when you check out.

Thank you for your support,

Dan, Justin and John
Founders, Unbound

Lily Poole

DAY 1

The wee girl went down in the slush, not hard in an adult way, but in that childish way, soft-boned and sprawling. Her clear grey eyes, close to tears, rested on John's.

Snowflakes clung like porridge to the leather uppers of his Doc Martens, blanketing his progress. Biting cold nipped at his feet through mismatched football socks. He scanned parked cars, luminous shells of white on light, and looked up towards Shakespeare Avenue, searching for the lumbering presence of an adult, or even the bundled-up spectre of an older brother or sister hurrying along to catch up with the wee girl. She tottered. He dashed the last few yards to help her and found himself lying on his back at her feet, snowflakes drifting down on his face. He laughed, which made her giggle.

He tried standing, but toppled forward. The wee girl squealed, her fingers, scrambling to help, grabbed at the coat-tails of his Crombie. He hooked her wrist, gripped her cold hand, holding her upright and keeping them both safe. She was barely up to his hip. He hunched down to her level, feet sliding sideways.

'You waiting for your mum?'

A shake of her head. No. Eyes downcast, chin tucked into her quilted anorak, she whispered something through chittering lips.

'You goin' to school?' he asked.

A nod of her head. Yes.

'Okey-dokey,' he said, standing up slowly, keeping her close, stopping her from falling.

Her black, shiny shoes were broad and flat-soled leather, which irked him – she might as well have been wearing skis. They slid towards a terraced house used as a dental practice on one side of the road. Then shaving the snow, uncovering the pavement and letting gravity do the work of walking, they worked their way towards a garage and high wall he used to kick a ball against on his way to school. She giggled as he made a game of it.

They got safely to the corner of Duntocher Road, which made it easier to shuffle forward and reclaim their feet. Kids sloshed in close beside them in weatherproof nylon. They were careless of their bodies, faces sunk inside igloos of duffle coat hoods. Adults bowled along behind them, collars pulled high and heads bowed in prayer to the elements. A Ford Capri stuttered and skittered, scattering mush towards the side of the road. It juddered forward, slipping and crunching gears, windscreen wipers shuttling backwards and forwards to expose a pasty face leaning forward in the driver's seat. Parents glowered at the car, resentment shaping blank faces, as if machinery was alien and a form of cheating.

'You must be new to the school.' John spoke to her in the milky-adult tone he adopted when talking to bairns or pets. He kept her small hand warm in his and helped her cross the road and find the lip of pavement. 'What primary are you in? Primary One?'

She nodded in a shy way, neck bent and exposed, face hiding in her hair, as if even that small exertion had been too much.

They shuffled onward without slipping. A wrought-iron fence separated them from the playground. The school children penned inside were delirious with the crop of falling sky, screaming and squealing in an ecstasy of stamping and running and jumping and hustling away patches of virgin snow. John let go of her hand as the school bell rang. But she didn't let go of his. She grasped at his fingers and held tight.

He leaned over her. 'It's OK darlin'. I won't leave you.'

She sheltered behind his legs.

'You scared?'

She nodded. 'Sometimes big people don't understand,' she lisped.

'I know darlin'. I know. But you better hurry up or you'll be late.'

She tugged at his hand, a signal to get them moving. They were only a hundred yards from the gates. He stood among the other bystanders when they got to the entrance to the school, watching her solemn face as she trudged across the playground. As she passed the school kitchen, he lost sight of her in a gaggle of other kids.

'You lost something?'

John whirled round, a daft smile still coating his face.

Mrs Cunningham's sing-song voice was unusually harsh. She religiously took her children to school and lived five blocks down from him. He had never spoken to her much because she had proper breasts and was

way too pretty to attempt anything more than a rudi-
mentary, grunting *hi-ya*. She wore a long black leather
coat and thigh-high boots. Snowflakes dampened her
dark swept-back hair. Her back was against the railing
that separated playground from pavement and she was
fisheyeing him.

John felt glad of the swirling snow that kept his
cheeks from flaming. He patted the plastic bag he had
rolled up and wore as a hat to keep the snow off his hair.
He thought maybe that had upset her in some way. 'No,'
he said. 'I was just taking that wee lassie to school.'

'Whit wee lassie?' Mrs Cunningham's raspberry-
coloured lipstick was a jigsaw of splinters on her mouth.
The lollipop man knocked the cleats of his wellington
boots off the bottom of the fence beside her. 'Charlie,
you see him with any wee lassie?' she asked him.

Some mothers slipped away. Others dawdled, pat-
terned-nylon scarves covering their hair, heads turning
one way then the other, waiting to pick over the bones of
gossip.

The lollipop man battered his cap on the top bar of
the railing and examined John through the smudged
lenses of black NHS specs. 'Drugs or drink,' he said.
'They're all on it. I was watchin' him.' He put his cap
back on, pulling the brim low so his eyes were shaded.
'Or glue,' he added.

Mrs Cunningham tugged together the lapels of her
leather coat making her breasts jump. 'That's whit I
thought. I've got two daughters at that school.'

'But the wee lassie—' John said.

Mrs Cunningham took a step towards him. 'Look, son, I don't like it when you keep harping on about wee lassies.'

'Or wee boys,' said the lollipop man.

They looked at each other and shook their heads. She tugged at her earlobe and a gold bubble earring. 'Look, son,' she said, in a more placatory tone, 'just don't let me see you back here again. I know your Ma. You come from a good family. Let that be the end of it.'

'But the wee lassie—'John said.

'Let that be the end of it!'

DAY 2

John's feet skidded as he tried to run on thawing snow outside his house. Deskbound clerks at the Social Security office on Kilbowie Road made signing on the dole hard work when people were late. He scurried down the shortcut at the dump, slush splashing from the branches of the rowan bush in great gobbets. Long grass wept snowfall and wind cat-pawed rain against his face. His gaze followed a memory of the dirt path, shuffling sideways and ducking down, throwing his body through the familiar gap in the chain-link fence.

'Jesus,' he said.

His Wrangler jacket pulled and snagged on the frayed edges of rusting wire. He dropped off the retaining wall, feet punching holes into the grass, and made up for lost time by galloping down the small incline onto the pavement on Shakespeare Avenue. Rubbing his right shoulder to check for bobbled edges and tears in the denim, he thanked God that there was nothing but a biro-type scratch. But the soles of his feet felt squidgy and waterlogged. He heard the spindrift of the car behind him as it followed the curve of the road. He stepped onto the pavement as water sprayed and sopped through his jacket, gluing one leg of denim onto his thigh.

'Fucking cunt,' he shouted at the metallic tail-end of a purple Escort, the red brake light dotting and dashing as the car slowed. A blond head and doughy face turned, briefly, observing him through the back windscreen. The car skidded to the left at the intersection of the hill where Shakespeare met Wells Street, and he hoped the frosty-faced cow would crash and burn.

Then he saw the wee girl again, clinging to Kerr's privet hedge, too scared to move. Hurrying, in case she would fall, he slid and slipped downhill, following the geography of the pavement to meet her. Her eyes shone bright as ball bearings. She was shivering, biting colour into the wobbly line of her thin bottom lip, the school blazer wrapped around her bony shoulders, little more than a prop against the biting wind. Her coltish feet skidded, babyish fingers grabbed at his denim jacket and clutched onto his side pocket.

He latched onto her reedy wrist and peered at her forlorn face. 'It's OK pet, you won't fall.' She made a present of her other hand for him to unmelt. He hunkered down and kneaded her fingers and palms in his own until he felt them stir and grow warmer.

'That's better,' he said. He stood up slowly, clutching her right hand, and kept her firmly in tow.

'You'll be awful late again,' he said, alluding to a feather-brained mum, but immediately regretted being so snide. She didn't seem to notice.

She had the same black shoes on as the day they met: smooth soles, useless for snow, and more useless in slippery sludge. He thought his feet cold, but hers must be ice-water. She slipped when he least expected it, when they reached the apparent safety of the flatter ground at the dentist's. He grabbed onto her hand, swinging, jumping her up into the safety of the air. 'Whee,' he said, laughing to balance out the fright the fall caused her.

Teeny fingers gripped his more firmly. He felt her elfin body relax, but noticed her thick socks had slipped around her ankles, making her shiver more. He patted the top of her head and she leaned into his thigh.

'Won't your mummy and daddy be worried about you?' He crouched down to her eye level, the eddying fog of their breath mingling. A woman stinking of stale fag smoke and wearing a fawn trench coat passed them. She glanced at John. When he looked back at her, her head whiplashed away. She cracked on, slowing to batter the heels of her green wellington boots on the salted ground where grey snow was piled against the wall of the dentist's.

He tried cajoling the little girl, pursing his lips and screwing up his eyes to indicate he was being adult and serious. 'Won't they?'

Her pale eyes studied his. 'No!'

He felt groggy and slack-footed. For a moment, her face seemed far away as if he was studying it through the eyepiece of a telescope flung out of focus. Then the image sharpened. He stumbled away from her, almost falling. Her chest bobbed up and down as if she was at sea, her mouth open and drunk on howling, calling him back, but she made no noise. Tears made her cheeks shiny and her face crabby.

'Jesus,' he said.

Rain pelted down, making rivulets on his forehead and cheeks. He looked up and down Shakespeare and along Dickens Avenue for help, some divine intervention, but even the snowmen were looking the other way. She clutched onto his thigh and he felt her rubbing her snottery nose on eighteen-quid worth of precious Sta-Prest denim.

'Yah little besom,' he said.

John picked her up and she locked her arms round his neck. The kirby from her hair scratched his cheek as she buried her slobbering head on his shoulder and her stubby feet scrambled for a foot-hold. He pulled her close enough to whiff breath warm as new-cut hay. Taking the plastic bag off his head and working it over her soft wet hair and icy ears, he tamped it down and created a makeshift crown. Pregnant with his charge he tramped towards the intersection at Duntocher Road, towards St Stephen's School. She settled, sniffling on his chest. Her head lifted and he squinted sideways, watching her studying the houses and gardens they passed. She squirmed as they crossed the road, a signal she no longer wanted to be carried. He placed her down on the pavement as if she was made of rippled glass. The school bell rang for playtime.

Ahead of them the janny shovelled pockmarked snow from the gateway onto a discoloured mound in the gutter. John grabbed her hand and tugged her into a slow, forward jig, stopping for a breather on the strip of pavement beside the school railing that had been cleared and salted.

Children's voices splashed into the air. Funeral browns and deep blues of duffels and coats ebbed out of closed doors, splurging into playground and puddles. She hiccupped a laugh as a walk became a run, and they raced against each other, matching each other foot for foot. The janny leaned on his shovel watching as they slowed and stopped at the school gate and John pantomimed being out of breath. He bowed over and his index finger chooked gently under the winner's chin.

'You want me to come in with you?' John asked her.

'Whit's wrang with you hinging about school playgrounds?' said the janny, eyeballing him from beneath the black plastic peak of his cap.

'Whit's wrang with you?' John replied, bouncing backwards, straightening up and eyeballing him back. 'Who are you anyway?' The janny looked levelly back at John, making him splutter. 'For your information I went to this school. Where's the real janny, Mr Barlow?'

'He died last week. The Big C.' The new janny shook his head at John as if it was his fault. 'I've been working this school on and aff for at least ten years and I don't remember you.'

'Well, I'm just taking a wee lassie to school,' John said.

'Whit wee lassie?'

John followed the orbit of her path, looked for her among a scattering of boys' heads, and gazed all around the playground. 'Ah – she must have nipped inside.'

The janny scraped at the ice and snow with his shovel. 'Aye, right,' the tone of his voice a sneer. 'Your card's marked pal. I know your sort. Fuck off. Don't let me see you back here again.'

DAY 4

High winds pushed and pulled at the metallic frame of the lamppost. Creaking back and forth, it sent foot-soldiers of shadows sniping up and down the ill-fitting windows of the ground-floor, four-in-a-block flat. Inside, Mary swung her legs out of bed. As usual, her husband Joey lay in a diagonal heap, snoring his face off and ruck-ing most of the blankets to his side of the bed. He flinched as the gap between husband and wife widened. In the inky blackness she tugged at the bedclothes, pull-ing them back and creating a space to sit up. The misshapen corns on the balls of her feet cold-stepped against linoleum, finding the worn pair of old leather sandals she used for slippers under the bed. She peered at the clock, but the luminous hands slanted behind the oval of the ashtray. Light seeped through the venetian

blinds and it was better not knowing how early – or late
– it was. Her fingers flapped around the curve of the
hardwood footboard of the bed for the ragged old coat
she used as a nightgown. She shivered as her hands and
arms wormed their way through the static of acrylic
sleeves. She stood for a second, eyes growing into the
darkness, the shape of her breath misting in the frigid air.
The hubbub of pulling the bedroom door open and shut
behind her blended with the creaking of prefabricated-
metal sheets on the outside walls. She brushed her
fingertips against the trim of the anaglyphic wallpaper in
the hall, feeling her way in the dark by the rough sleepers
and uniform lines. Ahead of her, the living room door
was lying athwart with a thin triangle of light visible. She
dunted the door open, but took a sharp left into the
toilet, not finding enough time to flick the light switch,
before she was squatting over the pan emptying her bladder. She ran her fingers under the cold tap before going
back to bed, but fretted about leaving the light on.

Mary's hand rested on the living room doorknob, and
she chivvied herself for an increasing absent-minded-
ness and also for leaving the lamp on in the kitchen. She
scanned the telly and fireplace. In her head she calcu-
lated whether the mess she had left behind when she
went to bed was the same mess she now faced. The kit
and caboodle seemed stacked the same, but a tapping
noise came through the wall from the kitchen. A faint
smell of cigar smoke made her want to gag and a low-
pitched moaning made the downy hairs on the back of
her neck prickle. Not a murmur was coming from the

bedroom nearest her; the girls were safe. Her son John was in the back bedroom. Fireworks exploding under his bed would fizzle and die before waking him. Then the moaning sound started again, quicker and louder, with a slapping sound. She bent away from the gamy smell, knowing what it was. Her right hand raised in defence, she edged forward, mouth pursed and ready to scream for Joey.

Mary pushed the kitchen door open. The faulty hinge Joey had been meaning to fix squeaked. She squawked in fright, but there was no answering cry from the other rooms, which was just as well. Lamplight illuminated her son. His sketchbook was on the kitchen table, a nude drawing of a prepubescent girl on the top page, the lips of her hairless vagina shaped to resemble an open eye, the pupil a smudged slash. His pencils were strewn across the floor. Her legs went wonky and bile gathered in the back of her throat. She clamped both hands over her mouth like a mask, breathing through her nose, her eyes watering, willing herself not to be sick. The stink of cigar smoke grew acrid. John was there and not there. He stood, head lolling like a question mark, one finger resting on the stem of a soup spoon, rapping metal against the flat ceramic surface of a plate. The tap, tap, tapping followed some kind of pattern, but only he seemed wired to understand the Morse. His eyes were closed, his face animated, chewing over the nuances of speech. She rested her hand on his arm.

The life-like drawings were something, but sleepwalking was nothing new. She had to be strapped to the bed when she was younger. Even then she ended up in some strange places and with some strange faces gawking at her. Auntie Teresa hooted with laughter when she recounted nightly conversations that she had with Mary answering in what sounded like Chinese. It reminded her of her own frustrations of being alien and not understood. Having no control over what happened. She considered slipping away, leaving him the dignity of the unobserved. She was sure the embarrassment of waking up naked with a hard-on – obviously he had been wanking – and his mum standing beside him on the cold stone floor, well that would make her weep for him. The noises he was making as he struck the spoon came to a sudden stop; a snap in the landscape of silence. But with no physical contact between the stem of the spoon and John's fingers the dispatch kept tapping out. Mary looked for an explanation, some optical trick.

His eyelids flickered and opened, the same heavy-lidded eyes, the same wash of green around the iris, looking into and mirroring her eyes. The silent stare – childlike. His hands dropped and netted his loins.

'Mum?' He gazed over her shoulder, tracing an arc around the ceiling, lingering on the plate and spoon on the table, darting away from his drawings, anywhere but at her. 'I must have—' His head shuttled from side to side, face aged by indecision and his mouth hanging open, 'I don't know what's happening to me. I get these terrible dreams. Nightmares about little girls. And I'm standing in our Jo's room, watching and waiting.' He slapped his forehead with the palm of his hand, the slapping sound echoing round the kitchen. 'I think I'm going crazy. Then when I think it was just a dream, I see what I've drawn and know it's no.' He sniffed, choking, trying to swallow his tears.

His penis had shrunk to a hooded mushroom, a small boy's toy. Mary slipped her hand round his smooth back and drew him in, letting him rest his head on her shoulder as she cuddled him. 'Shush,' she whispered in his ear. 'It's going to be alright. Shush. I know. I know. These kinds of things pass. You'll get yourself a wee girlfriend, settle down, and you'll no' have time for all this kind of malarkey. The important thing is no' to think too much about it. We used to have an Uncle Paddy that did just that. Thought about things too much. He was good to us when we were younger and had nothing. But he ended up so far up his own arse he would only come out on public holidays. And he ended up in one of those places.'

John wiped at his nose with the back of his hand. Shifting his feet, sliding away from her touch. 'Whit places?'

'Never you mind what places! The kind of places you see in black-and-white photographs. The kind of places you don't want to go to ... And when did you start smoking cigars?'

'Whit?' He looked perplexed. 'Don't know whit you're talkin' about.'

DAY 9

'He's no' fuckin' coming.' Sergeant Collins yawned, cupping his mouth with a fist and covering distended teeth discoloured by fag smoke. 'Fuckin' perv,' he spat out, mangling words with sour breath. Collins' bulk overflowed the passenger seat in the panda car and his presence sucked up all the air.

Constable Lodge was wedged into the driver's seat next to him. Lodge's cap sat on the dashboard. The engine was running and the fan heater was on full because his superior did not like the cold. He rested the side of his head on the cool glass windowpane to keep from falling asleep, the school bell clanging nearby. Lodge grunted a reply which might have been yes and might have been no. They were parked half on and half off the pavement, sheltered behind the ten-foot trunk of an oak tree creaking in the wind. The control panel of the Bakelite police handset between them crackled – a possible housebreaking on Boquanharan Road. He sat up straighter in his seat and looked in the rear-view mirror. 'That's not far from here.'

Collins coughed, sniffed, and reached into his inside jacket pocket for another twenty pack of Regal. Both of their uniforms were saturated by smoke. The pull-out ashtrays overflowing, he wound the window down, and dropped his dout into the gutter to be carried away by rainwater. Ahead of them the lollipop man glowed unhealthily in his luminous coat and leaned his bum against St Stephen's school gate. A stop sign was tilted against the metal railings and the peak of his cap was low on his head, slanted against the rainstorm, cutting his face in two and leaving only the suggestion of a faint grey moustache. 'Let's give it another five minutes.' Collins used the plug-in lighter from the dashboard to spark another cigarette. 'You know what it's like. I was like you, keen as mustard to get up and get on with things.' He puffed on his fag and grew philosophical. 'One of the first cases soon cured me of that. Not far from here. Had to guard a house in which a guy went crazy and killed his wife and two little kids. Always remember them taking the wee wans out on a stretcher. You don't appreciate how small and fragile they are. Just dods of blonde hair. I'll never forget it.'

Collins took a drag on his fag, before adding, 'Funnily enough, Chief Inspector Allan wasn't so high and mighty then. Open and shut case. But he was a bright boy. Had a way about him. Always destined for bigger and better things. Soon he was in charge of the investigation and promoted to Inspector.'

Lodge sagged back in his seat, elbow on the armrest, kneading his temple with one hand. He had heard a variation of the same story a number of times. Knew how it ended, with some old fart, a butcher, a baker, or candlestick maker hanging himself in custody. Good riddance to bad rubbish. And how that had saved them the bother and the expense of a trial. He studied the same desolate stretch of tarmac pavement, the same red-brick side of the chapel and its grounds, the same railings that could do with a fresh dab of paint. 'Sarge.' His voice was jagged. He leaned forward, ducking his head to check the wing mirror.

Collins sat up straight and angled his head to check the rear-view mirror. 'Whit the fuck's he daeing?'

'Dunno. But he's walking hell of a funny.' Lodge reached for his cap.

'Hang on.' Collins' voice was sharp, stopping Lodge from pushing open the door. 'The janny's an old Masonic buddy with Chief Inspector Allan. They can dress up funny in yon robes and bay at the moon for all I care, but you know what that means, them with their special handshakes? Masonic with a capital M. Muggins here's got to do the dirty work. Says he comes every day and stands outside the school gates, fuckin' perving at the kids in the playground. Keep an eye on him.' Their heads swivelled in unison as the boy passed them on the other side of the road.

'Are you sure that's him?' Lodge's Adam's apple bobbled up and down. 'He looks kinda harmless.'

'Look, son.' Collins' nicotine-stained fingers lightly slapped a warning on Lodge's hand resting near the gear stick. 'The quiet, gormless fuckers are the ones that you need to be watching. If you've seen what I've fuckin' seen then you'd fuckin' know that.' He squinted through the windscreen and shook his head as the boy stopped outside the school gate. 'Must admit though, he's not the fuckin' smartest. You'd think he'd fuckin' mix it up a bit. Go to the other schools roundabout here to fuckin' suss out other potential victims.'

Collins stubbed his fag out in the ashtray and pushed the door open on the pavement side of the road. The door slammed on the driver's side.

A sickly yellow Datsun slowed and then sped up, a hole in the exhaust making Lodge wince as it passed them. They crossed diagonally, falling into quick swishing step with one another until they reached the pavement on the other side. The lollipop man sidled to the side of the boy, holding his pole upright, his peaked cap nodding towards him as if to say plainly – that's him; that's the nutter.

Collins was a big man, but he moved quickly. His hands slipped round the boy's waist and flipped his wrist so that his arm locked. He wrenched his arm up his back and kicked at his right foot, using the weight of his body to butt them forward. The boy's nose clattered the railing, his forehead ringing and his head jerking back in recoil. His hair was fashionably long and gave a good handhold; Collins battered his face against wrought-iron poles.

'Seen enough?' Collins taunted him, only stopping when he felt his colleague's hand grab his shoulder and pull him backwards. Collins had almost no eyelids. The black rims around his irises blazed with a vivid light.

It took a few seconds for Lodge's words to reach him. 'Sarge. Sarge.'

The button brown of Lodge's irises had never looked darker. They darted sideways to indicate the perimeter fence and massed blanched faces of little boys and girls behind it, magnetised by the thrilling sight of policemen's uniforms. Now the school children were hiding behind each other and one or two of them were sobbing.

John lurched sideways; his head tilted and he vomited blood. His eyes were empty egg cups, but he made straight towards Lodge, arms out in appeal before he slumped to the pavement.

Shaking his head slowly, the lollipop man cleared his throat before speaking. 'You better get an ambulance.'

'No, we'll be alright!' Sergeant Collins spoke with authority, staring the old man down. 'Get an arm.' He signalled to Lodge, reaching down and pulling at the boy's denim jacket until he got a good hold under his oxter. 'And we'll get him back to the station.'

The school bell sounded behind them, playtime was finished. Lodge helped carry the boy across the road. 'Whit we goin' to charge him with?' the constable asked.

'Fuck sake,' Collins snorted. 'The janny said he was in the school last week and goin' on about searchin' for something or other. That's trespass in anybody's language. Don't worry. Just wait until we get him in the cells.' The boy struggled upright into consciousness and Collins tripped on the kerb. 'Whoops-a-daisy! See that? All that blood on my jacket. Police assault.'

DAY 12

Because it was a Friday, John was locked up in Hall Street Station over the weekend. It was still dark when the police released him on Monday. He was cautioned, but let off with a warning. The Town Hall clock clanged seven a.m. and the pavements clattered with the tramp of shipyard workers on early shift. John was fuzzy on his feet. A few bleary-eyed drunks held overnight filed soberly out of the side entrance of the police station. The tang of chlorine in the air from the swimming baths across the road hung like a bath towel draped over a warm radiator. Even though rain battered down, he was glad of the walk home.

Mary fussed and made him cups of tea that stretched day into night. His sisters cried when they saw his face, but when they came back from school they tried to make him laugh because they knew when he laughed he couldn't stretch his face properly – his head ached and his ears echoed sound like the inside of a Lambeg drum – and his facial contortions made them giggle. Then Joey came back from work, had his dinner and, saying nothing, retired into the cubbyhole of his room. Later, using the living-room door as a shield, he stood squinting at John for a long time. John warmed his stockinged feet off one bar of the electric fire, pretending Valerie Singleton on *Nationwide* was naked and he was the only person in the room that noticed, but it wasn't any fun.

It was quarter to one when John sloped off to bed, leaving his mum chain-smoking in the kitchen. The trickiest part of getting undressed was getting his jumper over an oversized head. Standing in his Y-fronts, waiting to jump into the welcoming warmth of bed, his bust nose presented a new challenge. It felt like under-cooked egg yolk ready to spill and spoil the whites of the clean blankets.

Usually he would have hauled the bedclothes up and over his ears to keep the heat in, but now he lay like a cocked rifle, with cold patches left and right of his body ready to catch him out whichever way he shuffled. The house susurrated and settled into closing doors and silences as those around him found sleep.

At first the sound seemed faint and hallucinatory, impossible to pinpoint in the darkness. The streetlight outside showed a meagre light. He eased himself up against the headboard to a sitting position to help him hear. The sound seemed to be coming through the walls. He wondered if his mum had left the telly on – there was something familiar about the sound – but he also knew nothing would be on but the Test Card girl. Dragging himself out of bed, his fingers felt in the space between bed and built-in wardrobe for the shirt and denims he had dropped onto the linoleum. They felt damp with cold, but he was glad to pull them on. He shuffled towards the door, listening to the drone of what seemed to be a nursery rhyme. As he approached the living room the chant was barely perceptible – *Frère Jacques, Frère Jacques* – and seemed, in his sluggish state, a strange choice for the BBC. It sank away into the lull of the wind pushing and creaking Murdoch's locked garage gates. He poked his head into the living room. The telly stood small and lopsided on its rickety legs in a way it would never have seemed in daylight, and the room had the late-night chill of the unoccupied. The faint smell of cigar smoke came from one of the ashtrays dotting the room, and he briefly wondered if one of his da's mates was visiting. He turned to go into the toilet, convinced it could just as easily have been Daft Rab's telly he'd heard – his living room was directly above theirs – or it could have been Douglas's telly through the wall, or Mrs Bell's, next door.

The shock of the swelling music made him spin round. Blood seeped from his nose. It was *Frère Jacques,* but with tonal distortions that sped it up and slowed it down, a spinning carousel that seemed to come from a great distance across the pin-light of blue stars and seeping through the thin spaces between tin walls to reach him. His head cocked to one side, frozen and numb with listening, the spattering of crimson blotches dripping onto the floor made him bolt. He held his nostrils shut and his eyes watered as he dashed to the bathroom for bog roll to staunch the bleeding.

Mary traipsed up the hall and stood guard outside the toilet. 'You alright in there?' The door was unlocked. She pushed it open and peered into the darkness, looking in over his shoulder as he crouched down near the toilet roll holder.

His voice sounded funny with paper up his hooter and blood running down his throat. 'That noise get you up?' He tried to make a joke of it.

She flicked the light on and stood him under the bare thirty-watt bulb, pushing his head back and forward, tilting his chin, assessing his first-aid work. 'What noise?'

'The noise. Jesus Christ. You must have heard it. Daft Rab must have hooked a set of stereo speakers up against the living room floor and turned them on full blast.'

Mary stroked his face and seemed satisfied with the job he had done plugging his nose. 'I only got up because I heard you moving about.'

'You never heard *Frère Jacques* played at fifty decibels?'

She pursed her lips, eyes briefly squeezed shut, as she shook her head in denial. 'C'mon I'll make us a nice cuppa.'

The kitchen smelled of damp washing, but it was a little warmer than the living room. John balanced with practised ease on the wooden chair with three-and-a-bit legs. Mary put the kettle on and turned on the grill to throw out heat, but the room filled with the aroma of frazzled bacon rind with little increase in temperature.

'You not sleep?' She yawned, and snatched up her packet of Embassy Mild King Size, while they waited for the kettle to boil.

John could still hear a tinkle of the nursery rhyme in the distance. 'I thought I heard something.' He searched his mum's face for some clue she had heard it too. She turned away to fill the teapot with loose tea leaves from the caddy. The stench of something putrefied caught him like a kick to the groin, bowled him over and brought the dry boak to the back of his throat. He tried to throw up.

Mary hauled the plastic bowl out from underneath

the sink and held it under his chin. His eyes streamed and his nose bled, but worst of all was a mouthful of something corrupt, like decomposing flesh. Just as quickly as it came the stench disappeared and he could breathe again. 'You don't smell anything?' He added wistfully, 'Cigar smoke?'

'Jesus, son. You OK?' Mary's fag had burnt down to her fingers; she flung it into the sink full of tomorrow's dishes. 'You in pain? Concussion? Want me to phone for a doctor?'

He shook his head, 'I'll be alright.' His voice jiggled like a lock with the wrong key in it, but as his mum was watching him so closely, he tried to make it sound normal. 'I'll no' bother with tea. I'll just go back to my bed. I just need a good night's sleep.'

Mary put her hand on his forehead. 'You're hurt. Seeing things and hearing things?' He was sweating and her hand felt cool.

'Nah, just tired.' He didn't want her thinking he was turning into another Uncle Paddy.

'You're boiling hot, maybe I should get the doctor out?'

His chair creaked and rocked as he stood up. 'Nah, Ma, I'll be fine. Just leave it.'

'We can get you help.'

'Whit kind of help?'

'The priest . . . a psychiatrist or something?' Her tone was light, an attempt at playfulness.

He snorted, forgetting how sore his nose was. 'Nah, Ma, just leave it.'

She gripped his forearm, her hand digging into skin. 'You'll be alright, son.' Her words were filled with a certainty John didn't feel. 'Just promise me you willnae go down that shortcut again for a while. You'll stay away from that school.'

Her eyes were backlit by tears, but he shook his head. 'Nah, Ma, I cannae do that.'

Her voice rose in protest, 'Why not? You're just being pig-headed like your da.'

'I cannae, Ma. There's a wee lassie, waiting for me every day. I cannae leave her standing there.'

Mary's voice dropped into a confidential whisper. 'I've had that nice Betty Cunningham at the door. She said she was worried about you. I'm worried about you too.' She patted his hand. 'If you just leave it for a while, I'm sure things will settle down.'

He kissed her frowning forehead as he passed her on his way to bed. 'Could you leave a wee lassie Ally's age waiting for you, standing on the street and not turn up? I cannae. Neither would you.'

'You've grown up, son.' Mary tamped down a rueful smile and reached for her fags.

DAY 13

John lay cocooned in the cosy warmth of his bed. He paid little heed to his mum getting up, trailing up the hall towards the toilet and then into the living room. About fifteen minutes later, he caught the careful tread

of her flapping slippers returning to his parents' bedroom. As she edged open the door, he heard the clink of
a plate clip the glaze of the mug. He whiffed burnt toast,
just the way his dad liked it.

Joey didn't believe in silence. Ten minutes later doors
banged open and shut. Radio Athlone blared from the
kitchen with reports of strikes, inflation and the impor-
tance of feedstock. Their toilet flushed so many times he
thought it must have been fishing for water and dried up
Loch Katrine. The front door slammed shut, shaking the
house as though it was made of plywood, the mark of
Joey's hasty exit.

There was a lull when John might have dozed. The
girls kept mainly to the warmth of the living room.
When he clambered out of bed, the house was on mute.
Mum didn't have time for the radio, or telly, or anything
much other than cleaning and smoking and sometimes
both. He sought her out in the kitchen and took a seat
while she scrubbed the bigger of the two sinks a shade
less jaundice with a wire pad.

'You want eggs with your toast?' She turned away
from housework; her eyes searched his.

Mary stood, taking a minute, her back pressed against
the sink, swilling mouthfuls of tea as she smoked. They
talked about their neighbours and Wilcock's pampered
Golden Labrador with a forced familiarity. She poked
about in the cupboard for eggs and stood at the cooker
watching the pot boil and slices of white bread brown
under the grill. They chattered some more, with his
mum suddenly turning American on him and adopting

an encouraging tone, trying to gee him up and hold him in place with small talk. She clattered a plate on the table in front of him.

His jaw still hurt. He chewed slowly, eating only because his mum had made the effort. He finished half a slice and the top half of an egg. Easing up out of the chair, he slumped back down, not sure what to say, wishing the telly or radio was on to fill the silence.

Her cheeks were puffy and she seemed worn and old. 'Don't go,' she said. Tears formed in her eyes.

All his fine talk of the night before washed away like Poohsticks in a fast-flowing burn. She leaned in close enough for the tang of disinfectant and cigarette smoke to make him feel uncomfortable, her white knuckles pinned to the back of the top bar of his chair, as if it was holding her upright. She mussed his hair and kissed him clumsily on the cheek. Her fingers wandered and pulled out a packet of twenty fags, and a box of Swan Vesta matches, from her nylon smock but found no hanky to dab at her eyes. She shook silent tears away and dashed off to get a bit of toilet roll. His Wrangler jacket was hanging on the ironing board in the alcove beside the back door. Getting up and pulling it on, he scarpered out the back door without looking back.

At the shortcut, cumulus hung low on the flat roofs like a stove-pipe hat, and the wind rustled the black fingers of overhanging branches, bending them backwards and forwards. The last of the snow had cleared. He studied the slippery-bowl patch of ground where other people had stepped on the long grass to avoid the muddiest parts of the path. He felt older and out of practice. Going down the steepest part, lurching one way then another, his feet sought the safety of a spongy tussock of grass; he was lucky not to end up on his arse. He climbed through the gap in the fence and dropped onto Shakespeare Avenue.

With no snow on the roads or pavements he convinced himself that the little girl would not waylay him. His feet slowed as he approached Well Street, despite a muddled belief his dad would be ashamed of him. As if his thoughts had taken form, hail, then rain, pattered down. It swept the road in great sweeping gulls of soft water washing clean everything and everybody in its path. And there she stood near Kerr's knobbly wooden gate, her blazer soaked an unnatural blue, hair flattened to two dimensions around an oval face, her arms folded tight across her chest to keep in body heat. She whimpered, teeth chattering; her bright eyes looked destitute of vision. He wondered if she had spotted him, running the last few yards towards her, watching water dripping barefaced from the end of her nose as she contemplated her black shoes, locked into solipsistic and tear-stained misery.

Mary snatched the hood of a coat off the door of the hall cupboard. She ran down the steep hill outside her gate, her fingers dipping into the side-pocket for her packet of fags before she realised she was wearing her eldest daughter Jo's worn-out school jacket. Her breath came in razor-edged gasps. It had been years since she had run for anything. The pelican coloured anorak flocked out behind her as she broke into something resembling a trot. Dickens Avenue was shaped like a horseshoe with Shakespeare Avenue curved inside the heel. Her son had a head start. She knew he had taken the shortcut that sliced through the horseshoe, but it was too wild and slippery for her.

Heavy rain dashed her face and made orange blancmange out of the halo of her hair. Her lungs burnt and her legs grew buttery, but when she got to the bottom of Ramsay Street, her prayers were answered – John had been delayed. He was cutting across the road. His dark bush of hair made darker by the incessant deluge, his Wrangler jacket collar was turned up in spikey protest against the weather. He was hunched over holding nothing as if it was something

Mary was not yet close enough to hear his chit-chatting, but he babbled to himself in the same way he had that night she had disturbed him sleepwalking.

Opposite the school, a police car was parked beneath the shelter of an oak tree. The words of a prayer slipped fully formed out of her mouth. 'Out of the darkness I cried to you, oh Lord.' A thin strap of a policeman leaned his bum against the bonnet of the car, his feet planted on the kerb, and Mary followed his gaze towards her son.

Mary was halfway across before the dull thump of the gear change made her turn her head. The bus horn blared, the updraft of wind fluffing her hair in its wake. She dashed the final few yards to the pavement on the church side of Park Road. The policeman standing beside the panda belly-laughed and wagged a finger in mock warning. A squall of wind and rain buffeted her body, halting her progress, but she closed the distance between her and her son.

John faltered and stopped a few feet in front of her. He spoke to someone obscured behind the facing brick pillar of the church grounds. Across the road, the thinner policeman adjusted his cap. As she got closer, surprise and relief choked her voice. 'Jesus Christ, Joey, whit you doing here? I thought you were at work.'

Joey's glance took in his wife's anorak and her dishevelled hair. Normally, he would have smiled, but his deep-set eyes narrowed to slits as he stared across the road at the policemen observing them. 'I wiz. Now I'm no.'

'You alright, Da?' John glanced nervously at his father.

The bitterness in Joey's voice and his scrunched-up face were sweetened by the sight of his wife. He shook his head as if he had forgotten something and fluttered his fingers airily towards the school. 'You take yer wee—' a splintered laugh escaped through his nose, trying to find the right word as he spoke to his son, 'pal down to the school.'

Joey took a deep breath, his chest swelled and he seemed to grow a few inches taller. His pupils shrunk further in his head, dark as new-cut anthracite, shiny dots sighted on the two figures on the opposite side of the road. He was deaf to the soft soap of his son's protracted goodbye-goodbyes.

Mary tugged at the shiny sleeve of the double-breasted dress jacket he wore over his work-worn boiler suit. 'Don't do anything daft, Joey.'

He stood unmoved and unmoving. 'Let a man be a man.' The skinny police officer looked away first, his eyes growing skittish and unsure as he glanced at his senior officer. Sarge rested his hand on the roof of the car, but looked over his colleague's shoulder and locked his body into listening to the jumble of messages coming from the car radio.

Joey's eyes were nailed onto the balloon-white faces above the collars of the dark police uniforms as he stomped forward. He cleared his throat with a rough grogging sound, spitting a slimy frog of a greener onto the slick, glazed tar. 'Fat lump of shite.' His voice was low, but a clear challenge.

The lollipop man stood sentinel at the school gates. He stepped in front of John and barred his way. His bristly moustache showed grey, but he had a firm voice. 'You might be a bit of a long-haired weirdo and a trouble-maker, but apart from that, you're alright. What happened to you a couple of days ago was well out of order. I said to my Maisie that'll no' happen again on my watch. Over my dead body will that happen again.' He tipped his head back, chin strap and smooth chin pointing at the police car up the road.

DAY 15

Canon Martin waited in the warmth of the day room for the housekeeper to bring the boy through. He thought of him as a boy – he had christened him John Joseph Connelly, a fine Catholic name, helped him make his First Confession and First Holy Communion. Such a lovely, quiet boy. His fingers fussed with the fuzz at the top of his head to help him remember. He had developed a shameful habit of expecting everything and everyone to remain the same and was perplexed that the boy he was thinking about was the one that he was expecting as a visitor. Now there was this terrible business with his mother, Mary. Sometimes the confessional box is little more than a pit stop for a certain type of woman. On the way to the pictures they rhymed off the usual list of sins and waited for absolution like one would wait for bubblegum to come tumbling out of a half-penny tray.

Mary was different. She was greatly troubled. Post-natal depression they called it. He'd call it a murderous rage. Shades of Herod's evil. He blinked through his thick glasses at the wooden crucifix above the rosewood cabinet. His eyes drifted down to a brightly coloured bauble, where the gathering dust grew heaviest, a statue of Joseph carrying Jesus. Then she saw the error of her ways. Grew more pious, as often happens. Made sure the boy attended Holy Mass and Novena, even if the father was a bit lax. His arthritic fingers found no comfort in the weight of rosary beads swaddled in his lap. He used his elbows to help him get up and untangle himself from the wing chair near the window. It was cold and wet outside. There was never enough natural light to read and those new-fangled light bulbs never threw off enough artificial light to compensate. It felt like walking through a world of shadows.

'One mustn't complain,' he muttered, his feet trailing as he made his way towards the door. His hearing wasn't what it had been, but he heard his housekeeper marching up the hallway before he saw her. Such a marvellous, capable woman, simply marvellous. He recognised the contours of her bear-like shape through the opaque glass door, inlaid with the images of swimming fish. Only God-in-creation knew what they would have done without her. She knocked before pushing the door and popped her head through the thin gap.

'Mrs Shields.' The canon's voice was high and whiny.

The housekeeper took this as permission to step into the room, bringing with her a whiff of cleaning fluid and beeswax. She wore a plain, acrylic blue dress, with gathered three-quarter sleeves and a round neck. Her breasts hung safe at her stomach and a black belt encircled her waist in case they got any lower. Teeth warred with each other at the front of her mouth, but with God's grace she didn't smile much. 'The Connelly boy is here,' she whispered.

Canon Martin peered over her shoulder. The boy looked like any other from that distance, apart from his hair, which gave him the appearance of a mangy lion. 'Best bring him in.' He turned, retreating. A Chesterfield with seats that sagged in the middle was positioned opposite his wing chair. He liked guests to sit there so he could see them properly.

'I'll bring a pot of tea and some nice digestive biscuits for you to dip,' said Mrs Shields.

The priest, once settled in his chair, gestured with his arm towards the seat opposite him but the boy, who had been at his back had already ensconced himself on the high pillows of the couch, suggesting a certain cockiness or nervousness. Canon Martin leaned forward to see if he could detect which it was. He decided to be direct.

'Your mother told me you're consorting with demons.'

The boy angled his head sideways as if he was talking, but also listening to what he said. 'She wouldn't say that.'

'She said, every day you meet with ghosts.'

The boy squirmed on the edge of the seat, his voice whiny. 'It's not like that.'

'What's it like then?'

'It's not like anything.' He pushed his back into the shine of leather and sat up straighter.

'Your mother's a good woman. She said she's tried to stop you, but you meet a demon every day and some nights . . .' the priest's voice trailed off.

Pink mottled the boy's neck and rose flushed his cheeks. He felt betrayed, and he felt he had to justify himself. 'It's only a little girl.'

'Ah,' said the priest. His mouth stayed open as he scratched at the loose flap of skin around his eye, up and underneath a lens of his glasses. His voice dropped and he spoke in a confidential tone. 'You admit it then?'

'It's not like that,' said the boy. 'I didn't want to meet her. She was just there. And now . . . And now . . .' He looked at the lustre of the gold bands on the white china plates in the cabinet and shook his head before continuing. 'I just don't know what to do. She's waiting for me every day. It doesn't matter if I miss a day, two days, or even three, when I go back she's standing waiting for me. And when I don't go I beat myself up about it and feel like a coward – and worse, because I know she needs my help and is all alone, at least I've got a family – and then I need to go back just to see that she's there. Just to see that she's OK.'

Canon Martin clacked his teeth together and wondered if Mrs Shields would be much longer with the tea. He harrumphed, clearing his throat before speaking. 'And what does your mother think of this distasteful business?'

The boy's face screwed up as he considered this, before blurting out, 'She doesn't think anything.'

'She thinks exactly the same as me,' Canon Martin said emphatically. 'That's why she asked me to have a word with you. The best thing for you to do is to stop this nonsense and get on with your life. You should take up a hobby like football or fishing, so that when you're not at school your days are filled. Then you'll be tired at night and be able to get a good sleep. Try and attend Holy Mass. Read your Bible every day. Say the Novena to our gracious Virgin Mary. Attend Confession at least once a week.'

'I left school about six months ago, Father. I've not been able to get a job yet.'

'Shame. Shame. That a young fellow like you has his life blighted like that.' He looked across at the boy and for the first time there was commiseration in his voice. 'I'll pray for you. But then again, if you're not working that means you can go to Holy Mass every day and pray for a vocation. Have you ever thought of becoming a priest?'

'Whit about the little girl?'

'What little girl? Ah ... the devil can take many forms. He is the great deceiver. He can quote scripture at you, but girls are naturally tricky beasts and little girls the trickiest of all. You are being tested, but through the Lord's Prayer you shall find strength and forgiveness. It asks for His mercy and not to be led into temptation.'

'Are you saying I shouldn't meet her?'

'Yes. Yes. A hundred times yes, you shouldn't meet her.' He shut his eyes, shook his head and opened them again. 'God commanded us in Leviticus not to seek out the dead. If she is simply a lost soul then— '

The door shushed open. 'Ah, Mrs Shields.'

DAY 17

To be alone, just smoking and looking out of the frame of the kitchen window was enough. There was not much to see – the drop of the house roofs in the street below and St Stephen's Church edging into view. The distant arboreal backdrop of Dalmuir Park was eclipsed by the squirrel-grey of clouds scudding across the sky, the sudden light filtering through, hinting at change, the smudges of brown and green shadowing the distant hills. Mary snatched another draw of her fag and narrowed her eyes. The yellow rayon curtains on the window were a mess and had to go. They had wilted. She took another drag, knowing pretty and functional had little relevance, they were just something to peg her thoughts onto.

The girls would be in soon. She didn't need a watch to sense the day moving on without her. She heard Daft Rab's clumping steps upstairs as he put on his dinner. Dogs barking. The vibrating echo of trains and the plaintive note of an InterCity horn, muffled with the window closed as if a sock had been placed over it, warning those on the metal tracks that it was time to move. Normal living sounds setting out the course of a day.

John, of course, pulled normality out of shape. But he had not been her first. She had been six-months pregnant when she had lost Joseph. There was no baby to hold. No baby to bury. She had just got on with it. That was what you did. Then a second life ten months later, John Joseph's perfect little hands and feet. The screwed up squall of mewling face, crying to be alive. Seconds before, but a lifetime later, her body had, in a literal and Biblical sense, cleaved to his. Something airy-fairy passed through her when she first held him to her breast and cradled the fragile skin of his wobbly head, an ecstasy and sense of fulfilment. It had soon been dashed into the Beelzebub pit of depression. The blind mirror of his dumb animal faith reaching for her allowed her to stick it out. She had not had that whirlwind with her daughters. She had cared for them, but that kind of consummation bypassed her at their births. A prickly, fierce, protective love only grew up later. She stabbed her fag out in an ashtray on the sill. The front door banged open. She brushed her thoughts aside along with the tendrils of cigarette smoke curled around her hand and face. A rush of staccato feet sounded in the hall.

'Oh, Mum,' Alison sobbed, using her mother's body as a climbing post, monkeying into her arms to be hugged and comforted. 'They're saying bad names about me and Johnny.'

'Who, Ally? Who?'

'Them at school.'

She had the head-on innocent expression of a red deer calf. Unable to say more, playground grief loosened Ally's thin frame. She shivered, holding herself lock-tight against her mum's shoulder. Baby-wool hair, white eyelashes and eyebrows contrasted with the angry red patches on her cheeks. Tears dampened the floral pattern on her mum's blouse. Her howling lips had an oddly naked look, as if they lacked a layer of skin. But she'd always been like that. At home they called her 'Band-Aid' because of her tendency to get yellow sties between her white eyelashes, and bulbous sores in her mouth. Always first to get a rash or an infection, she was also last to recover. Frail and clumsy, she'd earned all her Girl Guides' badges in scrapes, bruises and walking into closed doors. Her head tightly nestled in the comfort of her mum's body, her sobbing lessened enough for Mary to carry her a few steps and slump onto the couch behind the living room door. She allowed her a minute to recover before gently asking, 'Who was it?'

'Pauline Moriarty and Anne Gallagher started it.' Ally squeezed out another few sobs. 'All the boys joined in. They started shouting and making chimp noises – "John is a Mongo. Your mum's one too and you should go and live in the zoo."'

'And look.' Ally's eyes were bright with tears. Digging her shoe into the chewed-up sofa cushion, her kneecap shot up as she proudly showed off a red dot that might have been a scab. 'Someone pushed me into a puddle.'

'That's terrible,' said Mary, leaning over and kiss-kissing it better, until her youngest child's cheeks dimpled, followed by a laugh. She held onto her daughter's warm hand. 'I'll need to go down to St Stephen's and have a word with your teacher. Those bad boys shouldn't be doing that to you, or pushing you into puddles.' She gave the knee one last little peck. 'All better?'

Mary pulled her daughter in close to her hips, giving and receiving another buzz of warmth before getting up from the couch. 'We'll see what your sister says.' She knew how much Ally wanted to be like her big sister, Jo.

Many of Ally's problems at primary school would have evaporated if, after the summer, Jo had not left her behind to attend St Andrew's Secondary. Her elder daughter was a street cat, more like her dad, liable to spit and hiss when provoked. No tethered claws there. Her youngest daughter and oldest son lacked that protective membrane. The world and its ways got inside them and hurt them far too easily.

'C'mon.' Mary grabbed her daughter's hand. 'You can help me make the dinner.'

'What is it?'

'Mince and potatoes.'

Ally jumped off the couch, her face buckling with the weight of her grin. 'When do you think our Jo will be in?'

Mary looked at the clock on the mantelpiece and, settling back down on the sofa, pulled Ally onto her knee. 'Let's see if you can tell the time. What time's the big hand at?'

DAY19

John skulked in the draughty back bedroom, his warm feet tethered in blankets that smelled of soap-powder, his big toe worming through a hole in his nylon sock. He flicked through page after page of Commando comics – *Achtung!* and *Spraken zee Deutch?* – that had lain sprawling in dust-gathering bundles under his bed. His concentration was too shot to read a book. Each panel was a snapshot into childhood and happier times when there were only evil Nazis to worry about. He hoped the little girl would no longer be waiting for him – he had grown scared of what people said and did. He flicked another page – *Snell, Snell vee have ways of making you talk.*

Someone was chapping on the front door. He ignored it, knowing his Auntie Caroline would answer. She'd been round so often lately they'd made a bed up on the couch. John knew it was because his mum was worried about him and his Auntie Caroline was worried about her and him. Whenever anything happened in the family, his aunties rallied. Mary's parents had died when she was three years old; her eldest sister, Auntie Caroline, brought her up. Her two brothers had all but disowned them, emigrating to Canada or America, or some other far-flung place, where they could forget about being dirt poor and having eleven sisters. John remembered that when he was small he felt as though every woman in the world was an auntie of his, which made him feel very special.

His Auntie Caroline looked the spit of Vincent Price, but with fluffy grey hair. Her false teeth flapped about, too big for a small mouth, shaping saliva-flecked hisses into words, and eating was a nocturnal activity nobody had witnessed. The muffled voice in the hall sounded like her, but there was also an unfamiliar voice, high and lilting. He groaned, flinging down the comic on the bed and leaving the British officers inside their hermetic panels, planning an escape which would involve shooting everybody, and then flinging a couple of – *K-POWWW* – grenades just to make sure they were dead.

'John! John!' his Auntie Caroline shouted. 'I've got somebody here very anxious to meet you.'

He shuffled into the hall to meet his doom. The most he could manage was to twitch the side of his mouth in a nervous smile at Auntie Caroline. He offered a limp handshake to her friend, who was introduced as Gloria.

'I thought you got lost,' Mary said, making a joke of his presence, but continual absence, in his bedroom.

He had to tug his fingers away from Gloria. She kept peeking at him like a geography teacher mapping the San Andreas Fault line. His face flamed, and he searched for clues to her nuttiness to distract himself. Gloria stood slightly apart from them under the accordion-box shaped lightshade. Her make-up blended in with the texture and coral colour of the walls. She wore a dotted blouse with a floppy bow at the neck, tucked into a brown skirt the same colour as her long coat, which was normal enough. Her hair was shorter than it should have been for a woman of her age and fizzled around her face, its mucky brown colour torched with red at the tips and around her small ears. Her face was as pouchy as a hamster and her small teeth were uneven and stick-brown. It would not have surprised him if she had squeaked, but when she finally spoke she had a soft, feminine voice. 'Very glad to finally meet you John Joseph.'

'Em, likewise,' he replied.

They followed Mary into the kitchen. John parked his bum against the sink. The two guests favoured chairs either side of the table. Mary stood puffing on a cigarette with her back to the cooker, waiting for the kettle to boil. The teapot, caddy and the best china cups and saucers were already set up.

'I'm sorry about the state of the place.' Mary waved her fag towards two mugs hidden in the bigger of the two sinks.

'I do the same,' said Gloria. 'Leave everything to the last minute.' Her mouth puckered as if she intended to say more, but the kettle began to boil and Mary turned away from her.

John had nothing to add to the conversation. He endured the women's company, but was anxious to make his escape back to the world of men – *Snell, Snell*. Auntie Caroline grabbed at the brown-banded cuff of his ribbed V-neck jumper as he slinked past.

'Gloria's a spiritualist,' Auntie Caroline said. 'She can read auras. She's going to help you put this poor child to rest.'

Gloria puffed herself up in her chair.

He let that settle. 'Whit do you do for fun?' he asked.

He heard the swish before he felt the slap of his mum's hand on the back of his head. He rubbed above his ear. It was painless, but he made the most of his mum's apologies to Gloria, darting out of the kitchen and back into the safety of his bedroom. His stomach ached and he needed to sit on the toilet pan before he left to meet the little girl.

He pulled the front door shut behind him. Panic set in. He took the four steps at the door in one swoop, feet slipping on the slabs of the garden path. The border beneath the window was spiked full of ground elder, but it barely registered. Rain had settled in for the day, hard, slashing cuts across his face. He adjusted the spine of the plastic bag and netted his hair, but the deluge saturated the shoulders of his Wrangler jacket and the knees of his denims. He wondered if the little girl was getting soaked and what would happen on a dry, sunny day – maybe she would evaporate and his troubles would fade.

White-faced, he barrelled downhill, the futility of life's dark whimsy spilling across his mind. There was not much for the crows to pick over. He had left school as soon as he could with no O-Grades. He had even mucked up woodwork. And from what he had overheard from Jo, his pals were pissing themselves laughing at him now. He was Mr No-Mates. No chance of ever getting a girlfriend – not that he ever had a chance anyway with his stupid hair, big nose and feet. Everyone hated him, except the little girl.

'Wait on us, dearie!'

He recognised his Auntie's voice and he turned and looked back up the road. Auntie Caroline wore a red patterned scarf over her hair, noose-tight at the neck. Gloria had a matching blue scarf tied in the same way. Their long winter coats made them resemble competitors in an adult sack race. Acting deaf, John stumbled into a lopsided run, feet slipping and bouncing down the mud chicanes of the shortcut. Minutes later he reached the safety of the street below. He knew they would have to take the longer route and would not be able to catch up with him.

At the bend of the hill, he spotted the blue of the little

girl's blazer, the billow of her hair and white pallor of her face. She stood shivering in the same spot. He hated himself for his cowardly tardiness, leaving her standing there all morning.

The little girl peered at him with an owl-eyed intensity, making her body small against the hedge. Beyond the dip of the road, up and along Shakespeare Avenue, the red and blue headscarves of Auntie Caroline and Gloria came into view. He sprinted the last twenty yards that separated him from the child. She weighed about as much as a Christmas turkey and giggled as he scooped her into his arms. The echo of high heels clattered after them, but was overwhelmed by the hubbub of traffic at Park Road.

'Whit's your name darlin'?'

Her answer went unheard in the dash across the road. The police van was parked in its usual spot. He knew they were watching and waiting. He walked slower, pushing tight against the church railing.

She perked up, and carefully rearranged his plastic hat and his hair, to whisper her name in his ear, but instead she said, 'Big people don't understand'.

John was too distracted by the cops playing peek-a-boo to ask again. Even by the abnormal standards of lanky policemen, both of them were inordinately tall. They shuffled from foot to foot, within touching distance of the bole of the tree, trying to use leafless limbs as a shelter from the guttering rain.

John scanned the bend of the road at the dentist's, but traffic was intermittent, one or two slow-moving cars spraying up the slicked run-off from the road. John felt the cops' eyes following his progress. Women's heels clacked along behind him again, Auntie Caroline and Gloria sauntered into view.

The school bell rang, signalling playtime. Some part of him felt that when the little girl was inside the school gates and mixing with the other kids, she would be tagged den-free in the daily game of hide-and-seek. That was what she needed. He crouched, letting her scramble from his arms, using the sodden denim on his knee as a step down onto the pavement. The church wall acted as a temporary windbreak, but the rain danced around them like apaches taking no prisoners. Her back teeth chattered and her lips pursed in a shade of pinky-blue. John pulled her in close to his chest, offering what little heat and shelter his body could offer.

'Darlin', I'm not goin' to be able to take you all the way. Look!' Her hair dripped rainwater. She nodded and peered towards the school gates 'It's not far,' he said. He patted her on the head. Down the road the cops cut across to block him off at the school railings.

She got caught up in the calling and high piping of children's voices colouring the blank slate of the playground. His eyes followed her averted gaze. His voice was high and sweet as a chorister's. 'I'll watch you from here. See how fast you can go. Is that OK?'

The briefest of head nods. He stood up. 'Whit's your name again?' he asked as if he had forgotten it.

'Lily.'

'Right, Lily. Let's see you run as fast as fast as you can. On your marks. Get set. Go!'

She had an audience for her race. Kids dashed across the playground, snagging on the railings like windblown washing, eyeing the chequered blue and white of the police car. Pointed and padded anorak hoods, blue, green, brown and a smattering of red, a loose chain of elfin figures, wax noses poking through the gaps, they stood waiting for something to happen. Lily's flat shoes clattered on the immiscible glaze of oily water and tar; she lurched sideways, round the long, spidery legs of the policemen, close enough for those in the playground to reach through the bars and touch her, but she kept on going. A few of the smaller children's heads turned and followed her progress, but most focussed on the two uniformed cops. John got to his feet and craned his neck to look past the barrier their bodies made. Hand-clapping in an exaggerated seal-fashion, he shouted, 'Well done, Lily!'

Looking up into the cops' faces he felt the size of a child himself. One cop's long nose was too big for his face and his uniform too small for his body. He had the frown of a Millport holidaymaker who had seen nothing but God's good rain for a fortnight. The other had a sharp-whittled face, his features carved out of ivory. He spun John round by the shoulder. 'We're arresting you for a breach of the peace and for being a persistent pain in the arse.'

John offered no resistance, but the skin on his wrist nipped as the officer ratcheted the handcuffs too tight behind his back, pulling him backwards so that he stumbled into the cop's midriff.

'Shit.' The big-nosed policeman looked through the slanting rain at two bedraggled women crossing the road and bearing down on them. He held his hand up in crowd control mode, planting himself between them and the officer escorting John to the patrol car.

More children piled up against the school gates to watch them. Anonymous white faces, John thought, until he saw Lily twelve or thirteen railings along. A freckle-faced boy and brown-haired girl made space for her at the fence. John's feet dragged, jerking the policeman that pulled him backwards. A sour look passed over the officer's face.

John heard his Auntie's voice behind him. 'What are you doing to that boy?'

The walkie-talkie pinned to the sharp-faced cop's coat hissed and crackled gibberish – foxtrot and over – temporarily distracting him. Lily's hand shot out from between the railings and touched John's side. He felt his legs buckle and his arms flailing; falling, falling, falling. Rain battered down. John felt like a fish tugging on the end of a line and he heard the panic in the cop's lugubrious voice.

'Jesus, get an ambulance. He's having an epileptic fit or something. Get an ambulance!'

John's senses sharpened and he observed his body from above thrashing on the pavement. He dimly heard a sense of panic and concern in the jagged tone of the cop's voice. What worried him was how dirty his

Wrangler jacket had become in the muck and rain; how he couldn't afford to get another and, anyway, he didn't want another, he wanted that one and it wasn't fair. The officer fiddled impatiently with the handcuffs and they fell from his wrist. He caught a whiff of the cop's fear, recognised the dark shape, a nimbus hovering above his head.

A wailing cry of 'Lily!' came from outside his body and from his open mouth. The damp, cold pavement compressed an ear and stiffened the side of his face. Dry lips formed her name again. In the sparks a fire-bright lust burned, branding his soul; he became she, being plundered and ploughed and raped by a posse of strangers, and she became he, lying prone on the pavement. A cudgel blow came from nowhere and the tendrils of plants wound and poked through his rib cavity and hers. He understood Lily's body was calling him, calling her, back to the dry earth. Their bodies fused inside the tomb of a dark cellar filled with coal. Others who came before him were showing him the way, holding flaming torches in a clear winter sky, inviting him like an honoured guest to uncover the burning bowels of the earth. Light flooded through his arteries and veins. His mouth unlocked, opened too wide. He cried out for his mum at the light filling and spilling out of him, bleeding into the drizzle.

'Make sure you get his tongue. You don't want him swallowing his tongue.'

'Get something in his mouth.'

'He'll bite his tongue off,' shouted a dark shadow, screeching into a walkie-talkie for an ambulance.

The school bell rang. He felt a kiss on his cheek and looked up into Lily's face. A kaleidoscope of luminous colours hovered above the halo of her hair. Dark energy sputtered and reformed in shifting and pulsing patterns, covering each of the adult faces pressed close to his own, like a monk's cowl. Hate was an absence that dulled their eyes. Wetting the corner of his lips with the tip of his tongue, he mumbled, urging her away. 'Run, little girl. Run for your life.'

John dreamily lifted his head and watched her go back through the school gates. Her blue blazer merged with the damp colours of other coats, disappearing through the double-doors of the main school building.

Auntie Caroline bustled forward, breaking through the crowd of onlookers that surrounded him. 'You should be ashamed,' she said to the cop who had handcuffed him. 'Scaring the boy like that. He's never done anyone any harm in his life. Now, because you've got a uniform, you think you can go around beating up innocent young boys and bullying them.' She grabbed hold of John's hand to help him stand. 'Shame on you.'

Bent Nose looked as if he was going to say something, but the other cop's voice butted in with an officious tone meant to settle grievances. 'There's an ambulance on the way.'

John had peed himself. He sloped his back against the pavement as if hurt, glad of the distraction.

'Are you alright, son?' Rain slicked Auntie Caroline's

fluffy hair and stole colour from her face. She smacked of Vincent Price emerging from a twilight crypt, but it sounded like his mum speaking. The familiarity of her voice could have made him weep. He turned away with undignified haste.

'Aye, I'm fine. I just want to go hame.' He heard the wheedling, boyish note in his voice as he looked round at the policemen's faces.

The sharp-featured cop spoke to John, but he was really speaking to the other policeman. 'I'm sure that would be fine, but it would be best if you waited for an ambulance. We can't force you to. We've not formally charged you with anything, but you understand we've had a few complaints from the headmaster of the school about your behaviour.' He looked at Bent Nose for reassurance.

Bent Nose spoke bluntly. 'One of the top nobs has taken a particular interest in the case. You probably read a bit about it in the papers, or even seen it on TV. All those young schoolgirls going missing.' He looked across at his colleague to help explain it better, before blustering on. 'I'm not for a minute saying he's got anything to do with it, but better safe than sorry.'

An ambulance with klaxon and flashing lights cleared the streets of slow-moving traffic as it hurtled round the bend of Park Road, splashing up close to the kerb beside them. The passenger side window wound slowly down, allowing the medic to flick his dout onto the road before starting work.

'Where's the patient? Where's the hurry?' The ambulance driver was a balding, stocky man. He spoke in a jocular tone, looking from face to face, before settling on the sharp-faced cop.

The other medic, a small man with a short-back-and-sides, looked a bit like a soldier. He went round the back of the ambulance and swung open the doors. The bent-nosed cop nodded in John's direction.

A helping hand onto his back ushered John towards the waiting vehicle. 'I'll go with him.' Auntie Caroline fashioned herself into a prim lady, not showing too much leg, as she stepped into the ambulance.

John screwed his face up and shook his head. 'Nah, I'm not goin',' he said. 'I feel fine now.' But looking over at the cops' faces and double-checking, he decided the alternative might be worse.

'Best get you checked.' The ambulance driver ducked his head to get a better look at the patient over squarish glasses clouded by condensation and rain.

John allowed the medic to take his arm and guide him up the steps and inside. He perched side-saddle on a trolley, its wheels rolling towards the door. Auntie Caroline sat opposite him on another. The army-type medic got in beside them. 'Best if you lie down,' he said. 'It might get a wee bit bumpy.' John's body stiffened as he was strapped in. He looked with amusement at his black Doc Marten boots, the criss-cross stitching of yellow laces and his feet sticking out at the end of the trolley.

'Don't worry,' said Auntie Caroline as the back doors banged shut.

He didn't. He dozed, his body shuggling sideways with each corner the ambulance took. He felt the childish security of being firmly buckled in. No siren sounded. Fag smoke filtered through vents from the front of the ambulance, reminding him of his mum leaning over his pram, but with a whiff of danger as if they were balanced on the serrated edge of a cliff.

The ambulance men wheeled him on the trolley into Accident and Emergency, Auntie Caroline stalking behind them. The casualty officer had been arguing with somebody, another doctor, when they arrived, but the anger bleached away from his voice, blending in with a bouquet of strong disinfectant. He directed the ambulance men, with a wave of his arm, towards the corner cubicle.

John sat to the side of the bed, reading a *Daily Record* discarded on the chair, as if he was a visitor. A nurse pulled the wraparound curtains round the bed, but a man-sized gap was left pegged open on the waiting room side for him to escape through. Those who had travelled by public transport or car had already failed the first test of triage. They smoked and chatted, waiting on banks of seats bolted to the floor. Auntie Caroline stood near the vending machine chatting to a woman with an ill-fitting crepe bandage over one eye. The old man in the next bed coughed, and spat into a cardboard tray shaped like an upturned hat. John felt he'd throw up in response.

The houseman, a nervous-looking man, not much older than John, arrived with a swish of curtains. A nurse dogged his footsteps, a piece of crinoline confectionary perched on her head in the shape of a bonnet, signifying the position of matron.

'Does this light bother you?' the houseman asked, propping John's eye open with splayed fingers and shining a light into it.

He was in too much of a hurry to wait for an answer. He turned to the nurse, 'We'll send him for EEG. Keep him in overnight. Keep an eye on him.'

John was shunted into a wheelchair, not allowed to walk. A shaggy-haired porter sporting a dark dustcoat pushed his wheelchair to the lifts and took him up to his ward on level eight. Hospital corridors with their sharp turns were his world. He talked about Scottish football, by which he meant Glasgow Rangers. John nodded now and again, to show he was listening, though he noticed the porter had not bothered looking at his name tag. It seemed pointless telling the porter he supported Celtic.

The porter expertly parked his patient close to the partition window, across from the nurses' station, in a ward with five geriatric patients. They were shocked. John was shocked. The matron snatched his hospital records from the porter and snorted, 'You're meant to be seventy-one.' John thought she was going to box his ears. She insisted the porter take him to the men's ward on level four.

He shrugged. 'Sorry, Matron.' With practised impudence he slouched away and round the corner towards the lifts.

A student nurse with long brown hair tied tightly

back and black-rimmed glasses shuffled into the ward to get John settled. When Matron left she tugged the curtains on their rails round the corner bed. She allowed him two minutes to get undressed and put on a gownie with drawstrings at the back that covered everything but his bum. When he was decent the student nurse went to get him a cup of tea.

'What are you in for?' the man in the bed next to him asked. His eyes were bright, greyish-blue, with one eyebrow arched. He was corpulent and baldy with a piercing stare.

'I think I'd some kind of fit,' said John. 'At least that's whit I was told.'

There was a straining of ears from the three beds facing them. Then everyone relaxed into their own ailments, which they wove into the throw of their conversation. He was given lunch that seemed to him like a school dinner with mashed potatoes and custard for dessert.

Patients in the other beds made a fuss when the student nurse came back after lunch and tentatively held out a plastic bottle for him to give a urine sample. The grey-haired man, who was always getting up onto spindly legs and smoking out the window or sucking and clacking on endless peppermints, shouted: 'She'll soon be wanting more than a sample.' The other patients cackled together in appreciation. The student nurse's eyes slid away from John's and focussed on the extension-arm of the reading lamp at his head. A flush rose from his toes and sweat prickled under his arms. The red beacon of his face matched the student nurse's, provoking a 'hoo-haa' of delight among the older men.

After lunch, the day settled into a routine. A doctor arrived at his bedside to take blood. John did not know why he was doing it, nor did he ask. The doctor put on the tourniquet and John presented him with his flexed arm, but the whitening of his skin seemed to confuse the doctor and he was unable to find a vein. It took five attempts before blood swirled into the syringe, unnaturally purple, even black in the strip lighting. The doctor withdrew the needle before releasing the tourniquet and blood dribbled down John's arm. The doctor dabbed at the blood with a Steret swab and pressed down on the puncture wound with a ball of cotton wool. He indicated that his patient should keep pressure on it, before putting the syringe on a metal tray and hurrying away, leaving John's arm extended and smelling as if it had been lying in a medical cabinet.

'I don't like Paki doctors,' the ginger-haired man two beds along from John said. It was the first time he had heard him speak. He had spent much of his time sleeping with blankets wrapped around his head. Unlike the other patients, who were quick to discuss their ailments, he was clueless as to what was wrong with him.

The man in the next bed to John looked up from his book before his gaze dropped and his eyes scanned the page. His expression was neutral. John could tell he was irritated by the way he flicked through the pages a bit too quickly. The man caught John staring and his face coloured, but not nearly as badly as when they were teasing him about the student nurse. He covered it up with a question.

'Good book?'

'Pretty good.' He showed him the cover, *To Kill a Mockingbird.*

'I read that at school.'

He had worked out from listening to the ebb and flow of conversation that there was something wrong with his neighbour's fingers or toes. They tingled too much or too little and made him feel a bit stupid.

'It was a good book,' John said.

'Yeh.' He looked fixedly at the page.

John knew not to say more or ask any other daft questions. The ward was suddenly crowded with an influx of friends and relatives at visiting time but nobody came to see him, or the man in the bed next to him. He was constantly referred to as the youngest geriatric in the world, and grandchildren, less circumspect, stared directly at him. He took to hiding his head under the blankets, feigning sleep.

One of the nurses rang the hand-bell in the corridor outside as a signal that visiting time was over. John heard a muffled voice.

'Hiya,' Mary said to the man next to him. 'I hope he's not sleeping.'

John's blankets were wheeched back and his mum's lopsided, smiling face loomed above him. She set up base camp on the portable bedside cabinet with crisps and sweeties. He knew he was ill when she brought the bottle of Lucozade out of her plastic bag.

'Sorry,' Mary explained, 'the buses were murder.' She settled herself into a padded seat beside his bed and unbuttoned her coat.

'It's stifling in here,' she remarked to the man in the bed opposite him.

While other visitors drifted towards the exit, Mary and his neighbour talked over his head for few minutes. He picked up from their conversation that the man's name was Bert. Mary was always embarrassing him like that, making friends with total strangers. Even when the nurse came in to shepherd visitors out, Mary sweet-talked her into letting her stay for another ten minutes.

Mary was a good mimic and she kept him – and the other patients – entertained with tales about what was happening at home with Da and Jo. John felt as though he had been away for weeks and not just a few hours.

'Little Ally's got a new imaginary friend,' Mary said.

John laughed even before she got to the punchline. Ally always had imaginary friends whom they had to feed with balled bits of paper and make cooing noises at. Her worsted bear was worn thin and looked as if it had been chewed by a pack of hyenas, but O'Mally, as his Da called the bear, led a more charmed life than a sackful of cats.

'Oh, for God sake,' said John, laughing. 'Whit's her new friend called now?'

'Lily,' replied Mary, chuckling. 'She's quite the bee's knees. And even goes to the same school as her.'

The matron looked over the glass screen dividing the corridor from the ward.

'Got to go,' said Mary, kissing his forehead. 'See you tomorrow.'

John was stung by what his mum had said and couldn't settle. He turned over the possibilities like face cards, trying to figure if the Lily he knew was the Lily his wee sister knew. Then he felt like a busted flush, bored, not tired, but in the muggy heat of the ward, with mute lighting and the nurses talking in scratchy whispers, he must have dozed off. He dreamed he was back home, sitting in the chair near the living room window, his legs tucked up under him to keep his feet warm. Ally was sitting scrunched up on the rug near the fireplace, play-ing hide-and-seek, her face comically buried in her hands, as she counted down: 'ten, nine, eight, seven . . .'

Lily, who was hiding under John's bed, put her finger to her mouth to shush him into not telling where she was. In his dream, he could see them both clearly, even though they were in different rooms.

Ally's voice rose as she closed in on the chase. Her hands fell from her face, and she looked across at him, willing him to count down with her. 'Three, two, one, ready or not, coming to get you and you'll get caught.' She raced towards the door, hands flapping in excite-ment.

He got a whiff of cigar smoke, but could not spring off the soft chair quickly enough. Ally pulled open the living room door and flames engulfed the hall. His mouth opened to scream her name. A frothing river of water poured out instead, making him gag, but it was too late to quench the flames. His feet kicked and legs thrashed and he sat up in bed, the smell of cigar smoke lingering.

'It's not just me then.' Bert's voice was low. He was smoking a fag, and the muted lights seemed to isolate him, make him seem more vulnerable and less adult. 'That can't sleep,' he added with a smile.

'Sorry.' John was sure he had shouted something, but the other patients in the ward showed no sign of being disturbed as they settled into the bruised silences of sleep.

'Don't be daft.' Bert began coughing. 'It's just the smoking,' he said, speaking through the hawking fit and taking another drag. 'That's better.' He sighed and edged closer, so he could whisper, 'It's just when I can't sleep, I smoke.'

'That's OK,' he said.

'I'm sweating like a pig.' He fanned his face and the smoke with a hand. 'I toss and turn. Go to the toilet. Have another cigarette. Go to the toilet. Tell myself I'm going to kill myself if I don't get to sleep. Then in the morning, when everybody's getting up, I don't want to kill myself, I just want to get some sleep.'

'Can't you get something from the doctor?' John glanced at the patient in the bed opposite. He was sleep-walking, muttering gibberish, and searching for something in the bedside cabinet. His striped pyjamas had a wet stain at the groin and his cock twitched and snaked through the cotton flap. John blinkered his gaze and locked it onto the patient in the bed across from him.

Bert shook his head. 'I don't like to bother them.' His

voice adopted a jaunty tone, 'But what about you? You're young, how come you can't sleep?'

'I can,' he said, adopting the same devil-may-care tone. 'I've just had a bit of a nightmare.'

Bert asked what it was about. John tried telling him as best he could about Ally and Lily and his sister and his family, and everything that had happened. He knew he was talking far too much, but Bert didn't seem to mind. He asked questions, dotting their conversation with the light of one cigarette lit off another.

'I'd a little girl too,' Bert said, watching his reactions.

He confided in him just before the changeover, when the dayshift drifted in and settled themselves at the nurses' station, screeching chairs over the once-shiny floor, a war party round the desk, getting ready to hear the nightshift's handover.

'The thing about death is it's an absence, but also a presence. There's not a minute in a day I don't think about my Jamie.' Blotchy tears appeared on his face, rolling down his cheeks. He sniffled, making no move to wipe them or hide his grief.

John felt a surging anger growing in his throat and stomach as if he had been cheated. Bert had made him talk about himself because he needed some form of reassurance from him.

'I'm sorry.' He wanted to look away, hide his head under the hospital blanket and feign sleep as he had earlier, but the watery sorrow in the old man's eyes pinned him into place. Then he was babbling the first thing that came into his head, speaking quickly, trying to get it all out. 'When you go up to his grave, he's playin' football in the field beyond you. He's eleven now. And he tells his friends that he's got to go because his mum really needs him. He says the new house is nice, but you need to get a colour telly. A house is not a home without a telly. He's sorry about Mum and what happened between you. Don't be sad, he said, you'll meet someone nice too.'

The overhead lights buzzed as the nurses switched them on and they began their rounds, patrolling the wards. A frowsy older woman, wearing a blue hat at a jaunty angle, began mopping outside the entrance to their bay. They heard the thump and the slosh as she kicked her bucket, sliding it along with one dainty black shoe, until they could only see her shoulders moving from side to side behind the partition. A wet slug trail filled the air with the armoury of disinfectant.

'How dare you!' said Bert, in a scathing tone. 'I don't think you're right in the head. I've never heard such shite. I'd a daughter not a son. A daughter! Ya fuckin' eejit. And my wife will be up to visit later on.' He rose up out of his blankets straight-backed, his head turning, one way and then the other, looking for assistance, looking for something to throw, but he contented himself with stabbing out his cigarette in the cup he used as an ashtray. 'You shouldn't be in this ward. You should be in the fucking loony bin.'

The patients in the other beds were sitting up, struggling out of the cocoon of sleep and hospital-cornered blankets. The man with the bed nearest the window was already padding towards the toilet and stopped mid-step to listen. 'What's he done, mate? You know what these young boys are like! Tried to get in bed beside you and get his leg over?'

Bert turned his head, as he addressed the other man. 'You're nothing but a foul-mouthed, stupid old bastard. You should be ashamed of yourself.'

'Bert. Bert. Easy Bert,' said the man in the bed across from them. 'He's just having a wee joke.'

'Ha fuckin' ha,' Bert said. He pointed index finger and thumb at John in a warning shot. 'I intend to have a word with the matron and have you moved to another ward. In the meantime, don't speak to me, don't look at me and don't come anywhere near me. Is that clear?'

John's neck and cheeks flushed plum-purple. He nodded in agreement and stared at his feet entombed in clean blankets. He desperately needed to pee, but was scared to get up and go to the toilet with so many eyes on him.

Bert yanked across the curtains that separated their beds. John was cut off from him and partially cut off from the other patients. He vacillated between grateful and mortified, willing the nurse to come and provide a distraction so he could go to the toilet without any snide comments.

DAY 20

The auxiliary nurse mopped under John's big feet. He tried dancing out of the way to escape her attentions, but his chair was squashed in beside his bed, and she seemed to delight in hitting him. He had dressed for breakfast, put on his denims, but they smelled dank as fungi and felt damp on his legs. A discarded *Glasgow Herald* hid his face from the other patients; he peeked out from behind it as he flicked through the sports pages. Nobody was taking any notice of him, which made him feel better. The matron paraded through the ward; the student nurse, a step behind her, managed a scattergun look that rested on everyone except John.

'I'm leaving,' he told the matron, when she turned in his direction.

'Yes. I know.' The matron walked round the bed and tugged the curtain that separated his bed from Bert's. 'I've already arranged for you to be moved to level four, Men's General Medical.' She took a deep breath, the upside down timepiece on her chest heaving, before she continued, 'Where you should have been in the first place.'

He folded the newspaper and placed it between the plastic beaker and the glass quarter-filled with tepid water on top of the bedside unit. She had misunderstood. 'Nah, I'm no' goin' to level four. I'm leavin' the hospital.'

'But you've still to see the neurologist!'

A shake of his head infuriated her even more. The student nurse looked on the verge of smirking. The matron gathered in her expression and spoke in a monotone. 'Fine. I suppose technically you're an adult. I'll just get the forms for you to sign.' He watched her broad back retreat, the student nurse trotting behind her.

Outside the wind blew and there was a nip in the air, but the sky was cloudless and his stride lengthened. He followed the short leash of perimeter road, leaving behind the antiseptic, enclosed world of concrete and glass for traffic fumes, busy roads, wide pavements and hurrying pedestrians. He had no money in his pockets. It was a couple of miles walk home, but he didn't mind.

He got to Partick Station. Crossing over Dumbarton Road, he decided to jump on the next train to Dalmuir. Speed-walking through the station, avoiding the eyes of the staff behind the Perspex screen, he went safely up onto the railway platform. It was a familiar game. He got a window seat on the Balloch train. At every station, as the train slowed, he scanned the commuters on the platform for a ticket inspector. His luck had turned for the better; none got on. He prowled up and down the aisles in the smoking compartment until he saw what he was looking for – a used return stub. At Dalmuir Station, a bottleneck of passengers waited for the guard to take their tickets. He sloped in among the crowd, handed the guard the stub and brushed against a man in a gabardine coat as he hurried away. John took the stairs outside the station two at a time. From here it was a five-minute walk home.

The weather had held, but he was more than a day late meeting Lily. There was no heavy rain, no snow and no logical reason why she could not walk the last stretch of road down to the school herself. He trotted up the Cressie stairs, taking him onto Duntocher Road. He pondered what his mum had told him about Ally and Lily's friendship. The rules and roles, it seemed, had changed. Lily might be sitting waiting for him, waiting for them, at home. He dabbed his forehead, blessing himself, as he passed the front entrance of St Stephen's Church. Down the street the panda car was parked near the school gates. Up ahead on the hill, scant sunshine had faded into a memory of Scottish summer, and Lily was scuffing one shiny black shoe off the toe of the other, waiting for him. He felt confused, as if he had lost a hundred pound note and found a fiver, or the other way about.

He cut across the road to meet her and she ran down the brow of the hill shouting, 'Wehhhh!' He chuckled as she bumped into him, clutching at his legs.

'Sorry I'm late.' He rubbed her arm through the blazer.

'T's OK.' She thrust her hand into his and tugged him towards the junction of the road and the school. He pretended she was too strong and she had pulled him off his feet, and he staggered beside her.

They stood on the edge of the pavement and looked left and right with exaggerated care before crossing the road, swinging and looping their arms up into the air. He initially failed to notice, but her hair was different, it was tied in little pink-banded pigtails and not kirbies.

'Lily . . .' he said.

John leaned down to ask her about who it was that had helped her change hairstyles, but the doors in the police car clicked open and thwacked shut. The cops who had beaten him leaned against the car as if they were on home base.

'Bad men,' said Lily in a solemn voice, biting her lips.

He nodded, but kept a hold of her hand. They walked a little slower. 'You'll need to run very fast. No other kids are in the playground. But it's OK, cause the bad men only see me. Not you.'

She shivered as she looked up at him, but he was unsure whether it was the sudden gust of wind, the policemen waiting for them, or that she didn't know what he was talking about. He dithered and dragged at her hand so she stopped too.

'You don't have to go to school,' he said. 'You're late. I could take you home. Where is it you live again?'

Lily scrutinised his face and frowned as she considered this for what seemed the longest time. She shook her head and tightened her eyes in a way that indicated going home was beyond her. Her constant trust in him and her innocence renewed his belief in the goodness of life. The lightest touch of her little fingers in his, urged him forward, made him fall into line beside her. It picked apart the barriers between them and made her seem more his responsibility than before.

The policeman who had beaten John strode up towards them and made a grab at his arm. John shortened his shoulder and shrugged him off.

'Run, Lily! Run!' John shouted.

He felt his arm wrenched behind his back, forcing his head down, so he could no longer see her. He expected punches and kicks, but he was pulled across the road towards the waiting car. The sergeant put his hand on the crown of John's head and pushed him into the back seat. John looked out the window, he felt an old hand that had seen it all before. The panda slid past the white garages and boxed houses of the Holy City on Second Avenue. It was a journey he had become familiar with, but instead of taking a right down Kilbowie Road towards the police station at Hall Street they kept going. The siren was put on. Lights flashed. Cars and vans pulled into the side of the road. They took a left up the hill. John had no idea where they were taking him.

DAY 20 (AFTERNOON)

Janine had decided to kill herself so many times she was getting fed up with the idea of dying. She followed the other defeated shufflers from the breakfast room to the telly room, and hooked a chair to face reception. Nobody looked at anybody here unless they bumped into each other in the corridor. The telly was never off – it was the one consistent voice, filling in the corners of silences, an antidote to every condition but the human condition.

Then two policemen, Tweedledee and Tweedledum, delivered a new face to the ward. They looked at her out of the corner of their eyes, as if they wanted to eat her out. Uniforms. They were so predictable. Policemen made everybody nervous and, Janine knew better than most, nervous patients were hard work. She hung about watching the show. The consultant psychiatrist, Mr Williams, processed the boy, sectioned him with a mandatory twenty-four-hour stay, do-not-pass-go, and got rid of Tweedledee and Tweedledum in double-quick time. He was smart that way. Not that anybody ever did any work with the patients, but the idea was a good one, a sound one, clinically proven.

There was an empty room three doors down on Janine's side of the corridor. She waited to see who could be coaxed out of the nurse's office to escort the boy to his single berth, his new home, before she made her play. Just her luck it was her designated case-worker, Stephen, on the seven-to-three shift. Stephen's skin was the colour of mixed concrete. She hated his fruity smell and the stained and oversized shirt and trousers he wore as a uniform.

Stephen held his hand out, warding her off. 'Just give John here a minute to get settled before you jump on his bones, Janine.'

'Just give him a minute, Janine.' Her face twisted in disgust as she mimicked his poofy voice.

John glanced past the portly nurse at her, his gaze shifting to his feet, a firecracker lighting his cheeks.

Janine felt a tingling in her vagina as if a pilot light had come on. She melted into the pleasure of his kinked smile as he sneaked another look at her through long lashes, then back down at the floor. Excitement and protective tenderness spread under her skin, making her glow. She felt a tingling contentment in the timbre of her voice as she answered, 'I'm just goin' to my room to lie down for a bit.'

'You can lie down anytime and anywhere.' Stephen licked his thick lips as he spoke and proprietorially took John's elbow to guide him away from her.

Janine could have slapped Stephen, but the damp, boyish smell of John made her pause and mellowed her. She stood, watching the nape of his neck, the shape of his head, and remembered the form of his face, the crooked nose, eyebrows that suggested something dirty and bright, hooded eyes, which sheltered boyish shyness. Ballsy plans for his body made her stomach flip. She would make him worship her in the privacy of her room. But not in public. Not yet. God she was hot.

Nobody flaunted sex like Janine. If you did, you were cheap. And if you were cheap, you were written off as a nymphomaniac. Not worth talking about – though everybody did. Men held the answer to how to unslut a slut. They did that in chapel or church. Then a slut became a lovely bride. Such a loving mother. The poor thing. She hated that hypocrisy. Hated men. She hated herself most of all, but hoped she could play this one differently. She waited until Stephen passed her in the hall, going the other way, returning to his scrapbook of unlined A4 paper to write something trivially monumental about her in his report. He waved an admonitory finger.

Her room door was open. She could tell if somebody had been in, rooting about – nobody had. She stood at the window, let her hand slide into the top of her denims, peeled back her pants, fingers in her tush, and waited for a sense of normality to come along, to wash her away, in the same way that she waited for a bus. With her mind full to bursting with junk it took longer than expected. A glow radiated from the dark yellow curtains that looked gaudy in daylight. The window only opened three inches, enough to push a dout out, empty cartridges of make-up, or a warm can of Coke that had gone flat. Her eyes glazed. She fixated on the sandstone gable of the opposite ward and the grassy knoll with the wind whipping through a sprawling rhododendron bush. She shivered, shook, and bit down hard on a moaning sound. Sniffing her fingers, she loped out of the door to wash her hands.

He stood in that awkward way in the corridor, reading the fire regulations on the wall, avoiding looking at her. She wasn't having that. Nipping his bum, she made him turn.

'Hi,' she kept her voice low, friendly. His cheeks were lipstick red. She liked that, and she liked even more the apple-green shine to his eyes and the way they flickered away from her face. 'I'm Janine. I spotted you coming in.' She laughed and stuck her hand out for him to shake. That relieved some of the tension in his shoulders. He smiled back at her as he gripped her hand. She held it a few seconds too long, rubbed her juice into his thumb. 'Thought since no one else has, I'd show you around.'

'That'd be great,' he said.

'There's not much to see,' she said, in a mocking, confidential tone.

'That'd be great,' he said again, floundering, the way most men did.

She easily took the slack. 'What's that in your hair?' Her expression took on a perplexed look.

He patted at his head as if searching for a piece of lint and expecting a nit or bug.

'No, there.'

He leaned over and down. She moved her head sideways and ran her fingers up and down through his hair, marking him hers again and again.

'You got it?' He straightened up.

'Emm,' she replied, slipping her arm through his. She led him two circuits of the ward and threatened to blindfold him and see if he could do a third alone.

The pilot light was on, burning hot. After lunch, she pushed him into a chair in the corner of the day room, grilled him until she knew everything there was to know about him, and why the police had delivered him to her. She kissed him and made it seem as though it was his idea. He kissed her back. The pressing together of their lips, slipping and sloping their bodies against each other was a testing, slick and cool.

DAY 26

From their house the phone box was a two-minute walk. The inside of it was grotty and smelled of pee, which was just badness, Mary thought, because if anybody needed the toilet that badly they could have slipped round the

back of the garages close by. She had a stack of ten pences
– fifty-pence-worth – balanced on the chipped metal
tray. Her feet slipped on broken glass as she dialled the
number, waiting for the pips. She wanted news, any news
that her son would be alright.

Mary was glad Joey was out working when two
policemen had come to the door. She hadn't invited
them in. It gave the neighbours an earful and something
to gossip about. The older and fatter officer had said
they'd taken John to a place of safety. He mentioned all
the wee girls that had gone missing in recent years and
made it sound as if they were doing him a favour. As if
they were doing her a favour. She'd flared up at them and
told them where to get off; John couldn't abduct himself
never mind some stupid schoolgirls, but it all came out
wrong and she ended up making a fool of herself. She
knew what they meant. They'd put him in the loony
bin. She thought of her uncle rotting in some far-flung
institution for years.

Visiting time, she was dutifully informed, was usually
between half two and half three. The nurse on the phone
that first night said they could be flexible, but it was
better to leave it a few days to let her son settle. A casual
dismissal of the structure of the day worried Mary, but
she grunted, 'Uh-huh,' as if she understood.

Over the next few days she could never quite catch
the names of the nurses she spoke to on the phone.
When she directly challenged them, asking them in her
most polite elocution voice, 'Who am I speaking to,
please?' they mumbled something, skipped along the

pathway of a different conversation and made reassuring noises. Later, Mary heard one nurse, the one she thought of as Krinkly Crisp because of the way she talked, tell another staff member that 'It was that pain-in-the-arse woman on the phone again'. Mary banged the receiver back onto the cradle, and lit a fag to calm herself. She felt like getting a taxi up to Gartnavel and knocking heads together. When she told Joey later, he just looked over the history book he was reading in bed and laughed.

Getting Joey ready for the hospital visit was in some ways worse than getting the kids ready for their absence. That part was easily sorted. Jo was eleven, almost twelve. Mary told her to keep an eye on Ally for a few hours. If she had any problems she was to run next door to old Mrs Bell's. Jo had given her that squint-eyed look as if to say the world would end in a raging ball of fire before that happened.

Mary wanted to take John something, a book perhaps, but telly-logic dictated – and she had heard all kinds of stories – in the psychy wards they were just as liable to froth at the mouth and eat the pages. Anyway, she reasoned, John had little interest in books or reading. He preferred sketching, but God knows what he would have done with a set of pencils. Joey had already warned her that he couldn't take more time off work, which meant he wouldn't, because he didn't like hospitals, and he especially didn't like psychiatric hospitals like Gartnavel.

Before they left home she had settled on a set of

crayons and picked up his sketch pad. Flicking through it, a picture of a beautiful little girl in school uniform made her shiver, partly because she had Ally's eyes. But then she got distracted, noticed a scuff mark from work boots on the linoleum in the kitchen. She got a dish towel and ran it under the tap, scrubbing furiously at the grey smear, hating Joey for his carelessness and blindness. She wrung the rag out and hung it on the pipes under the sink.

'Nothing to worry about,' Joey had said, when she first told him where their son was. 'He's just gone a bit daft, like his Ma.'

Mary and Joey stood on the platform at Dalmuir Station waiting for the Hyndland train that would take them to Gartnavel. The trip took about twenty minutes, but for Joey the wait was unpaid work. He was dressed in his best navy blue suit and a diamond-patterned tie in a tasteful lime, the knot loose so it hung lopsided and low at his chest like a lasso on the hitching post of his neck. The top three buttons of his shirt were undone and the winged collar spread wide as a dove in flight. His chest was tanned from working outside and he thrust it out, a gold crucifix on a chain glinting in the light. He paced up and down Platform Two, huffing and puffing in exasperation, eyeing Mary, blaming her, when the red light refused to turn green. She ignored him, smoked a cigarette and struck up a conversation about the changeable weather with a stout woman leaning on a stick.

At Gartnavel Hospital, the nurse had a fixed grin on her face and held up a set of keys, signalling to them through reinforced glass that she was going to use them to open the door.

'Wow,' she said, pulling the door open, 'you're early.' She had puffed out blonde hair that curled and stopped halfway down her face, and a body like an American fridge-freezer crammed into a cream trouser suit, and sporting brown Doc Marten boots.

But their explanation that they were booked in to see the psychiatrist made it forgivable. She marched along the hall ahead of them and stopped to wait for them outside a closed door.

'There now.' The nurse padded off down the corridor and left them standing.

'It's in here,' said Mary. There was a nameplate – Mr Tom Williams – slipped into a slot on the door. She wondered whether to knock.

Joey pushed in ahead of her and flung open the door, an uncharacteristic jerky movement that showed his haste to get in and out as quickly as possible. Mary stood uncertain on the threshold, listening to the murmur that came from the day room, hoping to pick out Krinkly Crisp's voice. Someone was picking discordant notes on a piano keyboard. The caustic institutional smell of disinfectant and fag smoke bled from dank green walls. The room they entered was not much bigger than an extended lobby with a desk and a few chairs.

'Please sit down.' The voice was Oxford or Cambridge, plum years of education in Received Pronunciation; the beard was a Che Guevara and his doctor's coat a lived-in yellow. It was only apparent how Lilliputian John's psychiatrist was when he stood up, his hand outstretched to offer them a seat.

Sighing, Mr Tom Williams concentrated on the minutiae of John's notes rather than looking either of them in the eye. The seizure, if it was that, was just an aberration, a freak of nature. It might happen again. It might not happen again. If a pattern emerged, he reassured them, he was just the man to chart its progress. There were medications that could control, but not cure, it. They could manage it together. He got up as quickly as he sat down, briefly shook Mary's hand and nodded at Joey on his way out.

'What about his psychiatric problems, his—?' Mary asked.

He batted away Mary's concerns with thin pink lips that struggled out of his facial hair. 'Psychosis, isn't as bad as it sounds,' he reassured her. 'With the right help it's manageable.' He grabbed her hand again, cupping it in his own, his dark eyes looking into hers, showing he understood the shock she had been through.

'Can we see him?' Mary asked.

'Of course. Of course. Feel free.' He waved his hands about for emphasis. 'We're not a prison camp.'

They followed him into the corridor. He pulled shut the door behind him and locked it. 'Feel free,' he said again, waving them away towards the day room.

It was a large central space divided into two. A row of different shaped and coloured hairstyles were sitting in easy-to-wipe shiny chairs, their faces pointed at the telly.

Mary supposed these were the dribblers and jerkers and criers.

'Glad to meet you, glad you could come,' said a man wearing a snazzy blue blazer with a squarish head. His hand was cupped and held out. 'You got a fag for Eddie?'

'Sorry, don't smoke, pal,' said Joey.

A woman glided up from a chair behind a pillar. She wore a scratchy acrylic trouser suit with man-sized flares. 'C'mon, Eddie,' she said, leading him away. 'Don't bother the visitors.'

'Excuse me,' said Mary, waving after her.

Joey shook his head. 'Jesus. It's harder catching the eye of the nurses in here than it is catching Blind Bobby's eye behind the bar in Macintosh's at closing time.'

Mary saw John sitting at a low table silhouetted against the large windows of the room, the blinds partially shut to keep daylight from spoiling the entertainment on the telly. He was canoodling, a girl wrapped round him like a blood python. As they got closer he stood up, brushing her off, so that she almost fell to the floor.

'What's that she's wearing?' said Joey. 'You can practically see her fanny through it.'

'It's a nightdress,' said Mary. 'Who's your friend?' Mary's voice was tetchy.

The girl's hair was a botched dye-job, black, long and silky at the back and loose around her face in a feather-cut. Her nightdress, a corn-syrup colour, skimmed her body and died above the knee. She wasn't wearing a bra, but the flouncy material round her chest barely hid what girlish bumps she had. Her eyes were her most absorbing feature. Blue shadows made her darting pupils piggy-eyed, as if they were hiding something. Gold hoops dangled from beneath her hair and gave her a little rock-star chic.

'That's Janine.' John's face was a starburst of embarrassment and his eyes darted away from his parents.

Mary expected the girl to push off, or whatever the psychiatric lingo was for leaving them alone with her son. Instead, Janine arranged the chairs, pushing one over to Joey, dragging another across the floor to create a jagged star, suckering them in so they sat facing each other, hands clutched like they were holding rosary beads in their laps in their laps.

'You look nice.' Mary spoke pleasantly enough to the girl, scrutinizing the ton of make-up she was wearing.

'Think so?' Janine said. Her mouth, bloated with red clown lipstick, was off and running on a whine, telling them everything about her bad skin and how much foundation she put on and what kind of brush she used and how she had to get up earlier than everyone else to look that way. How she didn't sleep much at all.

'Sleep is for the dead or older folk.' She twitched her nose as if sniffing out the difference. 'After a while you don't know whether you're sleeping or awake. But it doesn't matter to older folk. Cause when you get to that age they all look like each other anyway. Made of papyrus, with their bad hair, droopy mouths and wrinkly, disgusting bodies.'

Joey laughed. 'You might have a point there.' He sneaked a look at his wife.

Mary lit a fag. The girl stared at her. 'What exactly are you in for?'

Mary found herself passing her lighter and fag packet across for Janine to take one, hoping that at least that would shut her up.

'I've got issues.' Janine spoke in a knowing way with a shake of the head that seemed to convey everything and nothing.

'And that psychiatrist . . .' Joey frowned and shifted about in his chair to give himself time to think of his name.

'Dr Williams,' Mary breathed his name out with a puff of smoke.

'Aye, him,' Joey's voice was a low growl. 'Whit exactly does he dae for you?'

Janine slipped the cigarette lighter and packet back to Mary, her hand drifting across and settling on top of John's. 'He's a bit like God, only smaller.'

Joey chortled at that, his eyes crinkling up, catching Mary's. His wife half-smiled in acknowledgement. John inched his hand away from Janine's. Mary watched the girl's thin white fingers spidering across the arm of the chair, closing the distance, reclaiming them as her own. He looked away into the dancing dust motes of the day room, not meeting his mum's eyes.

'I think what my husband means,' Mary kept her tone level, 'is what kind of medical treatment do you get?'

'Oh, apart from the usual stuff, none. Mr Williams doesn't believe in that. He believes in the laws of entropy and everybody finding their own fixed state.' She flicked her hair away from her face. 'Or not,' she added.

'Sounds like something McGinley would say.' Joey snorted through his nose at the idea of two people in the world, one a workmate in the yards and another a medical doctor and consultant psychiatrist, talking the same bullshit. 'Whit are they keeping you in for hen?' he asked Janine.

She licked her lips before leaning over, pulling the ashtray diagonally across the surface of the small table nearby, stubbing out her cigarette, the clear lacquer marred by fag burns. 'I'm not in for anything. I'm a voluntary patient.' Her voice rose and her eyes took flight. 'I can leave at any time.'

Joey nodded towards John. 'Whit about him then?'

'I'm sectioned.' John shook his head as if he had trouble believing it himself. 'There's nothin' wrang with me.' His body bristled and he sprung his hand from Janine's. 'The bastards.' The swear word was like an intake of breath. He had never sworn in front of his mother before.

'Seven days initially,' said Janine. 'Then they can double it to fourteen, or twenty-eight, or fifty-six. The bastards can do what they want when they get you in here.'

'What about you then?' Mary's voice was more forgiving, more muddled, a whisper. 'How can we get him voluntary status so he can leave?'

'Can't,' Janine said. The two women's eyes met with

some understanding. 'If you want out you're not well enough to get out.'

'I've never heard such shite,' said Joey.

'Try livin' it,' replied John, slumping into his chair.

Mary picked up her fags and shelled one across to Janine's lap, lighting hers and passing the lighter across. She began foutering in the bag at her feet, pulled out the drawing pad, and put it on the table with the packet of loose crayons and a bottle of Lucozade. 'I couldn't find your pencils,' she lied, guiding the conversation back to the tramlines of something she could understand.

'I've probably dumped them somewhere in my room.' He smiled at her. 'Don't worry, Mum. These are fine.' He picked up the bottle of Lucozade as if weighing it, then put it back down on the table.

Mary didn't think it was a good time to ask about his drawing of the little girl. And Joey was already huffing and fidgeting at her side in a way that suggested that it was about time they were going. Any time soon would be good.

DAY 27

John thought being locked up in the ward would be like being in the gaol at Hall Street. Pacing two-and-a-half steps one way, sharp turn, three the other, careful not to stand on your bed. He expected to be too psyched-up to nod off and sleep. But the staff had given him two little white tablets with a sip of tepid water, and it knocked him out as if he had been hit by an upper cut from Muhammad Ali. At first, in a woozy way, he thought he was back in his bedroom at home. Even when he tried focussing, a blinding flash of light pulsing from the middle of his head made his eyesight hazy, blurring the edges of the solitary chair near the window, remaking the square of a desk used for stubbing out fags and God knows what else. Wind beat rain against the windowpane. The radiator oozed a cosy heat, which delayed him getting out of bed; he imagined he could put it off forever.

Sheets sticky and smelly as a shroud on a battlefield were wrapped around his ears, muffling sound. He must have nodded off, because he became someone with the rabbit-pink eyes and blurred sight of an albino. A door opened further down the hall, and, 'See you later,' was swallowed by it closing. Bare feet squelched a few steps on the newly mopped floor, pausing outside his room. A blink of light. She hopped over the threshold and squeezed inside through the thin gap. He knew who it was by the way she breathed. She had told him to wait for her. His whole life he had been waiting for her – a flashing of neurons and dendrites, flushing across tender skin, tricking his blood, thickening his heart, everything focussed on the here and now of touch. A gibbous moon hung low bringing the outside in.

Pressing her bum cheeks against the sill, she lifted her nightie, flung her bare legs apart, skin gleaming like birch, she fingered the damp cloud of hair, making herself groan. Her fecundity filled the room like a bouquet of dying lilies. He needed to jump out of bed, move his legs, shift his arm, but the only movement was his cock pulsing and straining on the bag of bones that was his body. He watched her teasing and was caught in her playful delight. The phut, slip and slap of nimble fingers on oleaginous skin brought on the contralto crown of moaning, but when her hand brushed back the cowl of dark hair from her face, Lily grinned at him. 'Fucked you good, didn't I?' Her voice was high and shrill, but the red lipstick coated round her mouth was Janine's. He thought he was going mad.

Breakfast was porridge, cornflakes, toast, or a fry-up, served from behind a hatch in the kitchen. Choosing a seat proved a more difficult choice than what to eat. Most patients were still in bed. Those who were ambulant took a table intended for two, or even four, to themselves. With the mess they made smoking and sloshing food into their gobs it was easy to see why. He nipped in beside an older patient who looked harmless. He was immaculately turned out, wearing a denim shirt and jeans with the legs rolled up and hemmed to expose pristine Nordock white trainers and white socks, the type nobody would wear outside a locked ward. His hair was a rockabilly wave across his brow, perfectly neat, and he foot-tapped a beat as he chewed and gummed toast. 'Telegram Sam' blared out of the old-fashioned radiogram in the day room across the passageway, but the older man's body held its own tempo and tune. John dragged the sugar bowl across the table, which upset his breakfast mate. The old man made a break for it, knocking over a chair and leaving scattered cornflakes.

'Don't mind George,' shouted the woman behind the counter. 'He doesn't like his things moved about.'

'Sorry,' John replied.

Her snaggle of hair nodded in acknowledgement. She stirred a tray with a metal spatula. No-nonsense NHS glasses magnified her eyes as she scrutinised him picking at his cornflakes. She offered the only piece of advice he had received from staff since his arrival. 'Janine doesn't really do mornings. You got her on one of her good days. She's a mopey little piece – best avoided most afternoons too.' She scrunched up her nose and her mouth made a bridge for wrinkles. 'I suppose she's a night bug, swanning about till God knows what hour.' She sniffed. 'Never get her in her own bed,' she added, raising an eyebrow, clattering off a pot lid and shaking her head as if the contents disappointed her.

John showed no sign that he heard her. He stacked his bowl on top of a column of others at the hatch, and slopped food waste into a rectangular metal bin on wheels. Despite what the grumpy granny had said, he turned his head when he heard somebody coming into the dining room. It was a short man who limped as he walked. With a smug expression, and a twitch of her lower lip, grumpy granny lapped up his disappointment. Her plastic name tag said Nancy McMurty and the black font told him she was a SEN. He figured she had trained as a nurse with Florence Nightingale during the Crimean

War. He sloped off to the safety of the day room to hate her in peace.

Everybody had their own chair. He made himself comfortable, arms on the armrests, where Janine had sat next to him yesterday, with a good view of the corridor. The chatter and hubbub of other patients made him dozy. His head dropped onto his chest. Somebody kicked at his feet. He woke with a start, jerking upright. SEN McMurty handed him a glass of lukewarm water. She tapped two tablets from the bottle-lid into his hand. Swallowing them down with another gulp of water he asked her, 'Whit are they anyway?'

'Your meds.' She turned, nipping away to catch another patient sitting across from him with the same trick.

He must have missed lunch. When he opened his eyes, the opening or closing bars of *Crown Court* wailed from the telly, but he had no stomach for food. His mouth was like an ash pit. He needed to pee and get a drink. It was a good excuse to do a circuit of the ward, but he returned to his seat without seeing Janine.

He brought back his drawing pad and crayons from his room. It was impossible drawing with them, but with nothing better to work with than green crayon, he started a rough sketch of the woman with the scary hair opposite him. He kept tilting his head to take another gander at her, which frightened her away.

Flipping over the page and starting on a clean sheet, he sketched from memory; pausing, looking into the middle distance, his crayon almost slipped from his grasp. Janine waltzed into the ward. She wore a loose-fitting man's striped shirt and tan-coloured slacks. Her make-up was heavy on the walnut stain, which was good for a certain type of fence post, but not so good for a girlfriend. He held a hand up in greeting. She looked over and sneered, breezing past, leaving only a whiff of perfume. His mind did the jitterbug. He sat rocking back and forth, looking straight ahead, like a cat watching a bird feeder. His drawing pad fell from his lap onto the floor, bounced sideways, and settled face-up on the picture of Lily.

John sloped back to his room. The ground beneath his feet tilted. Neat stiches, selvedge of stone and Gothic spires blurred into view, and he was aloft. Whispers of earth and hedgerow. Sound and scent of battle, flags flying. Cries of living and dying. Then the world tightened itself. His skin burned with a strange knowing. Somebody inhabited his chair at the window, the stub of a foul-smelling cigar in his mouth, studying far horizons from beneath narrowed lids. The old man kindled memories, a warlord of his dreams. He was wearing a different costume of a butcher's apron, mottled specks of dried blood on the bib and rust-coloured cuffs, whether from dirt or blood it was unclear. On his feet, he wore black wellington boots. He unfolded himself from the chair with the speed of a slow-motion still. A scratch zigzagged across the back of his large hand, running rusty to his wrist; he spat the cigar out to speak. 'You've been a busy boy then,' he said in a low voice – part growl, part wheeze. 'Getting up to all kinds of naughty tricks.'

'Whit dae you mean?' John hesitated, looking behind him at the shut door. His belly churned and his hands shook. He mashed them into his pockets to tether them. Standing by the bed his teeth chattered and his legs became wonky. He avoided looking at the wildfire of his visitor's dark eyes and focussed instead on the space behind his shoulder. 'You better leave and go back to your own room.'

The old man stayed put. 'Me and your mother go back a long way. A good little woman. Nice little tits. Long, longer than you remember. You've got a brother, you know. Dearly departed. A good boy. Not at all like you.' He laughed, but it was a knotted, phlegmy honk and he sucked on the cigar for the longest time. When he breathed out there was no cigar smoke but the stench of putrefaction.

John took a step back, not caring what anyone thought. Ready to flee.

'Poor little Alison. She can never do anything right. She'd have been a real looker. Plenty of jiggy-jig in such a small body, but you'll know all about that.' He licked his lips. 'Some folk just can't wait.'

John croaked, 'I'm going to get a nurse to get rid of you.'

'No need for that, John, my boy. My old cock. Nobody likes a tittle-tattle. Boy, could I murder a drink right now.' The visitor stood up, facing him. A big man. A rook fluttered down and landed on the windowsill. Then another and another, flapping their wings, jiggling for space. 'We could be friends, you know. Work together. This is no place for a man of your accomplishments. Men like us. We could be out of here in a second. Just say the word, my old son'

He sucked on his cigar. John watched him with bitter fascination and found it difficult to look away – a fellow conspirator exuding an awful bonhomie and campfire-type wisdom.

'*Logos*,' he said, 'words spoken from the heart. Calling into existence nameless voids. The force of your dreams and desires seeding the future. Take your Uncle Alistair. He finds himself a dive called The Captain's Rest near the *Times* Building. After working a fourteen-hour shift he needs a bit of me-time. His wife Lottie is at home waiting, three bawling kids under five. That's not what he needs. He's still young – ruddy complexion, like you – got a bit of sap in him. Bit of a goer.

'Now let me tell you about poor Deidre.' He turned away from the window. 'Perhaps you should lock the door. This could get a bit graphic.' There was that laugh again.

'I don't want to hear about Deidre.' John gritted his teeth so hard his molars hurt. He swayed his legs buckling , and he stumbled and fell onto the bed. 'I want you to leave now.'

The old man looked over John's shoulder, past him, listening to something. 'Perhaps you're right. Poor old Deidre up from the sticks and wanting a good time. She sure did get it. Him and his pal Danny Boy, good old

Danny Boy, they held her down, held her legs open. She sure did get a good time. Perhaps not the adventure she wanted, but an adventure nonetheless. All kinds of wonders waiting in the wings. Loving. The best kind. The kind you like. The rough kind, rough and innocent girls like your mum liked. A bit of cock-a-doodle-doo.'

He strutted around the room, hen-toed, with jerky movements mimicking a cock. The rooks outside began flapping and cawing, their cries echoing off stone and ringing in John's head. The visitor waited until they finished before speaking again.

'That nurse is coming to get you. Looking for you. She likes you, you know. Karen, that fat nurse. Deary, deary, great pity you don't like her. Doesn't fancy herself much either, you know. And her husband – beats her for it. He can smell it.' He crooked his neck and sniffed the air. 'Look for the marks on her wrists. Son, there will come a time when you'll be all alone in the world too. Just call. I'll be waiting in the wings.'

'Fuck off!' said John. He rolled about the bed, holding his head.

'Oh, touchy!' said the old man. He unlatched the window, scattering rooks like gunpowder, and stepped out onto the windowsill. Corvine-like he crouched, cigar butt clenched between his lips, then stepped daintily onto uncut grass. A gust of wind banged the window shut.

Karen stuck her head in the door. Her pale, anxious face was a reassuring sight. 'You alright?' she asked.

John sat up. 'Did you see him?' He gestured towards the window.

'Aye,' Karen said. 'Somebody in a uniform, was it? Probably a hard-working nurse trying to get some work done. Like me.' She handed John his tablets and a plastic tumbler with lukewarm water in it. 'Get that down you! I've been looking all over the place for you.'

'You did see him, didn't you?' John put his medication in his mouth.

'Course I did.' She shrugged, made a face, turned to go, but turned back. She shook the window, checked it remained locked.

Janine wanted to be touched. She wanted to be touched very much. She passed John in the day room a few times before he noticed her. She knew they had hit him with the old uppercut of Valium and followed through with a knock-out blow of Largactil. Thinking was not good for you. It was too much like work. The medicine trolley came round regular as an ice-cream van in Drumchapel. She had gone to the trouble of putting her make-up on specially for him and what was the bastard doing? Head sunk down and dribbling into his chest. He was young, strong enough to get used to being slowly poisoned. She had planned to take him back to her room, or even his room, but all the loser would want to do when he got there was get his head down – which was a good thing if it wasn't to snooze. Loser.

She did another tour of the ward, scratching around like a chicken let out of its cage and looking for worms;

she met nobody but her designated nurse toting a brown leather briefcase like a placard at an evangelical convention.

'Hi, Janine,' he said in his poofy voice. No doubt he was on his way out to some very important case review or yak-yak-yak fest that would make him feel momentous.

She didn't bother answering him. He was only talking to her because he got paid for it. She'd wangled a swatch at her care notes a few times. Knew the kind of shite he wrote: *I tried interacting with Janine this morning, but she showed some hostility and a marked inability to engage.* Engage would be underlined three times and have an exclamation mark or two. Loser.

Giving up on humanity, she slipped into the chair beside her erstwhile lover. His drawings were lying near her feet. She put them in her lap and started flicking through them. She thought they would be childish rubbish, but was struck by his ability to show real things: an old motor car, the chassis sitting up on bricks, with wooden huts behind it; a phone box with a telephone pole growing out of it, the clouds behind – maybe that one wasn't so good –but the last few of a little girl were quality art. The repetition was disturbing. She flicked between drawings. The girl wore the same school uniform; her hair was tied back from her face by kirby clips and coloured bands. In one of them she was wearing a hat and smiling. Janine's hand trembled. In the final drawing her eyes were black-crayoned, childish scrawls. She flicked back a page, then two. Despite the cloying heat of the ward, she shivered. The little girl's eyes were the colour and shape of her own. The same as her dad's. The same as her sister Lily's.

She snaked her hand into his lap to see if that would wake him. Her fingers began circling round his zip. It woke part of him, but his eyes remained closed. They suddenly fluttered open. The horny bastard had been faking sleep those last few minutes.

He caught her wrist as she tried to sneak her hand away. 'Geez a kiss,' he said. Leaning over, his hair brushed the side of her cheek.

'No chance.' She pulled away from him, her hand up as a barrier between them. 'Your breath's absolutely minging. I think when you've not been drooling on your T-shirt all morning, you've been chewing dog-shit.'

He cupped his fingers a few inches from his nose and breathed into them. 'It's no' that bad.'

'No' that bad if you like the smell of doggy poop.' She playfully pushed his arm. 'Go and brush your teeth or something.'

He shook his head and his eyebrows slanted down. 'I mean, I've hardly ate anything . . . Maybe that's what it is.' His voice gained traction and ended on an upbeat note.

'Nah. It's your meds. That Valium. It rots you from the inside out.' She shook her head in dismay. 'All your teeth will probably fall out by the time you're twenty. And your tongue. And your hair . . . Nah, your hair will be alright.' She slapped him on the side of the face as if he was a dumb animal. 'Stick your tongue out.'

He stuck the tip of his tongue out. One look at her stern face and he stuck it out further, tried looking down at it.

'You fit right in here,' she sniggered, 'looking like that.' Sitting straight-backed in her chair, as an example to him, she reverted to her semi-serious tone. 'Could tell just by the way you were speaking. Doormat tongue. Feels like your tongue's swollen up and doesn't fit in your mouth.'

'How'd you know all that?' There was admiration in his voice.

She didn't want to admit she was a few years older than him. 'Been there. Seen it. Read the fucking book.'

Her eyes stayed fixed on his. He was first to look away and first to speak.

'But how . . . how can I . . .?' He didn't know how to put it and his body slumped into the chair. He stared at the swept floor in defeat.

The music from the telly swelled behind them. Janine picked open the cellophane in a ten-pack of Silk Cut. His eyes followed the fan of her fingers as she put the fag in her mouth. 'Give me a sec,' she said, 'I'll need to get a light.' She turned her head to check who was working.

Jocky, one of the care assistants, slouched down lower than a gut shot in the row of chairs behind them. His stomach was a beach ball under his shirt and he had a honking laugh that rose above his surroundings. He sat among those who watched telly as a therapeutic activity. Patients could turn to him with the meanest dog-end and he would give them a light, even if it was nipping their lips.

Janine draped herself over the side of his chair to get his attention. She knew he fancied her, but he wasn't her type. Not that she had a type. But if she did have a type, he wasn't it.

She lifted her chin, stretched her neck and leaned forward to show him what he was missing. 'Thanks,' she said, after getting a light. She blew him a little kiss, knowing he would be checking her ass as she returned to the seat beside John.

John seemed more upbeat. She figured the day might not be totally wasted and huffed out a smoke ring, letting it float between them. 'You ever watch those American cop films where all they seem to do on stakeouts is eat doughnuts?'

'Yeh.'

'Well, it's a bit like that in here. They don't really give a shit what you do. The only thing they're interested in is watching themselves get fatter and fatter.' He looked confused. She patted his hand, deciding to put it a bit more simply. 'You don't need to take your meds. Nobody checks. Nobody's interested. Just hide them, and if you're pushed stick them under your tongue.'

'Whit will I do with them after?'

'Give them to me. I love tranks, but I'm not that keen on Largactil. Doesn't matter. I'll give them to somebody.' She shooed him away. 'Now that's settled. Go brush your teeth.'

Watching his plodding step, she took another drag of

her cigarette. There was stiffness around her mouth. The fag dropped from her fingers, the lit end bounced on the floor. She opened her mouth to yell, to call him back, but her body was shaking and she could not breathe. It felt as though she had a pincushion in her throat. Suffocating. The blackened eyes of the little girl in the picture looked up at her and she was grinning in a familiar way.

There was a kerfuffle in the day room. A crowd of patients gathered round somebody, reminding John of backs-to-the-wall school fights in crowded smokers' corners. The stench of cigar smoke alerted him to the presence of the old man. His butcher's apron was piss-yellow with age and splashed with blood. His head turned and he grinned as he faced John. His eyes were sump holes. But the old man scuttled away through the throng. Rushing forward, he bumped past one of the taller patients, bent-back Alice, giving John a straight path through the loose circle of onlookers.

Janine was on the ground. A stained cushion was propped against her head, but she jack-knifed forward, rattling and wheezing, her mouth working like a goldfish and her eyes glazed, looking up at him and begging for help. He crouched behind a care assistant, as wide as he was tall – John could never remember his name. His hippopotamus feet bruised the drawings and in a gruff voice he coached Janine in the art of living.

'Breathe. Breathe. Breathe.'

With a choking sound she did, her head falling forward onto her chest, eyes closed, nodding and quietly sobbing.

'Good girl,' the care assistant said.

He turned his attention to Alice who was making a fuss, bawling at her, 'Shut-the-fuck-up!'

Patients and staff drifted silently away like cigarette smoke. John edged forward towards Janine. 'You OK?' She flung her arms around one of his legs. 'You'll be alright.' He helped her to stand. She glanced around the ward and seemed to regain her strength, shaking off his hand.

'Fuck that,' she said. 'Thought I was going to be a gonner there. Let's go for a good drink.'

John pulled her in closer and gave her a peck on the cheek. 'Where?' he whispered. Not sure what she was talking about, imagining her brain had been dunted about, her reasoning circuits scrambled.

'The pond.' She spoke emphatically.

Behind them the usual crew had returned to their seats and the second part of the afternoon matinee. He glanced at the care assistant, the telly droned on and he was too far away to hear their conversation.

Janine gripped his arm and squeezed. 'You alright?' She changed tack when he delayed answering. 'You're looking at me funny.' She patted the tan primer round her nose and cheeks. 'Is my make-up alright?' Her eyes gleamed. She ran a hand through her long hair, searching for tugs.

He kept it casual. 'Aye. It's just I'd love to go to the

pond for a drink, but I'm no' so sure I've brought my pocket money.'

'Silly.' She hung onto his arm. 'I'm paying.' Grinning, she swung his hand up with hers and let it fall in a childish game.

He let her drag him by the arms towards the entrance of the day room.

'Hing on.' He scurried back and picked up his drawings, which were scattered over the floor. He plonked himself down on the nearest chair, sorting them out.

He briefly looked up at her. 'I'll no' be a minute.' His tone was morbid. The drawings were torn and ruined. He heard her soft shuffling across the floor and felt the nearness of her body as she stood over him.

'They were really good.' Her voice was encouraging, as light as her perfume. 'I'm sure you can redo them.' She sat next to him, her knee nudging against his. Her voice had a nervous edge to it. 'That girl, reminded me of somebody, was that your wee sister?'

He laughed. 'Nah, that's Lily – she doesn't exist. So I keep getting told.' Janine made drawing, or art, sound like some kind of jigsaw puzzle, where you just put back the same pieces again. 'Aye. You're right. They were rubbish.' He jumped up and stuffed them into the nearest bin full of douts, plastic cups and plastic bags.

'I didn't say that.' She lit a fag. He flung himself back down in the seat beside her. 'They were really good. That good that they scared me. Reminded me of somebody.' She turned away from him, her hair shielding her face.

'Scared you? I come in and you're lying there dying.

Next thing you want to go for a drink and a swim in some pond.' His voice had grown louder and harder, making other patients turn and look at them. 'And then, all of a sudden, you become an art critic.'

'Fucking grow up.' Her elbow was on the arm of the chair, her fag halfway between hand and mouth. She took a drag and the swirl of smoke created a pause between them. Her eyes looking into his were unblinking, like a lizard's. 'For your information, The Pond is a hotel. It sells alcohol. I was offering to take you there because, yes, my nerves are shattered and, yes, I need a drink. Now. Not later. Or tomorrow. Or the weekend. Now. And yes. Your drawing did scare me. Something about the eyes, reminded me of something I didn't want to remember. Brought on a panic attack. Satisfied?'

'Sorry,' he mumbled.

'Sorry doesn't cut it.' She shook her head and wouldn't look at him. Her fag finished, she stabbed it out in the ashtray and sighed. She bent forward to get up and leave him.

'I'm sorry,' he said. 'I was scared as well. I love you and I thought I was goin' to lose you.'

She slumped back into the seat. 'Say that again.'

'I was scared.'

'No, the other bit.'

'I thought I was goin' to lose you.'

'Emm?'

'Love you. Satisfied?'

'Again.'

'Love you. Satisfied?'

'Again. I'll never be satisfied hearing that. And I can never hear it enough.'

She squealed and flew into his lap and kissed him, not caring that they were in the middle of the day room.

'Love you right back,' she said, when they got their breath back. Her bum wiggled, drilling his body into the chair.

'How in the hell are we supposed to go out for a drink?' John said, breaking for a mouthful of air.

'That's easy-peasy,' she said, biting at his chapped lips. 'Leave it to me.'

DAY 28

Cigarette tip glowing, Janine's pale hand was a beacon in the darkness of the night. John slept at a crooked angle beside her, his sweaty feet loosely entwined around hers. Another slippery wrestling match; two falls and an easy submission were enough for one night. Maybe one more bout would have been nice, but she had already decided to give him a rematch in the morning. Some dirty grappling would help wake her up and slow her down. She felt as if she was hurtling towards or away from the men in her life. Teasing a leg out from under his, then the other, she sat on the edge of the bed, watching him breathe and rousing herself to move.

She reckoned the cold space of her own bed might allow her to sleep, but a tingling behind her eyes and the fear of falling into the same kind of dream, over and over again, kept her awake. The details differed, but it always began with the smell of blood. Sometimes she would be a little girl. Sometimes an adult. Rarely, she would be the age she was now, or older, a suggestion that she would be able to escape from the event, but never the nightmare.

Red handprints daylight could not fade. Fingers, a fan-shaped curve, motionless, on the lower panel of the flaking, forest-green, paint of the front door. Her breath a Gobi Desert in her mouth. Unable to swallow until she pushed the door open. A woman's voice. A voice on the fall into extinction. It was Mum's voice drifting in a slow-moving fog down the hall. All she had to do was push the door open. Her hesitation meant she missed what the man said, what Daddy said, the brief adult conversation gave her time to clatter down the close stairs and into the safety of Mrs McGilvery on the bottom landing. The door creaked as she pushed it open.

'Run,' whispered Mum.

The police report said that it was impossible. Mum had been dead for hours. Little Paulie dead in his cot. Lily dead in the living room. All that blood lapping onto the good piece of rug at the fireplace and ruining it.

Daddy could not die. He was lodged in her disbelief but escaped every night, flew straight into her dreams, catching his hand round her mouth, shutting her up before she screamed. He was a big man, worked as a butcher for Nairn's, and he picked her up like discarded victuals. Biting down, she tasted the meaty flesh of his hand beside his thumb. He jiggled her like a baby rat, covering her face and mouth, he carried her over Mum's naked, eviscerated body, her right breast a flapping wound. Her hair, her beautiful blonde hair, running red, rusting red. None of that mattered. All that mattered was she could finally breathe.

Daddy did dreadful things to her, left her a whisper from death. The police report said vaginal and anal penetration, bite marks on her shoulders and neck, multiple contusions, bruising around the windpipe and throat. Her body stuffed down the side of the couch. Daddy sitting next to her laughing, looking into the unlit fireplace.

Night brought its own terrors for those trying to care for her. She screamed herself hoarse at bedtime until she spat blood. No relative could hold her or help her. No foster parents could tame her. The battlefields of children's homes hardened her, taught her not to show emotion, but she never slept, not for years, unless she was in school at her desk or on the bus – safe places. Hospital. Hospital was home. Drugs let her sleep without dreaming. To be half-alive and move through the murky shadows of the day was the real nightmare. She leaned over and pecked John, smacking her lips, licking the salty damp of his cheek and nuzzling into his neck. He was a real puppy of a man, she thought, bumbling about full of energy and good will. Completely harmless in his own way.

Yet his crayon drawings of the girl, and the likeness to her sister Lily, disturbed her in ways that made her dumb. He had got her daddy's eyes right. The depth of the black holes where his eyes should have been. Psychiatrists and psychologists had talked about his delusions and explained to her about Capgras syndrome. How her dad believed his wife an imposter that had to be taught a lesson and his children were aliens sent to listen to his thoughts and kill him. Janine had learned to agree, to be moulded by the professionals' superior arguments. To ooh and ahh at their brilliance; it was more than her life was worth to disagree. They had not seen his eyes, the void that they held was the darkness into which she did not want to fall.

She learned a strategy for avoiding the holocaust haunting her life. When lured deep down into the hard place in her dream, her hand on the door, her mum's voice heavy in her ears, she did not have to push. In her dream she could stand, waiting, Daddy on the other side, talking in that low voice, words she could not quite hear. He was waiting too. Waiting for her to push open the door. She imagined this was what purgatory was like. The distance between uncrossed territories. But purgatory was always better than hell.

The hallway in the ward was like easing on a comfortable pair of slippers, stepping onto familiar turf, temporarily denuded of people, but full of muted and comforting hospital din. She crept back to her room and stood by the window, looking out into the night. Out there was a girl that was the dead spit of her sister Lily, and had eyes like Daddy's. She held the key to locking away the devil that was their dad; the link to what happened that day; and most importantly the key to how to fashion an escape from hell. 'I double-dare you. Go and ask her,' she said, kissing the glass on the windowpane. A faint trembling flickered through her body, her mind slithering past something, or someone, standing behind her, moving just out of vision.

Hunted, running in his dreams, disorientated, scanning left and right; John's eyes blinked rapidly and opened. He concentrated on the scabby seat and desk at the window. A crock-necked stiffness told him that his arm had been a pillow. Outside, rain lashed down, made the day greyer and more difficult to tell what time it was. He rubbed his face and pawed the sheets searching for the warmth of Janine, but a frigid space existed where she had been. The murmur of the ward reached him through a closed door. He needed to pee, and pulled on a pair of sniffy Y-fronts, denims and a blue T-shirt shaped like an upside down sack. The need to get some clothes from home also became apparent, or he would be wearing Janine's print dress, or cast-offs from the wash-bin and their near relations.

He conditioned himself not to expect Janine to appear for breakfast or even lunch. The idea of them meeting later brought a hard-on, and he hurried to the toilet stalls. After breakfast he shot a couple of rounds of pool with Derek in the games room. His hair was silver-grey and flopped unevenly around a face that ducked and squirmed left and right to avoid being directly looked at.

Not providing chalk for the tip made every shot an adventure. The green baize was marked and scored, some of the pool balls were missing and the cue had a curved bow Robin Hood would have been proud of. The table had a tendency to run balls down the left-hand side off the bulk cushion and into the bag. Derek used this to his advantage for the first of several games.

The care assistant John had seen the day before stood for a few minutes watching and listening to the faux-ivory ricochet of ball. He looked as bored as a statue in a public park, and tutted after John missed an easy re-spotted ball. 'I'll go on next,' he said. 'Play the winner.' He let go of the door handle and slipped into the room.

John lost again. A sneaky black down the left-hand side bag sinking him. Derek's eyes flicked towards his, corroboration that the game was over and he had won again. John retreated to the door, far enough out of the way so the players circling the table were not jabbing the spear of the cue backwards into him as they played their shots. The new challenger used his big hands as a triangle to rack the balls. 'Right, Derek,' he said, 'you're in for a right good whopping.' The care assistant played well and shook Derek's hand when he beat him.

'I'm Jocky.' He nodded his head towards John, a rough acknowledgement that he was playing him next.

Jocky set the balls up in the same way, but before cueing off, came round the table to shake John's hand, as if it was a match tournament.

'I'm John.'

Jocky's handshake was a brief and brawny contest, a way of showing how tough he was. He nodded and laughed. Like Derek, he didn't say much. They played until lunchtime and John still hadn't won a game. Jocky and John both lost interest at the same time when they rubbernecked at Janine's pink-spotted blouse ensemble parading past. Her hair was tied tightly back, giving her a severe schoolmarm look, but she had her full war-face make-up on, which added glamour. John bolted from behind the door in the games room and caught up with her in the day room.

'Missed you.' He crashed down in the seat next to Janine.

Her eyes flickered towards him, but she chose not to answer. She gazed straight-ahead, cigarette smoke wafting towards him.

'I did whit you said,' he said.

'What?' Her voice was as flat as a Monday morning.

Leaning across, he whispered in her ear. 'I palmed those pills they gave me.'

'What pills?' She frowned, but with a shake of her head she perked up a bit. 'What did you do with them?'

He sneaked a look left and right, waited until Jocky had passed out of sight and taken a seat with the other patients behind them, before he made his move. He delved into the right hand pocket of his denims and edged up a bit of white toilet roll.

Her eyes drifted down then back up at his face, her expression locked in neutral. 'You've stole some bog roll?'

'Nah,' he spluttered. 'It's those tablets they gave me at breakfast time.'

'Give me them here.'

He checked again nobody was watching, curled his

wrist and slipped the rag of paper into her hand. She unpicked them from the tissue and popped both in her mouth. Her chin tilted up, stretching her thin neck as she swallowed.

'Jesus.' His voice bubbled up in shock and admiration. 'I thought you were goin' to gie them to somebody.'

'I did. My head's pickled.' She stubbed her fag out on the low tabletop, letting the dout fall onto the floor. 'I just need some time off from myself.'

'But you said you wanted to go out. Go for a walk or something.'

'That was yesterday.' Her head turned, and she glowered at him like a stranger. 'Haven't you got things to do?' She shut her eyes.

'Whit's the matter?' He patted her knee through the denim. It was a skirt with a wide slit that made it look as though she was wearing flared trousers. Her breathing was regular as if she was feigning sleep. He worked his hand up and under the slit, fondling the skin on her thigh.

Her eyes opened and she turned her head 'Is that all you want? Well, fuck off and go and have a fucking wank then.' She whipped her knee away, his knuckles banging against the arm of the seat.

Dim Denny's feet shuffled over to where they were sitting. He had a peculiar walk, one leg shorter than the other, compensated by the black iron of a built-up shoe. He doubled over and picked up the fag end, slipping it into a side pocket of his dress trousers and scuttled off in a wayward diagonal across the day room.

Her words were scalpel sharp. He lacked the armoury of her cutting ways and could not talk to people like that. He stumbled to his feet and followed Dim Denny out of the day room. Turning back to snatch a look at her, he spotted Jocky had stolen into the seat he'd vacated. He ghosted away to be alone in his room.

Hands tucked behind his head, he lay on top of his bed and, even though it was stupid, let maudlin tears run down his cheeks. He wanted to go home. Then a thought, a kind of panic, made him sit up. Janine had colonised his life. But the little girl, Lily, would be stranded. She had been depending on him, as a bridge, to get her wherever it was she needed to go. Maybe drugs did that, he thought, made you forget about everything but yourself.

DAY 29

The girls' bedroom door hushed slowly open. Mary had been sleeping as soundly as Joey's snores allowed her to, but her body was as attuned to the bracing noises of their house at night. She sat up straight, listening to what was on the other side of the wall – footsteps. She scrambled out of bed. Standing in the empty hall, her breath a puffy cloud, the linoleum was cold underfoot, and street light filtered through the window above the front door stretching the darkness into long blocks, and leaving gaps for an active imagination to fill. She heard the click of someone sneaking the sneck up on the front door, and the Yale lock giving, which scattered her thoughts and made her scurry round the corner to catch the culprit.

Ally, with her back to Mary, pulled open the door. She wore her royal blue school blazer, her grey skirt and white socks smartly pulled up to her knees. It was a virtue she usually seemed incapable of. One sock would be up, the other down. Some kind of sock semaphore signal that the effort of equilibrium was too much for a little body to take on board. Ally's hair was in tight bunches and the pink baubles that tied her hair were a mystery – Mary could not remember seeing them before. Her thoughts jumped, Jo must have brought them home and helped Ally bunch her hair. It was the only explanation, yet it defied common sense. Jo could not have helped her, would not have helped her because she was too grown-up, a granny in an adolescent eleven-year-old body. Mary caught a flash of Ally's face. Her eyes were closed as she pulled the door shut. She had not seen her. She was blind as a new-born. Ally was sleepwalking the same way her son had. Mary thanked God that at least her daughter was fully clothed. Thread-bare slippers were a hindrance, but she followed her daughter into the garden.

'Chooks. Chooks.' She called after Ally as if she were a sparrow cornered in a cage. She had heard stories of people taking heart attacks when suddenly wakened. She could just make out the sheen of Ally's hair on the other side of the hedge and walked towards her.

Mary wrapped her arms round her chest to keep

herself warm. Frost bit into unprotected toes. The street-light at the shortcut cast a glow. She craned her neck, and turned to listen. Muffled feet rebounded in the dank bloom of night fog. The fence at the bottom of the short-cut rattled and there was a thump as something fell. Mary followed, slipping on the steepest part of the path, banging her knee and rolling into a jaggy bush, her nightdress snagging and ripping. She sprang up. No time for decency or pain. Her legs regained a semblance of strength, and her shoulders heaved as she breathed in snorting and wheezing gasps. She knew the chain-link fence had a gap in it, but the fog grew a thick skin and her fingers only found connected threads. Her hand banged against the diamond-shapes, imprinting them on her soft flesh; she could have wept. The nightmare of her young daughter waking, and being out there cold and alone, kept her moving, kept her searching. The gap was there, and she fell against it, twisting her ankle as she landed.

Hobbling on her good leg, car headlights picked out the road and pavement in front of her as it scraped downhill. The driver was wearing a white top, cigar burning bright, clenched in his teeth. She wanted to cry out, to warn him to be careful of her child, but knew her voice would be like that of a rattling crow, coming too little and too late. The car turned by slow degrees at the corner, the arc of light picking out a blur of blue. Evidence enough for Mary that Ally was nearby. Her hand floated above the line of privet, and helped orien-tate her as she traced the path of the gardens bordering

Shakespeare Avenue. The edge of the pavement came as a jolt and she almost slipped crossing the road. The strained ankle would take its toll the next morning, she was sure. 'Ally, little Ally are you there? Mummy's here. Mummy's here,' she shouted. 'I love you very much darling, please, please wait for me.'

'Here, Mummy. Here.' The voice came from near Kerr's gate.

Mary staggered across, arms waving and floundering searching for her youngest child. Her hand found a head and hair, and she drew Ally into the snug of her torso. 'Jesus,' she said. 'You're ice cold.'

Hoisting her up onto her hip and shoulder, Ally grabbed onto Mary, her stiff wintery fingers making a choker of her neck. Mary shuffled back up the hill, as fast as her ankle and freezing fog would allow. Ally's breathing was soft and regular as a Persian cat's on her cheek and neck. Her daughter sank into slumber, heedless of their halting journey. Mary's thoughts turned to hypothermia – whether she should dial 999 at the phone box or warm her up with hot toddies, hot water bottles and plenty of blankets. Ally roused as she carried her up the shortcut, her head banging against Mary's cheekbone.

'I'm cold, so cold,' Ally murmured.

Mary hirpled faster. 'Soon be home.'

'Promise you'll never leave me.'

'Of course not.'

'Never?'

Mary held her closer. 'Never.'

'I'm cold, so cold.'

The front door was wide to the world. Indoors felt as cold as outdoors. Mary knew the electric boiler would take two hours before there would be enough hot water to fill a teaspoon. Ally needed her own bed and to be covered with the warmth of every available sheet, blanket and towel in the house. As Mary shoulder-barged through the door to the girls' room, Ally sprung down from her arms like a kitten.

Joey stumbled out of their bedroom. 'Whit the hell,' he said, trouser legs snaring his feet. He tried pulling them on properly and banged against the doorframe, almost falling. His hand felt about for the light switch in the hall and flicked it on.

'It's little Ally,' Mary explained. One breast flopped from a tear in her nightie and from the waist down, her body was woaden with bruises and cold.

'Mum! What about little Ally?' Jo stood barefoot in the door of their room, her voice weighed down with sleep and her tousled mane covering some of the fear and disgust in her eyes as she, like her father, scrutinised her mum's appearance.

Mary snapped on the light in the girls' room. Ally's blonde head was tucked up in bed. Her clothes for school were neatly laid out in the chair, untouched from the night before. Joey patted her on the shoulder as he leaned over her, checking out the room.

'Whit you saying's wrang with Ally this time?' he asked.

DAY 31

'Hi Sweets.' Janine met John as he shuffled out of his room. 'We'll need to stop meeting this way.' She laughed. He didn't join in. Instead he favoured a bruised and brooding equanimity, hurt that she had been avoiding him, his lip buttoned down, his eyes straying away from her face and finding an interest in Eddie pacing at the bottom end of the corridor, waiting for visitors so he could cadge fags off them. 'Your parents coming today?'

'Maybe.' His voice was cautious. He studied her face and lifted his shoulders in a half-hearted shrug.

'Hope so. You smell a bit ripe. Hope they've brought some of that Hai Karate.'

He tried on a shy smile, his fingers dipping into his pocket and pulling out a white square of toilet roll. 'Afternoon meds,' he whispered, and he ducked his head down as he slipped the package to her.

'Aw, a present.' Her voice was playful, palming and slipping it into the inside pocket of the pair of Levis she had changed into. 'That's a lot better than that other present you gave me.'

'Whit?'

She tilted her chin up, stretching her long neck and moued her mouth. She dotted her index finger round her lips and chin. His eyes tracked her posing. 'My mouth's rubbed to a dishrag by your kisses, and my chin's scraped raw by your bum fluff and your passion.' She reached for his hand and drew him in closer. 'Feel.'

His cheeks flamed and his arm jerked like Franken-stein reaching for a bathrobe, but his fingers were surprisingly gentle, circling and patting her mouth and chin.

'Sorry.' His hand flopped down to his side.

The fire doors were pegged open and they heard the tramp of feet. The first of the visitors were being ushered in by Karen, a stout woman who doubled up as a staff nurse on another ward.

'That's not the only place that's bruised and needs kissing better.' Her eyes met his, and he was drawn into her challenge, his head tilting and dropping sideways to meet her parted lips.

He kissed chastely at first. Then more feverishly, forc-ing her backwards, shoving her up against the wall with a gammy-legged urgency. How long they kissed, she was unsure –four or five minutes – she glanced sideways and pulled away, standing demurely. His head dropped, his eyes like something taken out of a kiln, he moved closer, the heat from his body like a physical presence. Her eyes darted towards the few visitors coming through the door. His mother was one of the new arrivals. She was stranded midstream in the corridor, her knuckles white as she clutched her flower-patterned bag against her stomach for protection as the last of the stragglers filed past her. Her eyes were fixed on them.

'I'll leave you to it.' Janine slipped away, back into her room, shutting the door firmly behind her. She dallied at the window, examining without any purpose the same old sights of trees and grass and the Gothic architecture of the hospital wards. Sitting on the bed, she slid open the top drawer of the dresser where she kept knick-knacks. The palm of her hand slid along the side panel to the back. Her fingers pried off the old black-and-white photograph Blu-Tacked, face-up, to the plywood top shelf. She took a breather, unwrapped the cellophane from a fresh packet of Silk Cut Jocky had slipped to her, and put the photo in her lap. A cigarette soothed her nerves, allowed her to inspect her once fresh-faced father looking up at her. His trademark cigar never out of his mouth, stinking the place up. He wore a shirt and tie and a pearly grey double-breasted suit. She was little more than a baby then, bursting with pride as she peered up at him, and clutched his hand as if she would never let go. Her mum wore a dated cloche hat, her hair peeking out like raven's wings. Janine had no memory of hearing her mum laughing, but she was smiling down at her in the photograph.

'Witch,' said Janine. The lit end of her fag hovered above the image of her mum's face. She burned out one eye, then the other. 'You knew. You knew and did nothing.' Janine's nose twitched in disgust. Her dad's eyes had already experienced the same surgical procedure, two black holes in a once handsome face. She blew ash debris off her remodelling work. Her eyes remained pinned to Lily's impish grin in the photograph, until the fag ash drifted down, greying the floor, and the side of her hand recoiled from the heat. She leaned across and stubbed the cigarette out, shaking her head at the mess she had made.

She hid the photograph. The Blu-Tack was losing its stickiness, but it held. What worried her more was she was forgetting what Lily sounded like, or even what she looked like. Her mind was also losing its glue. She flicked on the bedside radio and sprawled over the bed. The drone of chart-toppers Status Quo filled the room. In the rush to turn it off, she knocked the half-filled glass of water onto the floor. She giggled, dipping her hand into her pocket and pulled out the package John had given her. Swallowing both tablets dry, she swung her legs off the bed and sat waiting for the bandsaw buzzing of voices in her brain to stop chattering. She watched the drip, drip, drip of water falling onto the matted carpet by her bed. Outside her window, somebody screamed. A mock fight played out, with the raised voices of nurses jousting with each other before coming on shift. One of them was The Poof. Janine laughed and laughed and laughed.

John swept down the corridor to meet his mum, but his eyes skidded away from the concern in her eyes. She greeted him with a tight smile. 'We better go through here.' He addressed her like a stranger, guiding her along the corridor. They stood awkwardly for a moment, at the entrance to the day room.

'I've brought you some stuff.' She held out a brown-paper parcel bound by string.

'Thanks, Mum. I'll get you settled and go and stick it in my room.'

A few residents sat blank-faced with their visitors.

John guided his mum between them. He noticed it was like sitting on a bus. The corner seats away from the telly in the day room always had somebody sitting in them. The seats nearest the door were the last to be filled. They found a few spare seats beside a bluff old couple, both with cropped white hair, as if they attended the same discount barber. Morag, their daughter, had a tendency to wander away for longer and longer periods of time. He sat across from his mum, the bag placed beneath the chair legs. He imagined himself a prisoner, perhaps Steve McQueen in one of those prison heists. Mary let her coat drop onto her chair and lit a fag. Her face was composed, but tired. She looked over his shoulder before speaking.

'Your friend joining us?' The emphasis was on friend.

'Don't think so.'

'That's good,' she said with finality. She drew his hand across the table and squeezed his knuckles.

Something about the weariness in her voice, the way she sagged in the chair, bothered him. 'You're no' well?'

'Not the best.' The palm of her hand masked her nose and mouth. Bent over like a drunkard, she barked cough after cough, her chest shuttling up and down and her eyes watering. 'Ha-ah,' she sighed and took another drag of her fag, before stuffing the lit end into the ashtray. She pulled a white hanky the size of a horse blanket out of her coat pocket behind her and honked into it. It was swept onto her lap, hidden under the table, but kept stashed in her fist.

'Whit's wrang with you?' he asked.

'Nothing much.' There was a slight tremor in her hand as she picked up the Zippo lighter to light another cigarette. 'Probably just a bug.'

'You been to the doctor's?' He adopted the same stringent tone as his da.

She laughed at this through her nose and shook her head, her eyes lighting up in amusement. Fag smoke temporarily blurred the edges of her and she seemed better. Then the barking started again, and the hanky came up.

When she finished, he leaned across, swallowing down the lump in his throat. 'You'll need to go to the doctor's, Mum.'

'Calling him now would just be a waste of time.' She met his eyes. 'If I don't get better I'll call him.' She added, 'But I will get better.'

'Mum!' Even to his own ears it sounded like a child's lowing.

'Promise.' She squeezed his hand in a mini-handshake to seal the deal.

'But whit's the matter with you?' he asked.

'Nothing much. Don't sleep.' She eased back into the chair and tapped fag ash into the ashtray. 'I thought with you in here, I wouldn't need to worry any more about people sleepwalking, but it seems,' she took a long breath, 'it's a hundred times worse.'

'Whit?' His body strained forward, but her mouth stopped framing words, her eyes sliding past him. She smoothed out the lap of her dress as if she had dropped ash onto it and took a long drag on her fag.

The scent of Janine's perfume should have alerted him, but in the broth of ward smells and the low buzz of noise it failed to register. Janine's arm flung casually over his shoulder startled him, and her body clung to the back of the chair.

'Nothing.' Mary fixed on a tight smile.

Janine slid into the seat next to him, pulling it in closer so their thighs squished together, taking his hand in hers. She beamed a lippy grin across the table at Mary. Then turned to him and in a cocky, playful voice asked, 'Missed anything? Missed me?'

Mary's feet scraped across the floor as she stood up. 'I was just goin'. I've brought you some fresh pants and socks. That's the main thing.' She bent and lifted the parcel and shoved it across the table.

'Mum.' He tugged his fingers out of Janine's hand and stood looking down on her. 'You're just here.'

She covered her mouth to cough again. 'Ah, well.' Her eyes watered, making her seem feebler and older. She knitted the hanky round her hand and nodded as if that concluded the conversation.

'You don't like me,' butted in Janine.

Mary gave her a quick look. 'No, I don't.'

John expected kind words and evasions, some heeing and hawing from his mum, not the gunboat diplomacy of his da.

'That's alright,' said Janine, scooping his hand into hers. 'I don't like me much either.' She tugged him in close, perfumed shoulder to shoulder, her arm rubbing against his. 'But your son, well, he likes me well enough for both of us.'

'Mum's not been that well.' His voice had a fluting sound. He volunteered the information as a peace offering, the equivalent of a missionary directing the natives to the beads and baubles on offer. 'My little sister's been doing a power of sleepwalking and she's not been getting much sleep.'

Mary bent her head in the way he recognised when she was considering something important. 'How did you know that? How did you know about little Ally?'

'You told me.' He sat down, looked at Janine for support.

She shook her head. 'No, I never.'

'You told me that someone was having sleepwalking problems,' he said. 'And I figured it must have been Ally cause she's the most like me.'

'Has somebody been talkin' to you on the phone or something?'

'Whit?' John made a face. 'How could they dae that?'

Mary flapped her hands in surrender. 'Never mind.' She bent across and kissed him on his hair, above his ear.

'I'll see you out.' He rose from the chair, shaking Janine's hand from its grasp. 'And thanks for the clothes, I really needed them,' he added in a gushing tone.

'My mum sleepwalked regularly,' piped up Janine, stopping them both. She waited until she had their attention before continuing. 'Dad soon cured her of that.'

'Oh, aye?' Mary said. 'How did he do that?'

Janine clapped her hands together like a loud gun-shot. They both flinched. Morag had briefly settled at the table next to them. Her head shot sideways, and she banged her legs against the chair legs in her haste to get up and escape. 'A good clean shock. Never fails.' Janine laughed, but it sounded like a sneer.

'I feel sorry for you.' Mary's voice was low, without malice.

'Ditto.' Janine made that stupid showy-off sign with two fingers bent like antennae in the air.

On the train home, Mary thought she would have been able to shut her eyes and get a quick nap, but her chesty cough scuttled that idea. It spoiled her even enjoying a fag. Enough was enough. She determined to book an appointment with her General Practitioner. She realised Dr Fleming was quirky because, unlike most doctors, she could talk to him. She could mention John being in the hospital and ask for his help in getting him out. The argument was already framed in her mind and made her fume. All those people crying out for a hospital bed and he was taking up one – and there was nothing wrong with him.

The train jolted forward as it left Drumry Station. Mary started fussing in the open mouth of her handbag for the train ticket. But the bag was a fly trap. Her fingers snared on her frayed leather purse, her cigarettes, lighter, box of Bluebell matches, another lighter in case the first one did not work properly, a cloth hanky for emergencies, an unopened packet of paper hankies, Polo mints with two left, one of which had been half chewed, the other in the corner of her bag, a packet of Swizzles, a bent sixpence, a cloth badge with a pin at the back and a picture of the Virgin Mary on the front which had worked its way loose and hung like a button on its last thread, an opened packet of PK chewing gum that Joey had asked her to keep, a cardboard-backed photograph of Ally and her classmates wearing their school uniforms and sitting smugly on gym benches in three-tiered rows, with Mrs McGonagle, their teacher, as a bookend.

The old man in the seat across from her mirrored her smile. He had a buzzing hearing-aid the size of a brick wedged inside his ear. The train slowed as it pulled into Singer Station, and her fingers grew frantic, running through the different compartments of her purse. She checked her pockets again, felt a tear in the lining of her coat, and played her fingers through it like an accordion, until she picked out the outline of the missing ticket.

'Jesus,' she said, to the man opposite. 'That was close.'

He puckered his lips, nodded in acknowledgement and fiddled with his earpiece, fixedly staring out of the window at commuters leaving the train and others waiting to step on.

The doors closed, the guard's window at the back of the train banged shut and he blew his whistle. The train pulled out of the station. Mary clutched the train ticket, her hands restless on her lap. Through the perimeter fence, Singers' factory buildings flashed by. She had once hoped to get a job there, even as a cleaner, because it was regular, well-paid, work and that was you sorted for life.

Hot air blowing from the heater under her legs made her feel drowsy, but it was less than a five-minute journey to Dalmuir Station. Her handbag was wedged in safely beside her, below the low frame of the train window. The old man tucked his feet under the chair as she stood up. Lifting her bag, body rolling with the passageway sway and tilt of the train, she anchored her feet as the train stopped, then stepped onto the platform.

The train pulled away. Mary sat alone on the damp slats of the wooden benches in the shed on Platform One. The ticket collector, a small man, shivered, his cap peak pulled low over the expression on his rain-dashed face. He was watching her, moving his feet, blocking access to the stairs and the exit onto the flats. Her bag was plopped on the bench beside her. She stirred through the contents, pulling out the class photograph. Running her index finger along the rows of banked, smiling children, her finger stopped on a girl's face, front row and three along from Ally. A blackened circular burn mark obscured the face. But it looked too precise – as if somebody had held the pinprick of a lit match or cigarette to the picture. Smoothed out, it was little more than a grainy blip. Wind whipped through the shelter lifting her skirt. A drip of rainwater fell from the end of the ticket collector's nose, but he didn't move. Mary traced the pink bauble in the photograph that tied the girl's hair.

Light faded early in the winter months. The streetlights squeaked in the wind and formed murky, moving shadows. Mary hurried up the hill and into her house. The front door was unlocked. She had once joked if anybody broke in they would end up leaving them something, but there was more to it than that, it was a trust that nothing bad could happen to her family. God was in every room, hanging from every wall. His saints fought with each other to find an inch on the mantelpiece. She dropped her bag at the door, but kept her coat on.

Matching beds, side by side in the girls' bedroom, were tidy enough, the blankets with the creased edges of hospital corners. She flicked on the light to help her search. An oak-veneer chest of drawers with an oval swing mirror reflected back a wooden school ruler lying sideways. Two over-bright scraps of paper angel were abandoned beside a faded silver locket. Mary picked through a jewellery-box tangle that held no real jewellery. Kirbies that had lost their grip sprung out at her. A red and pink plastic headband. A frayed yellow ribbon, tied to a green ribbon. She breathed more easily. Clothing in the drawers was refolded. She found a spider playing dead in the bottom drawer, but no elastic bauble that matched the burnt-out face in the photograph. The wall cupboard near the window was flung open. Anorak pockets, duffle coats and jackets that had not been worn since they were knee-high, were turned inside out. She thanked God and all His angels in heaven the room was clear. Before she flicked the light off, she knelt down to probe under the beds. In the far corner, underneath Ally's bed, lay the red-pinky bauble. Ally's makeshift friend had blended so seamlessly into the house and into their lives, it was as if she had always been there. Sometimes, when Mary was on her own, she experienced an overpowering sense of being watched, accompanied by a whiff of vanilla overlaid with cigar smoke. Her hands shook as she lit a fag, waiting until the voices and the smell faded, but here was proof that whatever Joey said, it was not just her imagination.

DAY 32

Lying on top of the blankets on his bed, John flicked through a wash-stained copy of *Reader's Digest* he had trawled – and never thought he would read – from the bottom drawer of his bedside cabinet. He took a shine to a story about some old guy who took his son fishing, and a disembodied voice started calling to them. In the sticky warmth of the ward, he must have dozed off. In his dream he was the man's son, fishing in a free-flowing river – something he had never done in real life. His dad had gone missing, but a cry hailed him from over the next crag. He followed the dip of the stream and climbed up a steep embankment, but no matter how quickly he ran, the wavering voice remained the same distance away. Clouds of midges rained down on him. Something flicked at his ears and he woke up. The book had fallen to the side of the bed. Janine's halo of hair was above him and, as if she had just stepped out of the shower, she smacked of soap and shampoo. She giggled. 'Caught you,' she said, and poked a bony finger into his chest.

He had become a regular dealer wrapping his meds in toilet roll inside an old sock, then stashing them among his grotty shirts. But he was unsure whether to give them to her because she had been a pain in the arse with his mum. Something about her childish laugh, though, her bright eyes and lips, the way she was stroking through the stretched cloth of his Y-fronts, made his insides tumble like a fruit machine and all the answers to his questions came up YES, YES, YES.

Afterwards, when their breathing was shallow, they dropped off for a bit face to face on the single bed. He told her he loved her. Her eyes searched his for what seemed the longest time.

'Good.' She gobbled down the pills and turned towards the windowpane, where the splashing sound of rain playing drifted in from outside. He spooned into her back. Her tone was nonchalant. 'I'm going out later to pick up my Giro. You fancy coming with me?'

'Whit dae you mean?' he asked.

'I said I'm going out to pick up my Giro.'

He answered in an exasperated way. 'I know whit you mean, but you're talkin' shite.'

'That's why I'm in here,' she said. Sighing, she flung her legs out of bed and sat up. Her bra was on the floor and knickers puddled at her feet. She seemed taller and less frail dressed than she was naked. 'You want to come or not?' Her voice was harsh.

'Aye,' he said.

'Well, then.' Her ankle danced the twist as she pushed her toes into one shoe, then the other. 'It's no' any problem for me to leave. I can come and go as I please. But getting you out, when you're not settled, is a different kettle of fish.'

'That's whit I meant,' he said.

'We'll need to arrange a member of staff to go with us,' she said. 'And that's not easy. Cause they're all lazy bastards.'

'Some of them are alright.' He was arguing for the sake of arguing. Rolling over to his side of the bed he made a patchwork of dressing, pulling on whatever clothes were nearest at hand.

Her pitying look suggested he had a lot to learn. 'We'll need to work it so we get the right one,' she said. 'It's easier saying no than yes. And when it goes in the logbook, it's like a precedent in case law. If you're allowed to go out for a walk one day, you'll be allowed out on others. At first a member of staff will always be with you, but they're so lazy that soon they'll be waving you through the door nae bother.'

'Jesus. You make it seem as if I'll be here forever.'

'Suit yourself.' She patted down her pockets for her cigarettes. 'I'll need to get a light.' A fag stuck to her bottom lip as she edged towards the door.

'Hing on a minute. If they're so lazy, how are you going to get a member of staff to go along with you?'

She took the fag out of her mouth to answer, rubbing it between finger and thumb as if friction would set it alight. 'Easy peasy, I'll just agree to give them a blow job.'

'You cannae do that!'

'Well,' her eyes fluttered as she vamped up his discomfort. 'Obviously, I couldn't give The Poof a blow job.' Her eyebrows shot up, making a joke of it. Making a joke of him. Her hair framed a smirking face he wanted to slap. She continued in the same breezy manner. 'I don't do fat people, or the old fossils, so that rules out the female staff. That doesn't leave much to work with.'

She made it sound like a game of Buckaroo. She waited for him to say something, her presence taunting him. 'Yes or no?' she asked.

His body drooped in defeat, but he raised his head and met her eyes. 'No.' He shook his head in disgust, like a mangy dog throwing off fleas from its coat, and his voice grew more emphatic. 'Never.' Like her, he found himself adopting a dramatic tone. 'I'd rather die in here.'

'Suit yourself.' She stuck the cigarette back in her mouth, forgetting she didn't have a light for it.

Something about her actions struck a chord, brought back a memory. But he didn't know the right way to put it. 'Those fags. Jocky gave you them, didn't he? Every time I look up, he's always hinging about you.'

'You're such a child,' she said. 'Of course he's hanging about me. He works here. He's always hanging about you, too. You played pool with him. I don't go around accusing you of giving him blow jobs.' She pulled the door open. 'Fuck off,' she said as a parting shot.

<u>DAY 33</u>

In night visitations, over and over, Janine was haunted by the reek of coppery blood and cigar smoke. Her hand was framed on their front-door panel, but she felt safe as long as her dad stayed one side of the closed door, she the other. A fragile awareness grew that on the other side of the threshold she no longer heard her mother's pleading voice. The sound of the traffic outside no longer worked its way up the stairs, and the shocks and spills of tenement life were muted. Her ragged breathing was the only sign of life. Dad had crept up the hallway. His ear was flattened against the other side of the door – listening. Pee gushed down her legs.

She woke with a start and flung her legs out of the warmth of her bed. Yanking down her knickers and crouching over the waste-paper bucket, urine sprayed over blackened douts, a *Daily Record* and Malteser wrappers, pooling in fag packets and collecting in darkened grime. It seeped out of the bottom and drained onto the carpet by her bed. Crinkling her nose at the stink and the mess she reached for a packet of Silk Cut on the chair beside her bed. Her breath caught in her throat as she picked it up and shook it, thinking that the carton might be empty, but there was one left. A life saver. The only way to start the day. All she needed was a light.

Sitting alone at a breakfast table, with nothing but a cup of strong black tea, she enjoyed the solidity of cigarette smoke around her face. Most of the regulars had already been served, a few tables cleared and stacked away. Lulu's 'Shout' was screeching on the tranny behind the serving hatch. John sat a few seats across from her, elbow crooked, protecting a plate with sausage, ham, egg and fried bread. An empty cereal bowl had been pushed an arm's reach along the table to make room. The matching ceramic white cup was positioned closer for swiping emulsified gook and quaffing hot tea after a few mouthfuls of grease. His eyes batted back and forth towards her, but the more he peeked, the slower he chewed. He finished eating, mopping his plate with fried bread. His chair legs screeched across the tiled floor. Standing slightly bow-legged, like a man frightened of farting, his hand perched on the top bar of a nearby chair, he allowed himself to notice her and to smile a lopsided grin.

'I hope we can still be friends,' he said.

Her cup rattled, leaving a red lipstick stain below the rim, as she placed it down on a plate. The mouthful of tea that she had been sipping was cold, but her voice was warm and upbeat. 'Guys only ever say that when they want to screw you or dump you. Sometimes both.' She raised one plucked eyebrow and shrugged her shoulders. 'Which is it?'

He laughed, conscious of the nurse behind the hatch and an older patient, a balding man, staring over at them. His cheeks flamed and sweat seeped from his pores. 'I'd just like to be friends.' His knee knocked against the chair closest to him as he lunged past it for the door.

Janine turned her head, watching him scuttle away. She dabbed carefully at the corner of her mouth with a paper napkin, her eyes watering as she giggled. A dull morning looked more promising.

She stayed in her room, avoided meeting him again until she was properly dressed. She stood at the entrance to the day room waiting for him to rediscover her. Long fingers were jammed inside the flaps of her oversized checked mohair coat. A Cossack hat flattened her head. But he had acquired a pad and a biro and was either writing or drawing. Eventually, when he did look over, she nonchalantly waved goodbye to him. She paused to pick at the flaked pink polish on her thumbnail with her index finger as she trudged, in matronly shoes, towards the nurses' office.

'Where you aff tae?' John stood behind her, his body weight on the back heel for a quick getaway.

'I was just going to get some air.'

'That's nice.'

She slipped her arm through his, looking up at him. 'Why don't you come?'

'Aye, I'd love to.' He tugged his arm listlessly away, but he was grinning.

She wrenched him closer. 'I'm serious.'

'I think we've been through this wan before.' His glance wandered over her shoulder to the poolroom.

She plucked at his arm until he was minding her and not something else. 'I can get you out of here.'

'How?' he whispered. He looked up and down the corridor, to see if anybody was watching them, but apart from a few patients hanging about nobody showed any interest in them. Day staff were ensconced in their office near the exit to the ward with the door shut.

'I'll make you invisible,' she said.

He snorted. 'Chance would be a fine thing.'

Her hand was held up in front of his face, her fingers making childish twinkling movements. 'I can, you know. Make you invisible. Get you out of here.'

'Whit are you? A witch or something?'

'Wicked Witch of the North,' she cackled.

They laughed, clutching each other's arms for support. She was first to pull away, straightening up her coat, but still clenching his wrist. She whispered, 'Just promise to do exactly what I tell you.'

'OK.' His face played it as a joke, but he sounded half-serious.

'Right.' She was Boadicea, slapping his arms so he stood straight as a soldier. 'Follow me. And remember, don't hesitate. Do exactly what I say. When we get there and they open the door for me to leave, I'll give you the nod, and I want you to kiss me as if your life depended on it.'

'That shouldn't be too hard.' He fell into step behind her, until Janine pushed him backwards, tilted her hip and flapped her hand fantail, signalling he should remain where he was.

He watched Patricia, the charge nurse, jingle the ward keys on the chain before selecting the right one to let Janine out. He tried to outguess Janine, keen to work out what kind of conjuring was going to track him round the nurse and smuggle him outside and into the grounds. He crept closer, stood within spitting distance of the office, leaning against the wall and trying to blend in. He knew that made him stand out like a banana in a packet of Wotsits. But he factored in the reverse logic of special pleading. Crazy people were allowed to stand out; if they did not eclipse their surroundings, there was something more seriously wrong with them than first thought. The charge nurse marked his position, but knowing she could take him out with one arm made her slack. She unlocked the door and held it open for Janine. He was deaf to what was said. Their utterances were brief. But they looked across and Janine promenaded towards him. She took one of his hands in hers, then the other, and pecked him on the lips. Her arms went round his neck and she pulled him close enough to taste perfume, whispering in his ear, 'Remember what I told you.' Her next kiss was forceful and mannish. She skittered along the corridor towards the exit with him pulled, whirling, in her wake.

'For God sake, gee that a break.' Patricia sounded squeamish, but more amused than upset.

The closer they got to the door, the more passionately Janine kissed him. He wondered if her plan might have included using his hard-on as a battering ram to help them escape. She let go of him at the door, the plan, whatever it was, stalling and breaking down. The charge nurse held in her stomach to let Janine pass, but she teetered on the threshold. The pull of his attraction seemed too much for her. She hooked herself to him like a life support-machine, closed her eyes, and spun him in a snog fest. Tottering, he stumbled as she shoved him backwards and pushed him through the doors.

'Push off! Run!' she cried. It was the kind of efficient voice that belonged in the wards of maternity suites, not a psychiatric unit. There was no arguing with her. He legged it through the double doors and into the grounds.

Janine scrambled out behind him, the doors flapped shut behind her. She was laughing so much she could hardly walk. Low sunshine sparkled and shone on acres of grass, and he filled his lungs with its musty green miasma. Taking her hand, they made their getaway like two drunks tagged together, past the lights of other windows and the graveyards of other wards. They were caught between two seasons. The trees in the grounds had lost their rustle and it was cold enough for sleet or snow. Wind whipped behind and between them. After being shut inside the Mediterranean heat box of the ward for so long he came unprepared in a thin T-shirt. The tarmac path curved in a half-moon towards Great Western Road and Hyndland Station. Leaf mould clogged their feet and sleet dampened their ardour.

'Where are we goin'?' he asked, teeth chittering.

'Back to mine,' she replied.

Shackled together they squished through broad leaves gathered on the bottom lane of the hospital. Two-storey houses locked in by rusting fences helped act as a windbreak, and Janine opened her coat out in invitation. They briefly clung to each other until they got to the low stone wall of the shallow pond. He dutifully tugged himself away from her, letting her gather her coat, button it up to her neck, and conserve heat. They were leaving the hospital grounds before he felt it safe to ask, 'Whit do you think they'll dae?'

She kept walking, her pace quickening. 'They'll do what they usually do.' Her voice held no rancour. 'They'll do nothing and hope it'll turn out alright, but they'll be shitting themselves and working out a story about who to blame and how it wasn't anybody's fault.'

He tried to laugh, but it was too cold and his jaw ached. 'Will they no' go to your house right away lookin' for you?'

She slowed to consider. They walked hand in hand to the Pond Hotel. Her voice was level. 'They'll not be looking for me. They'll be looking for you.'

It took him a second to realise what she was talking about. 'Whit will I dae then, should I go back?'

'You're just out! And you want to go back already?'

'Sorry.'

'Stop apologising.'

He nodded in agreement, drinking in traffic fumes as the traffic lights turned green and cars scooted past.

'I'll just nip in here and make a phone call,' she said. 'Let them know the lay of the land. Tell them that you were feeling a bit homesick and you'll only be away for a few hours. They'll like that. "Home visit" will already be sketched down on some bit of paper, ready to be endorsed as an official entry on your care plan as if they thought it was a good idea and authorised it. They'll not want to contact the police just yet, cause then they'll feel stupid. Whatever you do, don't ever make them feel stupid. Cause they always get their own back on you.'

'Aye.' He hadn't listened to half of what she said. Snow drifted, gathering in their hair. 'Can you just hurry up, so we can go somewhere?'

'We'll go in here. I'll make that phone call. Back to mine. Then . . .' her eyes shone.

He grunted his assent before she finished speaking, imagining what would come next. He imagined the unimaginable – not sex, just feeling warm.

'Then we can go and see this little girl you keep nattering on about.' She smiled, showing yellow teeth. 'Perfect conditions.'

She made it seem like going for a game of golf. But he nodded. He would have agreed to anything.

DAY 34

Four customers queued in Partick Post Office, a large cavernous room, but only one stood in front of Janine at the pay window. She was an elderly woman who reeked of clammy clothes and got flustered about what she had done with her change. She muddled between the purse on the counter with notes in it and another purse in a plastic carrier bag. Janine sighed and studied John as the man behind the counter patiently coached the old woman through what she had done with her pension book and money.

Janine thought her boyfriend – if he was worth calling

that – looked shifty as a gang's look-out, which might have something to do with the long, fur-trimmed Afghan coat she had given him to wear. It was the only thing that fitted him from her wardrobe and seemed, if not presentable, at least not too tight on the hips. But it left him looking like an unconvincing transvestite. He slouched, nose plugged to the door, peering out at the pavement, watching snow curling down and pedestrians stomping through the slush, ready, at a moment's notice and a nod from his gang leader, to turn the sign on the door from Open to Shut and hold the place up with the sawn-off concealed under his coat.

The post office assistant peered through the top of the metal cage at the rectangle of Janine's face. With a prac-tised movement she uncurled the pen from the bird's nest of elastic bands and scrawled her name on three green-printed Giros. She pushed them together through the box gap between screen and counter. The assistant's fingers flew to circular metal trays, divvied up the sum she was due and pushed it through the wicket to her. He leered at her with teeth like slag heaps and eyes filled with inky blackness. She did not bother checking, hurry-ing away, stuffing notes and coins into her coat pocket.

Gentleman John held the door open for her. She slipped her arm through his, dipping her hand into the pocket of his coat to keep warm. The pavements were slippy. Black bags and bins dotted the shop fronts and spilled into the gutters of Dumbarton Road. An elderly couple, arm in arm, weaved grey-sludge trails and jos-tled for space on the pavement. Janine and John crossed the road, wobbling as if they were half-cut, and faced down a hackney whose horn had them giggling and sprinting the last ten yards to the safety of the pavement.

'I'll need to go in here for ciggies.' Janine dragged him towards the chippy. Two mophead schoolkids pushed through the door, unwrapping newspaper, joshing and howling laughter. The smell of vinegar and chips made her suddenly ravenous. 'You want chips?'

'You payin'?' he said.

'Course. I'm loaded.' She coughed, leaning into his body for support. Her eyes watered and she held up a hand, flapping it in a shallow wave to show that she would be better in a minute. 'Jesus. Something went down the wrong way.'

The chip shop doubled as a café. They found an empty table near the plate-glass window and ordered. Janine sparked a fag and offered advice. 'You'll need to see the social worker in the hospital so that you can get your money sorted.'

John rubbed condensation off the window to peer out. 'I'm no' that bothered. I don't plan to be there that long.' He repositioned the place mats and the red and brown sauce bottles.

'But it makes sense. Doesn't it?' she said.

'Yeh,' he conceded, leaning back in his chair, so the frizzy-haired woman serving them could push in and plonk their order down.

Janine did more smoking than eating, leaving half a plate of chip fat congealing round the tomato sauce.

He finished his pie supper and started spearing her plate with his fork. 'Whit you want to see Lily for?'

'Who?' Janine was caught with her fag halfway between her mouth and the ashtray. Then she caught herself. 'The little girl? It's just,' she explained, but her eyes drifted away from his face to a hurt inside herself and she could not vocalise it.

From outside the window came the plaintive toll of a train horn. The vibrations of the train arriving into the station above played on the plates and cups. There was no more to be said. Janine paid the bill, and they caught the next train.

They camped snug inside a smokers' compartment. Cigar smoke filtered in from the corridor from a man standing with his back to them. Two sisters with the same blue-wash perm sat across from them, and went to war over who could best set the world to rights. *Miners were lazy good-for-nothings. Always on strike. Paid more than astronauts.* Their droning voices and the shuggling of the train, made John dopey and he shut his eyes. *And who would have believed it? Her a teacher. Him a lawyer. From Bearsden. Bearsden! Their wee lassie found buried in an old air-raid shelter at the bottom of the garden. Shame on them. Bearsden! What about those wee lassies from Dalmuir that went missing? Everywhere you look there are perverts. Everywhere! Would make you give up on humanity.*

Snow lay piebald on the ground outside Dalmuir Station.

A companionable smog of fag smoke trailed behind passengers as they eased themselves into the cold and wandered off to find a place to stand sentry on Platform Two. The dented bottom plates of Dalmuir Station's waiting-room doors flapped open and shut, the rubber chamfers making shushing noises. A man with a boozer's nose the colour of a turnip rattled through one set of double doors and, avoiding the beagle eyes of the ticket collector behind the screen, shot through the others, onto the concourse.

Janine perched on the end of a wooden bench. Cold wind whipped against her face, reddening the tip of her nose. She searched her coat pockets for the outline of her fag packet and lighter, sighing with pleasure as she lit one and inhaled. Smoke hiccupped from her nose and mouth, choked her recollection of the expression on John's face when he realised that the little girl, Lily, was not waiting for him. He had peered into gardens and examined privet hedges as if she was playing hide-and-seek among bare branches. And he thought he wasn't mad. He didn't know what to do.

She explained how the world worked to him and fashioned a plan. They had to go back to the ward. At least he had to go back to the ward. As a voluntary patient, she could do what she liked – which was to go back to the ward with him. She took a long drag of her fag. Leaning forward and favouring her right foot, she turned her face sideways into the wind and studied the broad, square back of a black gabardine trench coat. The frumpy woman standing a few feet from her could have been anywhere between thirty and fifty, but Janine would have swapped places with her in a heartbeat. She was normal. Her brooding revolted her and it was getting worse, pterodactyls nipping each other as they circled around her head, ready to rip apart the cardboard props of equanimity and leave her bawling. Gartnavel was the only place where she could be herself and feel safe.

Tracks squealed as the points unfroze and rail moved against rail. Forged and flanged metal wheels turned heated axles and the Airdrie train clanged into the station, each carriage lit with a cosy glow.

The sound of the train caught John flat-footed. His head was buried tortoise-deep in the fur collar of his Afghan coat, his hands slugs in his pockets, while he kicked over the crowns of sludge. Other passengers made their way to the edge of the platform, waiting for the train to come to a stop. He weaved his way through them and stood facing Janine, hopping from foot to foot as he fashioned his lips into a wan smile. She flicked her dout into the salted bank of piss-yellow snow and got to her feet, clutching at his coat, straightening up and sliding her arm through his.

When they got on the Airdrie train, Janine slipped into an empty window seat in the carriage to the right of the door, her head resting against the No Smoking sign. Coorie in together, they were content with silence and holding hands as they passed through the first few stations. The conductress at Westerton clipped their tickets, but forgot to ask Janine, or the elderly man sitting behind them, to put their fags out. Hyndland was the next stop. The battlements of Gartnavel came into view, framed in the train window like a still life of a mediaeval castle on a frosted hill.

Few other passengers got off the train and those who did hurried away. Janine and John stood isolated beneath the vandalised hands of time on the station clock, watching the back of the train bend away from them, the wind hunting for weak spots in their clothing, scouring their faces. With a jerky movement, Janine gripped his wrist, holding him back as he made to trudge forward, but her voice was soft and cajoling. 'Give me a ten-minute start to get into the ward and have a word with the staff.'

'You mean I should wait here?' His tone was petulant and his bottom lip curled like day-old lettuce.

She pecked him on the lips. 'Aye, it's for the best. Probably best no' to mention you spent the night with me, or even you spent much time with me. Some folk in there get awful jealous. If they ask you just say we split up outside the hospital.'

'But I'm wearing your coat,' he said.

'Don't worry, they're a bit daft. They wouldnae blink if you walked up wearing bright red lipstick, a Doris Day wig, false boobs and a pair of size twelve high heels. They're all mental in there.' She snorted at her own joke and crossed her eyes trying to humour him.

Before leaving, she forewarned him again. 'Just remember to say how sorry you are for causing them all that trouble. You know the script. It'll never happen again and you'll live happily ever after.' Her fist opened in a wave. She disappeared down the steps and into the darkness of the pedestrian underpass.

'I'll get you in there,' he shouted, but he wasn't sure she had heard him.

He retreated to the shelter of the waiting room. A Helensburgh train came in one side of the platform, and he pondered jumping on it and returning home, but he dallied too long, the doors slid shut and the vibrations of its departure travelled through the brick island of the concourse. He squatted on the wooden bench, positioned himself underneath the orange glow of the two-bar heater in the waiting room, his body growing slack and his eyes closing.

John recognised himself in his dream as older than at present, but also much younger. The boy he once was ran pell-mell with his classmates into St Stephen's dinner hall. The wooden floor allowed it to double as the school gym. Mr Galloway, in his thick tweed suit, stood timeless as an unsmiling Buddha, in his usual spot. Because he'd only one leg, he propped his backside against the stage to supervise the class.

'Right, get the mats out,' he said in a gravelly voice.

The gym mats were piled in the dusty nook between the end of the stage and windows. John was in a race with Matt Gibbons and Sammy Doak, pushing and hauling at each other to get to them first. He squealed in delight, diving and getting his hands on the top mat. The losers stood aside, dejected. Sammy Doak and him hauled it away to the far end of the hall, near the entrance to the kitchen. That was the signal. Unleashed, the boys in his class tumbled their wilkies and did all kinds of tricks that had never in human history been performed. Cloth beanbags – red, yellow, blue, green – enough for everyone to head, kick or fling, enough for everyone except the girls in their class. Sneaking a look at the stupid girls, he saw them playing with their stupid skipping ropes. He checked who among them paid him no mind, and who was watching him, following how good he proved at bucking and jumping. He would show them.

But a moan escaped from his throat and froze in his mouth from the frost-binding chill. He held the palms of his hands out, they were blackened to the wrist and stunk of cigar smoke.

The rasp of his breathing caught in his throat and filled the brooding silence of an empty hall in which he could not move. Dirt and dust from underneath the crawl space of the stage swirled and gathered around him, became filled with darting lights and the rhythmic beat of skipping ropes. Lily gradually took shape, holding one end of the skipping rope. Another, older, girl with darker hair, who he didn't recognise, held the other end. Girls with blondish hair similar to Lily's eddied from beneath the stage and formed a human chain, skipping to a quickening beat, and fusing into a blinding light that hurt his eyes. They clapped their hands singing:

Not last night but the night before,
Four rapists came knocking at my door

I asked them what they wanted, and this is what
   they said:
Dancer do the splits, the twist
Then turn around and touch the ground, and out
   the back door
Dancer please come back, back, sit on a tack, and
   do not look,
Jump with eyes closed, everyone counting out loud:
   1, 2, 3, 4 . . .
until you're missed.

Ally took a turn in the middle. She skipped and
jumped between the ropes, squealing in delight at not
being caught out. He watched as the skipping rope beat
faster and faster. He felt his heart racing in time to the
rhythm. There was a buzzing in his ears as the girls rose
into the air and condensed into a ball of light that shot
through the roof leaving behind the choir of their voices
and a temporary darkness. The stink of cigar smoke grew
stronger. He recognised his mum by the way she angled
her body, slightly tip-toe, though she wore widows'
weeds and a black lace mantilla covered her face. Mother
hen to the girls, she stood guard in Mr Galloway's position at the edge of the stage, staring directly at him. She
pulled the veil aside and opened her mouth to bawl a
warning. But the inky blackness of a crow flew out of her
mouth and straight at him. His head jolted backwards as
it smashed though his body and pierced his heart.

   He jerked awake and gazed at the retreating heads of
the passengers from a train leaving the station. Taking a

deep breath like a man that had been under water too long, he went outside into the bracing, clean, cold air.

The damp tunnel beneath the station echoed with his steps and led into the grounds of Gartnavel Hospital. He avoided the thicker patches of snow, but his socks grew wet. It took about five minutes to reach the stuffy discomfort of the wards and the sentry smells of fags and bleach fogging over pissy ammonia. His coat hung ragged like a sack over his arm, bending down he stared through the reinforced glass, hoping he would spot Janine. Eventually he rang the bell to be let in. It was near lunchtime and he was hungry. His body readjusted to hospital time even in the way he stood and then slouched, morphing into patient mode, slowing down to the pace of hospital life. He waited a minute and rang the bell again. A white snail-like shape loomed opaque on the ward side, the key jangled in the lock and the door jerked opened.

'Oh, it's you.' There was no surprise in the psychiatric nurse's gruff voice. 'We were wondering when you'd get back here.'

DAY 35

Ally was inured to the lingering presence of cigarette smoke on the cold night air. She heard, without really listening, canned laughter from the telly in the living room, reminders of a brightly-lit world outside sleep. Wind blew through gaps in the window frame, nudging the crayon-yellow curtains, and the lampshade swayed in sympathy, spilling light onto the worn linoleum of their room.

The sisters' beds shared a dark narrow corridor between them, and these were the life rafts Jo used, jumping from her own bed onto Ally's to lean across and flick the light switch off. Ally's job was to say the Lord's Prayer as quickly as she could so that the monsters didn't reach their bony fingers up, grab her by the ankle and pull her down underneath the floor to the great pit. It was a weighty responsibility. Once, Ally got stuck at 'Give us this day our daily bread'. She kept repeating it, her voice fragile, near to tears, but God was waiting. The room light was out and Jo wasn't safely tucked up in bed. Monsters piled out of the darkness, jumped from the clothes cupboard beside her bed and sneaked out of the dressing table drawers to attack Jo. She had to squeal and fight, kicking them all to hell, bouncing up and onto Ally's bed to put the light back on. Mum had shouted at them to keep the noise down or they'd get what for.

The only thing worse than forgetting the last bit, Jo had told her, was saying the Lord's Prayer backwards. Then the devil would swoop down straightaway with his big claws and all that would be left would be the sound of your last cry. Ally didn't want to think about saying it backwards, forwards was bad enough, but found herself asking, 'What if you made a mistake? Would the devil understand?'

'As long as you said God kissed it and the devil missed it,' Jo told her.

Ally snuggled up with her dolly and went straight from praying to sleep. Jo took a bit longer, blankets drum-tight, the faint light from the streetlight outside enough for her to see her breath. Sometimes a car would run round the bend of the hill and the headlights would dip and run across the space between the top of the cupboard and the wall. What if, she asked herself, there was a crash and a husband and his pretty wife were flung bleeding from the car, screaming for somebody to save their baby who was trapped inside? A few of their neighbours would mope about not quite sure what to do. They would try and hold her back because of the stink of petrol and the flickering flame under the bonnet. But she'd escape their grasp. The baby's mewing would be coming from the back seat. She'd burn her hand on the locked door. A fire engine's siren would be heard in the distance. There'd be no time for that malarkey. She'd rip the car door from its hinges and toss it to one side – God was always good for helping with things like that – and she'd pluck the baby from the back seat and, sheltering it in her arms as the car exploded behind her, run towards its mum and dad. She'd be modest, of course, and not want any kind of reward or anything.

The flickering light of a Clipper lighter woke Jo. Ally was waving it from side to side like a sparkler, illuminating her blonde bubble of hair and the deep pit of passageway between their beds. The light went out and Ally giggled, a foreign sound in the darkness.

Jo sat up in bed, her eyes nippy with sleep. The light sparked again. She swiped at Ally's arm, hissing through her teeth, phrases running together, 'Where did you get that? Mum'll plum kill you. Gie me that. Get to sleep or I'll kill you as well.'

Ally's head moved left to right, the flame a shield held out in front of her, hair glowing in a nimbus, her face in shadow. 'I'm cold, so cold.' Her voice rose and fell with the flame flickering and dying.

The chill in the room caught Jo like a slap. Her fingers gripped onto the flounces at the arms of her nightie and her body slipped under the blankets for heat. Her sister's low voice filled her head with worms. She couldn't think, didn't want to take her eyes off Ally, but a feeling in her stomach told her not to stare. The lighter blinked on and off. That gave her courage. 'You better stop that.'

'I'm cold. So cold.' Ally's voice see-sawed in a whine. 'Can I come in beside you?'

'We're too old for that now.'

'Just tonight. Just once. Big people don't understand.'

Jo snorted. She tugged a handful of blankets with her and shuttled over facing the window. She rapped on the other side of the bed.

The mattress creaked as the weight of her sister's body slotted in beside her. Jo recoiled from a casually flung foot resting against her bare leg and the arm flung over her midriff to cuddle in. Limbs that were arctic extremities.

'Ally, you better stop acting it.'

'It's not Ally. It's me. Lily.'

The breath on the back of Jo's neck smelt sickly-sour. Jo turned her head and sprung out of bed screaming. A glimmer lit Ally's empty eye sockets, the smudged colour of mud.

Jo sprinted up the hall, smacked the light on and plunged into her parents' room. Mum was already up and out of bed and caught her sobbing body. Da was slower, falling from his berth, but, realising he was naked, he slid back under the covers.

'Mum. Mum,' cried Jo. 'Can I sleep in beside you? Little Ally's turned into a ghost.'

'Jesus Christ,' said Joey, fretting. 'I've got work in the morning.'

'I'll tell you what we'll do,' said Mary, stroking Jo's face. 'We'll bring Ally in here beside Daddy and I'll sleep in beside you for a wee while.'

DAY 36

Ally's head felt fuzzy in the morning. A musty, old-wallpaper pong made her eyes flutter open. She had been sharing a bed with Jo and now she was in her parents' bed. Da struggled to sit up. Her nose lay squished up against his bare back. He broke away from her with a cough, and sat at the edge of the bed, with his feet on the floor. He sensed her looking at him. In the gloom of the room, he turned to peer back at her, the hedge of his eyebrows lifting. He reached across and caressed her curling legs through the blankets. His knees cracked as he leaned across the bed, kissed the side of her hair and whispered, 'You'll be alright now, beauty.'

She giggled, because Black Beauty was a horse on telly, and she wasn't a horse, but Da could sometimes be funny. Mum had an arm roped around her waist, pulling her body tight into the pillows of her breasts. The familiar cloud of fading talc and cigarette smoke enveloped her. Ally sleepily turned towards her mum for warmth and a cuddle. But she had moved away a tad, then another. A gap appeared between them, and Ally's fingers curled like seaweed fronds round the space where her mum had been.

'I'll need to get up too, darling,' said Mum, but her voice sounded wintry.

Ally puzzled over what she had done wrong before she found an answer in sleep.

She scrambled out of the gloomy bedroom, with her chewed teddy bear for company, to piddle in the toilet, and scurried through to the cosy warmth of the living room. Jo traipsed out of the kitchen, balancing a soup bowl stacked with a mound of cornflakes. She patted Ally on the top of the head like a spaniel and stole the best seat by the two-bar electric fire.

'Mum. Mum. I wanted that seat.' Ally's bottom lip made an island and sulked, her eyes on the edge of tears. She stamped her feet, but her mum didn't come rushing to comfort her or tell Jo off.

Ally stumbled into the kitchen with her grievance up for renewal, her teddy bear bumping behind her from carpet shine to dull linoleum. Surrounded by a girdle of cigarette smoke, Mum stood in the corner, her back pressed against the smaller of the two sinks.

'Mum. Mum,' said Ally again, but was stopped short. Mum clattered briskly across, meeting her at the door. Crouching down on her knees, her hand resting on the back of Ally's head, she jerked her daughter's body in close, the girl's mouth sandwiched against her shoulder, muffling the intake of breath and unfinished sound of sniffling.

When Mum spoke it was with a whispery sigh. 'Is Lily with you today?'

Ally had to wiggle her head out from underneath her mum's oxter. 'No, Mum.'

Mum lifted and carried her, plonking her bum down on the wooden chair at the kitchen table. Her spoon and cornflakes bowl were already set out for breakfast, slightly elevated, a bit too high for Ally's liking, but she dutifully picked up the spoon. Mum's head listed to one side, heavy with sighs. 'Well, you tell Lily from me,' Mum sniffed a few times and took a deep breath. 'You tell Lily from me, never, never, never to come back here again and bother us.' She leaned her head down, her face an angry knot that Ally failed to unravel. 'You got that?'

Ally's fingers loosed and her teddy bear slipped and fell to the floor. Tears smudged her cheeks. 'Yes, Mum.' She dipped her spoon into the bowl, but there was no space in her belly for cornflakes; her mouth tightened into a question, but she didn't know what it was. The spoon clattered onto the table, bequeathing a stodgy silence neither of them could fill.

'Bye.' Jo peered cock-eyed into the kitchen before leaving for high school. A few seconds later the sound of the front door banging shut reverberated through the house.

Mum resumed her sentry position with her back to the sink. She chain-smoked, one cigarette lit from the other, put the kettle on the ring, twice made tea that remained untouched in its cup and then swirled it down the sink. 'You finished?' she asked, watching Ally playing. She was spooning milk and dropping bombs of it back into the bowl, but Mum's voice was icy and her look inky. 'Remember. You hear me? You see that Lily, you tell her from me.'

Ally's head fell into her chest, her eyes grew big as tea plates and she dared not look upwards. 'Yes, Mum,' she lisped, lips barely moving, a cloying loneliness in her throat. She was scared to move from the chair, scared to breathe. She watched Mum duck into the living room. Ally's legs were jammed together, knees knocking, but her bladder was tighter than both of them; a trickle, then a flood of pee pooled where she sat, soaking through the nylon fabric of her nightie and dripping onto the linoleum. She shook her head and cried. When she looked up Mum stooped over her, studying her, her arms by her side. 'It wasn't me, Mum. It was Lily that did it,' sobbed Ally.

Mum's hand shot out and cinched her wrist, jolting her off the chair. Ally's body sagged, but she stood bare-toed, the front of her nightie wet and her face blotted with shame. Mum gripped her lower jaw, kept Ally upright, jerking her face from side to side. She stared into her daughter's eyes. Her grip loosened, allowing

Ally to squeal and fall to the floor. 'I'm sorry, Mum. I won't do it again. I promise, I promise to be good.'

'You won't get her without a fight.' Mum yanked her to her feet and marched her through the living room and into the hall. Ally, unable to keep up, slipped, but her mum swung her body around and dragged her towards the front door.

'I'm sorry, Mum. I'm sorry.' Ally's pleading voice was a mixing bowl of hair and snot. She slumped at her mum's feet at the alcove beside the front door.

Mum reached up to a shelf covering boxed-in pipes that ended in a ledge and brought down a medicine bottle filled with a clear liquid. 'Our Father, who art in heaven—' Unscrewing the lid, she sloshed holy water over her daughter's head. 'Hallowed be thy name—' She made the sign of the cross on Ally's forehead, reciting the Lord's Prayer again and again.

DAY 37

John expected more fuss to be made about him absconding from the ward. A few of the nursing staff made inane comments as if he were a wean of five that had stolen a chocolate biscuit, not a grown man of nearly seventeen. Listening was too much like work for them. He had clamped his lips shut, acted suitably chastised, and the natural law of hospital inertia reasserted itself and brought him back into the bonkers brigade. He made a quick circuit of the ward. Nobody took any notice of him. Many of the chairs were imprinted with the bodies of the patients he had left behind.

He also expected to be in the same room, but it had been allocated to a stoop-shouldered woman who would not meet his eyes. His relocation to another room was punishment enough. It had been cleared of a crazy dance of chairs with three legs and tables that tipped and dipped, and it was next door to the continual flushing of the communal toilets. The walls were a sickly, mildew green, the radiator broken, the window frame was lopsided and locked open six or seven inches, letting the wind whistle in. His cack-handed attempt to improve matters made it worse. The frame creaked and shifted as if it was going to topple, fall to the ground and smash the windows. He was already tainted with the stigma of absconding, and explaining how that had happened to a roomful of greeting-faced nyaffs made his gorge rise. He clambered outside and shoved the frame back into place before scrambling safely back inside. It remained shoogly, but held.

The loss of a room he could stomach, but the realisation Janine was not back in the ward sat less easily. He needed to find writing paper, an envelope and stamp so he could write her a letter, but although he was sure he could have found his way back to the street and flat where she lived in Partick, he did not pay any attention to her address. He sat on his bed, looking out the window, and thought about what he had done to upset her, but came up as empty as a bottle of Da's Bell's whisky at Hogmanay.

As a consolation he had sneaked into Janine's room. Staff had not touched her stuff and it still felt lived in, haunted by the sweet scent of perfumes and lotions. Checking out the expertly made bed, his cock stirred and grew in his denims. He bolted from her room and into the decompression chamber of the corridor outside.

After lunch he moped about the day room and dropped into his – and her – padded hospital chairs, the slow carousel of ward routine moving round him. He had even stashed medication for Janine as a memento, like Blackpool rock without the sticky bits, and thought about just popping them into his mouth and gulping them down so that the day without her, which stretched endlessly, passed quickly.

He picked up the stub of a bookies pen and an old *Daily Record* somebody had left lying aslant on the shiny floor beneath the visitors' tables. It was neatly folded and the crossword section was face-up with the word 'cleave', four down, spelled out. He looked at the pointer for a clue, and the answer marked in black biro did not make any sense. One seat up, two tables across from him, a grey-haired man rocked back and forth, the tic in his jaw working to a different rhythm, and John snorted at the idea of crossword clues making sense in a place where nonsense was the argot. Doodling around the edges of the newspaper, inking in adverts, he created a cartoon world of the ward staff and patients and time speeded up.

Somebody said something, startling him and making him sit up straight, but it was difficult to make out what it was above the blare of the telly. He glanced up to see Myra, a nurse he liked, leaning across, curtsying her body to get a better view of his etchings. His hand slid sideways and covered over a straggle-haired sketch of a Venus figurine with grotesquely ballooned buttocks and breasts in case Myra thought she was being mocked.

'Whit?' he half-smiled, in what he hoped was a friendly way.

'Mr Williams wants to see you.'

'Whit does he want to see me for?'

She sighed, her eyes straying to the television and she answered in monotone. 'Dunno. The police were looking for you. He probably wants to make sure—' A barrage of dramatic music came from the screen and her voice trailed off. 'Doesn't matter. He wants to see you.'

Yawning, John got to his feet and stretched his arms behind his head, loosening the kinks. Meandering through the day room in the direction of Mr Williams's office, they zigzagged past old hands who had taken up hiding positions near the stucco-grey pillar. Their faces were working over the equation of whether he was worth tapping for a fag.

They missed their chance.

Isolated in harsh ward light, Janine leaned against the door jamb of the pool room. Her hair was tied tightly back from her face and smoke rings clung to her skin. She looked jaded. He dropped back, out of step with Myra, but the nurse did not notice. His throat clogged as he got close enough to whiff cheap perfume, and he waited for his brain to catch up with his body. He knew he sounded aggrieved and a bit stupid, but the words came tumbling out. 'Fuck sake. Whit happened to you? I thought you'd already be here.'

Her lips tightened and she chugged on the filter of an Embassy Mild, before answering, 'I'm here now. What more do you want?' Her eyes settled on his face, but she looked at him like a stranger.

'I mean . . .' John said.

Myra stood at the consultant's door, looking back at them.

'You going to see Williams?' asked Janine. Then she whispered, 'Just make some shite up about your family, your wee sisters. He eats things like that up.'

'Right.' His face buckled into a smile, glad of her new-found sympathy. 'I'll speak to you when I get back. Tell you how it went.'

She pooh-poohed, her ciggy burning down in her fingers, in a model pose of couldn't-care-less.

He hurried away from her, towards Myra. The staff nurse knocked, then put her head in the door to say they were waiting.

Williams was reading some dry old file with such concentration he looked like one of those blokes who wandered around in words and got lost in sentences, for whom real life was an intrusion. John wondered if he should clear his throat or if Myra was going to use professional practice and push the small of his back to bully him forward into the room. Williams's sharp face turned towards him and his eyes narrowed. The sound of Myra's feet squelching off along the corridors made John feel isolated, and he realised with a start that it had been his file the psychiatrist had been reading.

'Come in.' Williams raised his arm, flapped his wrist effeminately and curled his fingers into an invitation.

The narrow office space smelled lived in. Williams flicked shut the folder on his desk. Gripping the underside of his cushioned seat, he rocked backwards in a segmented circle. John squeezed past him. The psychiatrist's chair faced his and boxed him in. John cradled his hands in his lap, making sure their knees did not touch. Their eyes met briefly and Williams cleared his throat. John expected him to ask, in his nobby English accent, why he had run away from Gartnavel, but he surprised him by asking a different question. 'Why do you think you are here?'

John frowned and after a few seconds of Williams's intense gaze, shrugged his shoulders.

He rephrased the question. 'Why do you think you are in this ward?'

'And not another?' John said, his voice fluting.

The psychiatrist gave this throwaway remark more attention than John expected. His white coat stretched at the back, biros in his front pocket threatening to fall to the floor; he scrutinised John's face as if by candlelight, his hands pressed down on his knees, lips puckered in concentration. 'Well,' he said, after an age, 'one of my favourite films is *Harvey*.' His salutary nod included John, as if they both knew what he was talking about. 'Harvey was a six-foot rabbit,' he explained, 'that few people could see.'

'I don't see six-foot rabbits.' There was a hiss of exasperation in John's voice.

Williams held the palm of his hand up in a placatory manner and continued. 'Harvey had a friend Elwood P. Dowd, who he sometimes lived with and they liked to go out for drinks. They didn't really bother anybody and were well liked, but soon people began to talk.' He paused, and his index finger flicked towards John, to emphasise the point he was making. 'What does the world do with an Elwood P. Dowd?'

John felt as though he was in one of those Bruce Lee movies when the opponent had swept his feet from under him. The fluorescent light above their heads buzzed and clicked. He took a deep breath, chewed his lips and shuffled his feet as he tried to think and explain. 'I don't see big rabbits. I see a little girl.'

'What's the difference?' The psychiatrist's eyes softened and the wrinkles around his mouth crinkled into a smile.

'Well,' John smirked, 'one's a rabbit and one's a girl.'

'How do you know that?

John shook his head. 'I know the difference between a girl and a rabbit.'

'So if you were walking down the road and met a giant rabbit, you'd find that strange?'

'Yeh,' John laughed.

'But if you met a little girl that no one else could see?' Williams tapped him on the knee. 'What's the difference?'

'Dunno.' John shrugged, sick of being caught out and the psychiatrist's stupid games.

'Well, then,' Williams said, 'why do you think some people get so exasperated with you seeing a little girl?'

'Dunno.'

They sat in silence for a few moments that seemed to go and on. John found himself saying, 'You mean the police?'

Williams's fingers played with the wisps of hair underneath his chin and throat, but he said nothing more, waiting for the patient to speak.

'They probably think I'm doing things to the wee school kids.'

'What kind of things?'

John's face flushed and he studied the gnawed nail bed round his thumbs. He felt as if he had swallowed a fistful of pebbles from Rothesay Beach; they were rolling about his mouth before he was able to spit it out. 'Sex things.'

'And did you?'

'Naw. Don't be daft.'

His voice had climbed a few octaves. He stared across at the consultant, suddenly bold, challenging him. Williams's head bowed slightly – whether this was in acknowledgement of John's outburst he was unsure – but the gaze of his dark eyes remained level and his jaws loosened into a little smile that disarmed John.

'So you've never hurt, or had sex with, an underage girl or boy?' His words were very precise, as if he'd been reading it from a legal document pinned to his patient's forehead.

'I would never dae anything like that. No. Never.' John looked away, but Williams seemed to catch some inflexion in his voice. When John met his eyes, he knew that he knew, and he bumbled on, 'I sometimes just have these mad dreams.'

'Tell me about them.'

John faltered, not knowing what to say or how to put it. 'I know it sounds daft, but sometimes when I go to bed I sleepwalk.'

Williams shook his head and blinked rapidly. 'That's not daft at all. In fact, it's a relatively common occurrence.' He made a joke out of it. 'I've even been known to sleepwalk myself after a few too many Glenfiddichs.'

John stifled a yawn and gave him the kind of tired smile that his joke deserved. 'I hardly ever sleepwalk,' he reassured him. The psychiatrist nodded back at him and John's face grew serious, and his tone more solemn. 'But when I do fall asleep I have these weird dreams. It's as if I leave my body. And it's me lying in bed and not me getting up out of the bed.' He couldn't explain it better. 'You know what I mean?'

Williams shifted in his seat, his expression was difficult to read. John tried a different tack. 'Before I fall asleep, I get this buzzing in my ears, angry voices and snatches of songs from some faraway place. I hear breathing and it comes closer and this fat squelchy thing sits on my face and chest. I can't move, not even to brush a tear away from the corner of my eyes. Then I pull away, escape, but I'm still lying in bed.'

Williams paid heed to what he had said, but waited

for him to continue. 'Although it's dark, there's enough light to see. I pull open the room door and steal into the hall. I can hear my da and his snoring.' John grinned at the familiarity of home.

'My ma is a light sleeper so I've got to sneak past their door.'

'Why should that matter if you're dreaming?' the consultant asked.

'I'm no' sure.' The memory made him screw his face up like he was chewing sour plums. 'Anyway, I glide down the hall. Put my head against my sisters' bedroom door. Listening.'

Mr Williams held his hand up in a stop sign. 'You said "glide" in your dreams. Have you got feet, do you walk?'

'Aye,' but when John thought about it for a few seconds he had to admit, 'I don't know'.

John stuttered and started the next part of his recollection, his face getting redder as he spoke. 'I'm listening at the door. I've got to be careful. Once my mum caught me standing bollock naked in the kitchen, and it's as if there's a force goading me on and another holding me back. I try the handle, but it's never locked. I slowly push it open. My sister Jo's bed is nearest the windae. She turns over in her sleep, a bump of dark bedclothes and frizzy hair. Little Ally's bed is nearest the wall. I stand at the end of her bed watching her. She moans, wriggles up out of her bedclothes. Her wee face seems fragile as a dandelion clock's in the darkness. She sits bolt upright, looking straight at me, as if she'd been expecting me all along. I pad round her side of the bed and kiss her on the forehead. Whisper for her to shush. I slip under the covers beside her, as easy as slipping into a shallow pool of warm water. She turns her back and moves away, flat as plywood near the wall. There's a draught between our stiff bodies. But she knows the drill. I shirk up her nightie and tug her pants down and she lifts her feet off the mattress so she can step out of them. I hook her pee-pee with a finger and reel her in close, let her writhe up against my chest. Clamp her knickers to her mouth so she doesn't squeal too much. And if she's good and she likes it—'

'What do you mean by "pee-pee"?' the psychiatrist asked.

John looked at the top of the desk, and muttered with his chin tucked into his chest, 'I think it means vagina.' Sweat ran down his forehead and stained the underarms of his T-shirt.

'Go on,' Williams said.

He found it more difficult to continue after he had been interrupted. 'I ride her,' he spoke as matter-of-factly as he could.

'Go on,' Williams said.

'That's it.'

'Is it?'

'Yeh.'

The consultant's fingers pawed around his chin. 'What about Jo?' he asked.

'Whit about her?'

'She's in the next bed. Doesn't she hear you?'

'Nah.' Then it occurred to John. 'She's too scared.'

'What's she scared of?'

'Me.'

'Why's she scared of you?'

John pushed his chair back and stood up. His voice wavered, on the brink of tears. 'In case I do to her what I was doing to Ally.'

'Do what?'

'Fuck her.' Tears calved and splintered like blocks of ice in the back of his throat and he sniffed and gasped to hold them back.

'And did you?'

'Yeh, I fucked her back and front.'

John lost control of his body as he hunched howling over the desk. Williams watched him. He was so composed, sitting with one leg up over the other, clutching at his ankle, John felt a keen hatred towards him. It travelled like a bolt of forked lightning through his body and his tears dried. He thought the psychiatrist better watch out.

John found his voice. 'She wouldn't listen. Said she was goin' to tell. I had to kill her.'

The chair creaked as Williams dropped his ankle and his fawn desert boot banged down and scuffed the floor. 'Who?'

'Little Ally,' he said. He felt cleansed by tears and sat down, facing him. 'She screeched, and I put a pillow over her face to stop her and she widnae stop. I had to press down harder and harder, until she did.'

'You raped and killed her?' Williams asked.

'Yes.' John shook his head. 'And no. When I lifted the

pillow from her face, I knew immediately that she was deid, but it wisnae our Ally's face. I put the pillow over her face again. Every time I pulled it away it was a different deid girl lying beneath me and looking up at me. But the last time I did it the girl's eyes blinked opened, and I screamed, but she hooked her arms round my neck and forced the slug of her long tongue into my mouth to shut me up. She was only a wee thing, but I couldnae get her aff. Then I blacked out. Found myself bollocks naked outside, up Dalmuir Park, in the woods at the Golfie. That's when I heard the wolves.'

Somehow, in a short time, they had grown used to each other, or at least John had got used to Williams sitting listening to him. Telling him the next part was easier. 'I was dying with the cold and it was pissing down. But you know what it's like. Stars and clouds for company and I'd my hands down protecting my shrivelled cock and balls. To begin with I kept to the long grass, but it was too jaggy. Sore on my bare feet. I hopped, skipped and jumped onto the fairways. Something, or someone, was watching me. Rustling branches. Something in the bushes made me skedaddle sharpish. A gigantic crow, an evil looking thing, lifted its black cloak of feathers off the branch of a rowan and cawed, once, twice, three times, as if signalling, and circled overhead and flew higher and higher. In the murky light, I was shiteing myself. I hunted the verges for a big stick, or even a small crooked stick. I ran onto the nearest green taking the metal pin and flag out of the hole and waving it about. I wasn't sure if that would be enough. Below the wee drop a ragged line of wolves padded to the edge of the thicket, or at least I think they were wolves. All I could see was the low orbs of their yellowish eyes, lit up, like slow blinking Very lights. Even though it was no good and I couldn't escape, I sprinted away from them. But I could hear them gaining on me. Even as I felt the thump on my back, knocking me down and into the mud, my mind was trying to work out whether you played deid for bears and wolves, or was it just bears?'

Williams kneaded his knuckles, waiting for him to say something more. 'What makes you think they were wolves?' he asked.

John shrugged. 'Dunno. I usually just wake up at that point.'

'Interesting,' he said. 'Freud, of course, wrote about his treatment of a wolf man.' His pink lips grimaced through facial hair and he sank backwards into his chair. 'You do know who Freud is, don't you?'

'Course I do. Fat guy. Liberal MP. Good for nothing.'

'Har har, good for you,' he said in his plummy accent.

John chuckled at having caught him out. They were silent for a few seconds. The psychiatrist fidgeted in his chair and John got the feeling that their chat was done for the day.

'One more thing,' Williams said. 'It would be remiss of me not to ask, you do have sisters Ally and Jo?'

'Yeh,' he replied.

He nodded as if he already knew that, then his phone rang. 'You don't mind if I get that, do you?'

John was out of his chair before the psychiatrist picked up the receiver. Williams drew in his legs and shuffled the chair tight to his desk to let him pass. He hung onto the phone, waiting for him to leave, facing the frayed Post-it notes he had tacked up on the office wall. John clicked the door shut behind him.

The ward looked the same, but he felt different, drained, as if he had taken an oral examination in a subject he neglected, in a tongue he couldn't speak. It was still early, but he needed to go and lie down on his bed. Nobody in the hallway even looked at him or tried to tap him for a fag. It felt like being a ghost in one of his dreams.

He blundered in, not thinking. The curtains were closed, but there was enough light from outside to show that the patient who had been assigned his room must have been dozing. When he crashed through the door she sat up screaming and shrieking. He checked out the corridor and dashed outside to make his getaway. Janine was standing at her door smoking an Embassy King Size with an amused look on her face. Her elbow nudged the door to her room open and she gave a throaty laugh and motioned him inside.

Janine closed the door behind them. He paced at the foot of her bed and eventually turned to her.

'I didn't do nothin', he said, in a pleading tone.

'Don't worry,' she said. 'That woman's fuckin' crazy.'

She edged past him, patting his bum, her long hair falling over her shoulders. Tipping her head to one side, she sat on the edge of the bed, glancing up at him, her blue eyes glistening. She arched her neck so that his eyes fell on her throat and drifted down. Her shoes were eased off with a slapping sound and she stabbed her fag out in an ashtray beneath the bed. Ashtrays dotted the room – on the window, on the bedside cabinet, under her bed.

Her mouth broke into a cruel grin, showing a red lipstick mark on her lower canine. 'All the women are crazy in here – *specially me.*' She started screaming too, really going for it. She batted his hands away as he tried to shut her up. They rolled about her bed and she kept shrieking. He put his hand over her mouth and she bit him hard. He pulled his hand away and shook it to see if it was bleeding. Her yelping grew louder, more frenzied. He pinned her arms with his hands and used the weight of his legs to pin her torso to the bed, lying on top of her and shutting her up with his mouth on hers. Her hips writhed beneath him. He knew she would be wet, aching for sex.

Myra burst into the room. They looked up at her. She looked over at them then quietly closed the door leaving him with the crazy woman.

Janine found his zip and opened a library of the senses. They slapped and slid against each other, the bed springs squeaking faster and faster, their bodies sinking and falling and there was a shifting and a giving and taking.

'Don't come inside me,' she whispered, through clenched teeth. 'My jag's overdue. I'm not on anything.'

'OK,' he said, too late. He did stop, dead, mid-thrust,

her back arched and his insides stuck together like a box jellyfish. Something about the way her hair was lying, and the tang of sex reminded him of one of the girl's faces he had seen squashed under the pillow in his dreams.

'Fucking hell,' he said.

DAY 40

Outside it was getting dark and the children were still held captive in school. Mary shut her eyes, a Silk Cut dangling from her bottom lip. The kitchen stank of disinfectant and bleach. It was just a reflex to smoke between jobs and sometimes when she was hoovering, or washing the dishes, or making the bed, or peeling the spuds, a fag would find its way into her gob. It was as natural as breathing, but they were getting a bit pricey now, up to almost forty pence a pack. She promised herself that if they got any dearer she would stop. It was a stupid habit anyway, but it was the only thing that gave her enough energy to keep going. To show she meant business she turned and nipped it, stubbing burnt tobacco out in the overflowing clay-pot ashtray on the windowsill and leaving an acrid aftertaste. Something moved in the periphery of her vision.

Wind whipped rain through the branches and boughs of the trees in the gardens below, the treetops a swishing and swirling net of spidery dark wood against the wire fence. A murder of crows lined up on the orange-tiled roofs, flapping and strutting, their beady black eyes darting from one thing to another. The one closest to the gable looked straight at her. It raised its oily slick shoulders, scolding the wind and rain, tightened its talons and took off. Glassy black pits of corvine eyes tracked her movements, and the sharp hook of its beak cut through the sound of the wind as it cawed and she stumbled backwards, away from the window.

'Jesus, Mary and Joseph,' Mary muttered to herself. 'I thought that thing was coming straight through the window.'

Cagily, she edged forward, craning her neck, peering up at the mottled whitewash on the ceiling as if she could look through walls and wood and metal and the roof of Daft Rab's house above to see where it went. The front door banged open and shut, a quick one-two, and she heard Ally's feet scuttling up the hall. She sighed, reaching into her apron pocket for her fag packet. When she glanced out, the sky was dark and empty, rooftops bare, the crows gone.

'Happy birthday, Mum!' Ally dropped her school satchel inside the kitchen door. She was breathless from running, strands of blonde hair plastered to her forehead. Her anorak was unzipped but snagged on the bottom rail of the metallic casing, half-on, half-off, and her sweaty blue shirt was tucked half-in and half-out of her grey skirt. Hurtling herself at her mum she flung her arms around her legs and waist and pressed the side of her face into her midriff.

'Ally, I'm smoking.' Mary flagged the hand holding the

cigarette to one side as if wearing a plaster cast, and shoved her daughter's head away from underneath her chest. Ally stumbled backwards, and Mary's expression softened at the hurt in her daughter's eyes.

Ally sniffled. 'I've got you a card.' Clutched in her hand was a yellow piece of cardboard, folded over once, with gold and silver glitter and the word 'Mum' in red crayon with an orange smiley face and blue crayoned kisses surrounding it in the shape of a love heart. She held it up to show her mum, a shy smile flitting across her face. 'Happey' was spelled with an 'e', which had been scored through, and partially coloured over.

'That's nice.' Mary nodded in acknowledgement. 'Leave it on the table, I'll get the dinner on and I'll look at it later.'

Ally's head drooped like a winter daffodil. She turned her back and flung the card face down on the kitchen table, but it fell onto the chair and then the carefully cleaned floor. She left it lying as she trudged into the living room, flicking the switch to put the telly on, pulling her anorak hood up over her hair and standing before the dusty, dull screen, waiting for the set to warm up and the dot to tune into the voices of cheery children's presenters. Turning her head, looking back into the bright light of the kitchen, she saw her mum bending, scooping the card up and opening it. She held her breath as the telly came on; her mum stood looking through at her with the card in her hand.

'Turn that down a bit, will you, darlin'?' Mary shouted, turning away to rinse a cloth in the sink.

The card was still folded neatly in her hand when Mary came back and stood in the doorway. Ally had settled like sediment into the cushioned framework of the chair near the window, just a face and feet poking out. 'Thanks for the card,' said Mary.

Ally scrambled out of the seat and, like a puppy begging for attention, rushed head first at her mum. 'You really like it?'

'Thanks. It's great. The colours are so bright and you're so clever. And there's lots and lots of kisses. I'll need to collect them all later.' She made kissy-kissy noises with her pouted lips. 'But one thing, darlin'.' She held the card pinned between her thumb and fingers. 'Who wrote on the inside of it and signed it with all these kisses?'

'I signed it. I signed it,' squealed Ally. Behind her mum the pots on the rings bubbled and one overflowed.

'Give me a minute, darlin'?' Mary placed the card on the seat. She turned, fiddling with the gauge on the rings with one hand and, with the other, manoeuvred a fork to joust with the pot lid and flip it.

Ally tiptoed into the kitchen and stood looking at the open card and the crayoned unwavering lines, the consistent way letters were evenly spaced, the uprights of the letters not touching, writing, which was not her own. Her shoulders heaved up and down, like newly hatched birds' wings, as she cried. 'I'm sorry, Mum,' she mumbled into her chest. She felt a warm hand on her shoulder.

'I'm sorry too,' Mary said. 'I'm just dead-beat all the time.'

'Whit's moany face greetin' about now?' Jo stood in the living room, peering in her short-sighted way first at her mum, then at Ally for an explanation. 'Happy birthday, Mum,' she shouted, without waiting for a reply. 'How many dumps have I got to give you now?'

Ally looked at Jo and they smiled complicity at each other.

'Thirty-four,' said Mary.

'Jeez, you're really old,' said Jo, with a note of admiration. 'That's nearly as old as Dad. And he's as old as the moon.'

Mary unlatched the window and pushed it open, letting in fresh air which dissipated steam from the pots and took away the sour tang of over-boiled meat and veg.

Jo sat at the kitchen table in the chair behind the door, a school book propped open, fork mid-air between dinner plate and mouth, a damp, blue cotton towel from the pulley above making a turban for her head. Her eyes scanned the pages of *Little Women*.

Mary thought all books were homework and avoided asking questions and getting one of those know-it-all faces. Mary had effectively left school and started working at fourteen –Jo acted as if she was going on forty – but she was proud of her eldest daughter, reasoned that if she could stay away from boys, then she had a real chance, and might even stay on at school and get an O-Grade in something.

Mary leaned across the burn of the cooker and stirred the mince. The tatties were simmering on the back ring with the lid on to keep them warm for Joey. He ate more than the three of them put together. He would be in soon. She knew he would stop off on his way home, go into Birell's and buy her a box of Black Magic and a card for her birthday. She just hoped that he would avoid birthday cards with racing-car drivers or footballers on them. He was vain about his short-sightedness, so wouldn't wear his specs, and had a tendency to pick up the first thing that came to hand, covering it all up with his war cry, 'That'll dae, that'll dae'.

Later, when the mince had stuck to the bottom of the pot, she knew he had gone to the pub. And by the time she had put the girls to bed and went to bed herself, she knew what his alibi would be: he'd say he'd met so-and-so who'd met so-and-so and would you believe it, they knew so-and-so? When she heard the door slam shut, she turned her back, pulled the sheets up over her ears and feigned sleep.

After banging about, opening and shutting the living room doors, parading up and down the hall and going to the toilet a couple of times, he finally figured out whose house he was in and where the bedroom was.

He skulked into their room stinking of whisky, beer and, although he hardly smoked, cigarettes. 'You awake, Mary?' he said in a muted voice, but loud enough for those in the bedroom upstairs to hear.

The stupidity of men never failed to flabbergast her. 'No,' she said. 'I'm sleeping.'

'I've got you some Black Magic,' he said.

She heard him stumbling against the dressing table and dropping them. She risked raising her head from the pillow. Joey was swaying and peering at the floor beneath the bureau, but the Black Magic had disappeared. He scrambled to get his working gear off, standing stork-like, working out the wonder of taking off socks without falling over.

He fell into bed beside her and patted her nightie down like a novice cop on drug detail. She skelped his hands away, inching closer to her side of the bed. The calloused hand fondling her hip went slack. He was lying on his back, snorkelling between snores, as if he was running out of air. She shoved him on the shoulder, then nipped his nostrils together, but he was out cold and there was no moving him. She soaked up the warmth of the bed for a few seconds with her eyes shut before flinging her legs out into the cold, and her feet into worn-out slippers, she hurried along the hall.

She barely made the toilet bowl before she was retching. There was little to bring up; she had not been eating much lately. It always started that way. Soon her face would be like a razor blade and there would be a little soft bump on her belly, and Joey would be overjoyed because he was daft and it was proof he still had it in him. She cooled her cheek on the white curve of Shanks' best porcelain and rubbed her stomach and thought about starving the baby out. But she knew babies were tenacious wee buggers and were quite prepared to mash her bones up to get the nutrients they needed. And all that baloney about hot baths and bottles of gin – she spat the sour taste into the pan. Her bony legs and feet were adapting to her fate and looked sickly white. Before she flushed, she thought she heard knocking coming from the girls' room. The light from the bathroom cut across the hall and splayed against their closed door.

She was too tired to care. The front and back door were locked and the keys hidden from Ally in the tea caddy. Stepping into the hall and cocking her head to eavesdrop, she sighed in relief. The noise was coming from Daft Rab's bedroom, situated above the girls' room. Somehow, God knows how, he had managed to get himself a girlfriend dafter than him. The two of them were playing pass-the-parcel with their sticky bits. And anyway, she thought, it was still too early in the night for Lily to make an appearance. She usually popped up about half two to half four, her timing impeccable; just at the moment when Mary's eyelids fluttered and she began to dream, her eyelids would pop up like a toaster and she would sit up in bed.

Mary sneaked back into bed. She had been in the bubble phase of a dream where she was driving an articulated lorry, being guided in by a man in uniform, zigzagging and reversing a trailer stacked with children's white coffins backwards through St Stephen's Church gates and into the closed double-doors. She waited for the crash of wood and glass, and the grinding of facing brick. It was an impossible fit. The reality was that she had never been behind the wheel of a car, never mind a heavy goods vehicle.

Ally's presence beside the bed woke Mary. Silver moonlight breached the venetian blinds. Ally's blonde hair was a foggy woolpack, and Mary inspected her daughter's appearance for clues about whether she was Ally or Lily. Her eyes glittered and were unblinking as distant Mars. Mary reached out and touched her hand.

'You're freezing,' whispered Mary.

'Yes, Mum,' replied the little girl, in a voice Mary had come to recognise.

Joey stirred next to her, but was soon snoring again. He harrumphed now when she mentioned anything about Lily. Lying in bed drunk beside her, he was useless. Sober, he was also useless.

She shook her head, a kaleidoscope of dreams and waking thoughts, her brain regaining time – tiredness left her feeling jammed on the wrong setting. Using her bum and elbows to slither out from under the blankets, she hunkered against the backboard and a creased pillow. The little girl turned and darted into the hall. Mary stared into the Stygian darkness, half wondering if she was still dreaming, hands patting for her fags and toppling the bow-legged, circular table.

She had played hide-and-seek with Lily, following her from room to room, the last couple of nights and reckoned tonight would not be any different. Plucking her housecoat from the bottom of the bed, she put it on, tucking her packet of Silk Cut into her pocket. Closing the bedroom door behind her, she turned the light on in the hall and listened to the shifting silences of the sleeping house. Branches buckling and groaning in the wind made it difficult to be sure what she had heard. She was no longer sure what she had seen and had a nagging fear she would end up in the loony bin beside John, which made her smile.

She checked Ally was not in her bed, then the hunt for Lily began. She searched every room, even kneeling and looking underneath John's bed. Standing in the living room with her eyes closed to help her think, she tried to figure where Lily would be. Logically, she had to be inside the house; the doors were still locked, and although it was kids' play to climb outside the window, step onto the metal ledge and jump down onto the two-by-two slabs, the lock of the window handles remained in position. *Think*, she told herself. But the gorge rose in the back of her throat again, and she rushed into the bathroom to hover over the toilet bowl, waiting for and willing herself to be sick. Ally watched her from the doorway, but before Mary could move the apparition was gone. She spent about fifteen minutes throwing up.

Outside she heard a childish voice singing *Frère Jacques, Frère Jacques, Dormez Vous, Dormez Vous*. She opened the window and let the cold wind wash sweat from her body. Leaning out into the night, she peered into the darkness. Her mind buckled at the thought – Ally, in her thin nightdress, had got out and was running barefoot in the street below.

Mary found Joey's key in the lock, the front door open, and the wind whistling through the hall.

Wind tugged her hair as she sloped along in damp house-slippers up towards the old folks' home at the top of the street, her nightgown falling open and her nipples erect through the rayon. A few windows were lit up, giving the appearance of a ship sailing through the night. She forced her heels into the trodden-down backs of her slippers, giving her a rolling gait, then bounced down the steps and followed the path onto Shakespeare Avenue. Panting, she stopped and looked up and down the road. A shape – it was difficult to tell what or who stood underneath the arc of smoky sodium streetlights – moved behind the shop opposite, onto Overtoun Road. Council houses running parallel to the road were shadow-filled flags. Then she heard the chime of *Frère Jacques* again and mocking laughter.

No traffic on the roads gave the empty streets a dreamlike quality. Her head jerked right and left, searching front and side gardens, looking for a crouching body hiding behind a Volkswagen, or one of the old Fords, or the work van with a cement mixer lying in the back. In an upstairs room a dog growled and barked, the sound, amplified, wolf-like, in the settled streets, taken up by another dog. She hurried on past the golf course, the oaks, elms and birch trees of Dalmuir Park a spectral presence, swishing back and forth in the wind. She dithered, unsure whether to go left or right.

'Mum! Mum!' Ally's voice squealed from the golf course below her.

Mary scraped along the sides of the hedges that ran up and along Clarke Street. Fifteen-foot high blackthorn, holly married to hawthorn, formed boxed battlements she was unable to see through or over.

'Mum! Mum!' The voice came from further away.

Twisting low at the branching base of the hedge, rain made Mary's eyes into slits as she peered into the murky night, picking out a distant figure framed by the reflected lights of Littleholm high flats. Thorns snagged her clothes and scratched her face, ripping her arms and legs, and she bit down on squeamish thoughts and forced her hips through the gap below the pavement and between the bowers of branches. She plopped stillborn, wet and bloodied, onto the terraced pasture and rough grass of the golf course.

Her knees were blotchy and felt shaky, but the down-hill terrain and the short drop to the fairway was easier on her feet. The bright silhouette of Ally's hair bobbed up and down in front of her as she barrelled forward. Her daughter was close to the bridge, too close to the tumbling swell and bruising rush of the burn, partially hidden from the road by the windbreak of another, higher, hedge. But she was not alone. A man stalked her, a luminal naked presence in patches of broken light and blackness. Ally rushed to meet him, shanking her nightie up around her waist, exposing her naked bum. She clung onto him, her arms round his neck and they shrieked with laughter.

Mary's slipper worked loose and she fell, skidding along the turf and twisting her left knee. Dazed, her mind warped and bent, she scrambled up and hobbled down to the dirt and stone path that ran parallel with the first green. They had flown. She recognised the man's hair, and the way he stood and laughed, but she forced away the thought like a wilful child spitting out a floret of broccoli. Her son was locked up in Gartnavel Hospital. She was sure when she got back home, Ally would have come out of her hiding place and would be sleeping snugly in bed. Joey would get into another one of his rages if she mentioned her misgivings, he'd call her the daftie, say she was sick in the head thinking about such things, he would have woken up and been the first to notice if something was wrong with his best baby girl. Mary cried like a wain, globs of tears and snot, not caring who saw her. Her feet hurt. Her knee hurt. She hopped rather than walked. Lately, everything always seemed to be her fault. She was no longer sure that wasn't the case. Her mind felt like a prison camp made of primordial, shape-shifting sludge, in which she played the role of a warden, patrolling the corridors alone, late at night. She just wanted it all to end, so she could get a decent sleep.

DAY 42

Janine thought sex was sex. Men slept afterwards. Those were the rules. Sheep counting was for country yokels; she counted the calories she had burned off. She stretched. If she was a cat she would have purred. Medication made the day a little fuzzy around the edges, a bit groggy, the lines of the window leaning in, eyes closing, and eyelids blinking. Her mind straightened out the angles of the window, the desk, the covers on her bed, until they started unravelling again. Sleep was a package she did not want delivered.

The night before she had involuntarily catnapped for a few minutes before falling into the dream. The room had been too stuffy. When John tilted the window open he had fiddled with the locking mechanism to keep it from banging shut. He was good with his hands, but not very mechanically minded. Mr Fix-It was super-horny afterwards. The pounding, fucking, lovemaking had left her nerve endings without any more spark and a mercurial sheen on her skin. With her head on the pillow, feeling the heat from his body, and the comforting nuzzle of his cheek on her neck, she fell asleep with her feet locked between his – she was a mermaid going under, no longer able to keep to the world of matter and consciousness.

Her da was here in the room. She tried to turn round, but she was dragged by an invisible force. Pulled through open doors into the void, into their old tenement block and up the stairs. Someone had left a wad of grey gum underneath the railing on the first floor landing; her legs looped and crabbed round the handrail. She screamed until her lungs burned, but nobody listened and nobody heard. Her legs and arms were stretched and racked until she let go.

'Onwards and upwards,' she heard him say. The stairwell stretched ahead and wound around marble steps, the gas lamps with spidery mantles shimmering onto the burnished cherry-wood of the banister. She hoped and prayed – to God knows who – for it to end, but each step was a stretched second, a little infinity, of waiting for something to happen – not yet, not yet, not yet. The house door was open and her da waiting for her. The smell of blood hung like a butcher's bib. She fell to her knees gagging until watery phlegm dripped onto the stairs and the knees of her denim. He gazed down at her and folded his arms across his chest. He grinned, his face was handsome, the way it had looked before he tortured her. Tortured them. He whistled off-tune through a gap in his teeth, *Frères Jacques, Frères Jacques*, and the song squealed and dipped and burned her insides like mustard gas. She was aware of a coldness creeping up through her feet and a pool of darkness that was not locked inside the house with her da, but waited outside, shape-shifting, taking possession of her body, mind and soul.

'Don't touch me. Don't touch me. Don't touch me.' Her arms and legs jerked and pulled and kicked, but she discerned an implosion of listless surrender in her limbs she had never felt before, even when her da was raping her. She whirled round, tumbling and falling down the stairs onto the landing. The shadow thing had taken form and was lying on top of her, pinning her legs and suffocating her. Her da was now outside the front door, looking down at her, looking down at them. The rules had changed. He had not been let out of the house before. And he was triumphant. A cackle started in the back of his throat and crowed higher. She was punching and kicking to get away. 'For fuck sake, John, let me go,' but the harder she struggled, the further they sank, deeper and deeper into a fissure of the marble floor. Below them the bright eyes of her wee sister watched with her hand over her mouth.

'Run, Lily! Run, Lily!' shouted John.

Janine's eyes opened as she heard the crash. John had fallen out of bed. His hair was tousled and he looked up at her in that woolly way he sometimes did, which infuriated her.

'Sorry,' he said. 'Must have fallen asleep.'

She reached across to the bedside table for her cigarettes, pulling the blankets up and over her breasts, stretching her fingertips for the lighter. He pulled back the cover, a sudden draught on her stomach, ready to slip back in beside her. 'I'm tired.' She lit her cigarette, blowing smoke out in front of her, and sat up straighter, patting the blanket and tucking it in under her. He stood, undecided, his body bow-shaped like an old man's, gripping a corner of the blanket. His cock was already rising and getting hard.

'Sorry.' He let go of the blanket, forcing his cock downward and sideways, like he was trying to fold a piece of origami into the shape of a stork. He held his free hand as a screen whilst scrambling for his pants under the bed.

'Careful, you might hurt yourself.' She jested with him, using her elbows to work her way higher up the bed. He was kneeling, peering under her bed and reaching for a sock, his denims or a stray shoe. She took another drag, watching his nakedness and measured movements as he gathered his clothes into a pile. 'I'm a bit sore now and I'll need to go for a pee, but you want a blow job before you go?'

He had his Y-fronts on, one sock over his ankle, and was standing on one leg trying to put the other one on without falling over. He looked over at her. She could almost hear his brain ticking like a parking meter. Tick. Tick. Tick.

'But you're smoking,' he said.

She nodded, blowing out a mouthful of smoke. 'Fuck off.' She waved him away, dismissing him. 'Go and play with yourself in your own room.'

Her fag was almost burning her fingertips when he finished dressing. She watched his shuffling uncertainty, wondering whether to come to her for a final snog or just leave.

'I'd this mad dream,' he said.

She gave him no encouragement, looking at him with blank eyes. But he continued talking.

'And some guy with mad-starey eyes,' he said, 'with a gap in his teeth. I've seen him before.'

Janine flinched, but he failed to notice.

'And I think Lily was there too.' His eyes crinkled as he tried to think. He shook his head.

She yawned.

'Sorry, I'm boring you. You'll be tired.' Then he made his run, darting across and pecking her on the cheek as though she was his grandma. 'You'll be wanting to get a good night's sleep.'

The bedroom door shut behind him.

DAY 43

Mary was first out of bed, but Joey said the porridge was lumpy, he complained about his tea being cold, said she was smoking too much and her hacking cough was keeping him awake. He made no mention of her being up all night with Ally again. He was like most men – selfish. His response was to grab for the covers and snuggle further into their bed.

The kids were at school and she decided to have a catch-up nap, but it made her more unsettled. Outside it was dark and sodden, wind swishing through the trees in the gardens below and the long, drawn-out keening of a herring gull. She experimented with burrowing under the blankets with her nightgown on and a thick pair of Joey's woollen socks, darned at the heel with the wrong colour, yellow, wool. He was meticulous, almost military, about taking care of his feet. He would have a nannyroony if he knew she was wearing them, but she would just fold them and stick them back in the bottom drawer and he would be none the wiser. She decided to have a fag to help her settle. Her nose wrinkled in disgust at the ashtray next to the bed, but she figured it would be best to empty and clean it out later. She reached for her lighter, but it was out of paraffin and would not spark. The flint gone. She reached across, dangling her hand. There was nothing but junk in the top drawer of the bedside cabinet. Batteries that might come in handy someday; a blue Matchstick car, from when John was a boy, with three tiny plastic wheels caught in a set of rosary beads; a black-and-white wedding photo and, thank God, a packet of Swan Vestas. She rattled the box. Satisfied there were a few matches in it, her body relaxed. She lit a fag, plumped herself up on the pillows and idly lifted the photo, daring herself to look. A lungful of smoke hanging in front of her face helped veil the threat. She felt an old woman now, hair suddenly threaded with grey, shadows like horses' hooves around her eyes, always panting and out of breath, a whinger and whiner, shapeless as a flagpole and always tired.

But there she was, glowing in her white dress, her arm through Joey's, floating on a misty veil with the discovery of him and herself. Her sisters had all said how beautiful she was and she hadn't believed them, not then. She held the lit end of the fag over her face in the photograph, tracing an arc from left to right, darting in and out, like an old school game of dares, daring herself to do it, burn and obliterate that dreaming girl. The arc widened. She took another draw and waved the fag-end over Joey's face. He looked just the same as he did now, she thought, because he was spoiled and got to sleep soundly every night. His eyes winked up at her, sporting a smile so wide it would split the stars, stocky, bursting out of his shiny double-breasted suit, tie shoogled to the side to give him a bit of breathing space. Joey thought she was a virgin. But she had been with a married man. Handsome enough to turn a girl's head, but he reeked of the slaughterhouse. God's punishment, he raped her on the first date and blackmailed her into seeing him again and again. Joey, with his temper, would have killed him. Killed them both. But then the rapist disappeared and life was so sweet after John was born. She convinced herself John was Joey's, kept looking in the blind mirror of the baby's face for a sign there was something wrong with him. Soon the only face she could see was John's. She did not mean to, but with not sleeping, the foggy tiredness in her bones, and her thoughts so far apart a double-decker bus could park between them, the burning smell startled her. Joey's portrait was singed. She flicked at it and harrowed away his face with chewed fingernails.

'Jesus.' She sat upright, looking to see if anybody was watching her.

Her fag was forgotten, left smouldering in the ashtray. She rolled out of bed and into her slippers like a sailor on shore leave, the photo pincered between index finger and thumb. The air was colder in the hall and warmer in the living room. Fairy liquid stood sentry on the sink and the pile of unwashed dishes were a reminder of how lazy and sluttish she was getting. In the kitchen hallway, she tugged the back door open and a gust of wind flashed into the house.

Snow lay on the grass outside, soft and melting into silhouettes and circular smears of grey footprints where a neighbour had walked. She pulled her nightgown round her, bunching the material and clipping it closer to her chest, the photo sticking out of her hand like a used ticket. Her slippers flopped about on her feet, but she was careful of the slippery stretch on the back stair-well and stairs. Below her was the spire of St Stephen's and, next to it, Ally's school. Above her was the thrum of a plane with cloud hanging low and cloaking its passage. Snow cotton-woolled the noise of traffic and trains. The quieter sounds were allowed to breathe, the drip, drip of water falling and slush sliding from roofs and garden huts.

She knocked snow from the top of the bin. Before chucking the photo in, she scanned the windows in the four-in-a-blocks to check if any neighbours were nosey-ing out. For a fraction of a second she thought she saw a man with a cigar clenched between his teeth looking down from Daft Rab's house, who winked at her. But she was havering. She put the vision down to tiredness.

Tearing at the photo she ripped it into pieces, letting it fall like confetti among crumpled newspapers, potato and turnip peelings and the empty, crushed shells of peas and bean tins, all covered in a layer of fag ash and empty cartons of Regal King Size.

When Ally came in from school, Mary knew from the set of her shoulders, the way she kicked her shoes off in the hall and let her bag drop from her shoulders and, in particular, the slide of her bottom lip, that she was in a strop.

'What's the matter darlin'?' Mary asked.

That was enough to release a cloudburst of tears. 'Nobody wants to talk to me or be my friend,' she cried. 'When Mrs Hone asked us to split into groups for maps of the world I was left sitting by myself.'

Mary took a drag on her cigarette and switched hands so she could pat Ally on the head and make cooing noises. She bent down to lift her up and let Ally bunch together the capped sleeve on her blouse and play with the split ends of her hair. She took another nip of her fag, her daughter's head flopped over her shoulder like a beanbag, when the front doorbell rang repeatedly, with somebody in a hurry to get in.

'Don't answer it, Mum.'

The tone of her voice made Mary shrug her daughter from her torso. It sounded like Lily speaking, but Ally's red-rimmed eyes looked up at her. She was no longer convinced which was which or who her little girl was.

'Don't answer it, Mum.'

'Don't be a silly billy,' Mary tried to adopt a jocular tone, but the words snagged.

Uncle Lonnie stood at the door twisting his fingers, sweat running off his blubbery face. There was no good pinstripe suit, not today, just a blimp of dark, work-worn trousers and a long black coat with stains on it that smelled goatish. A hackney cab was parked half on the pavement with the engine running and the door wedged open.

'There's been an accident,' Uncle Lonnie said.

Ally pushed away from her mum, so he could see her and give her ten pence for sweets.

'A terrible accident.'

Then he bent over as if he had been gut-punched and started bawling. 'Ah,'m sorry, Ah just cannae believe it. He's deid.'

'Who's dead?' Mary asked, and he slumped into her, hugging her hip and gripping her shoulder to help himself stand and steady himself, his jaw in a turnip-faced gurn.

'Who's dead?' Mary repeated.

'Joe.' He wiped the sweat off his forehead with an oily rag plucked from his pocket as he looked at Mary for what seemed like the first time.

Jo came up the path, sloshing through slush, and the way she walked showed she meant business. Her squinty eyes missed nothing: the idling taxi; Uncle Lonnie going from being hugged to hanging on to her mum, holding her upright like a telly aerial; Ally squawking and greeting because her mum was howling, a noise that seemed to come from a cave-dwelling animal; the upstairs neighbour, Daft Rab, with his nose speared against the window as he tried to find out what was happening.

'Whit's the matter?' Jo said.

'Your da's been in a terrible accident,' Uncle Lonnie said. He peered over the top of Mary's head. As she sunk into him, he had grown taller and he tried a gumsy grin to reassure Ally.

'If it was an accident, maybe it wisnae him,' Mary said. 'Maybe it was somebody else.'

'No, it was him alright.'

'But how do you know?'

'Cause I was standing beside him when it happened. He pushed me out of the road.' Uncle Lonnie waved a fist at the taxi driver who had wound down his window, signalling that he would not be much longer. 'One of the slings on the cranes snapped, dropped a steel beam.' He shook his head and took a deep breath. 'He didn't stand a chance.' Then his voice grew angry. 'Ah'd take the-bastards the whole way.'

Jo sobbed, 'It's not true. It's not true. It's not true.'

The taxi driver tooted his horn.

'Let's get inside,' Mary said.

Shutting the door behind them, they heard Uncle Lonnie shouting and bawling at the taxi driver.

'What am I gonnae dae? What am I gonnae dae?' Mary said. Her body crumbled, and head sagged onto her chest, her neck as wobbly as a baby's. The girls unable to bear her weight, stepped aside. Mary reclaimed her feet. Drawing them into her arms, and her maternal warmth, the scent of fag smoke, was a long remembered perfume; these were the stamps of reassurance that everything was going to be as it was.

DAY 44

John lay on top of his bed, fingers a wickerwork bassinet supporting his head, his weight creating a frown in the plumped pillowcase. He yawned, tired of being tired, longing to be outside the hospital and to be home. The light bulb hung off-centre; somebody had looped two knots in the cord, a practise at suicide. He watched as twilight was chased from the window. The darkness out-side reflected the darkness inside the ward and crept up the faraway wall. He was determined not to think about

Janine. Her mind games were making him screwy. He rehearsed scenarios in which he might love her, or even like her, wondering if there was any difference between the two. His feet were getting cold as he had taken off his socks. He had become lazy, wriggling his bum to scratch it rather than move. His armpits reeked of hospital decay. The skin on his arms and even his fingers was growing flabby. He scratched behind his ear, hair now a matted, unwashed Brillo pad, while trying to figure things. The problem was the more he tried not to think about her, the more he did. She was like one of those Japanese knotweed plants that rooted itself under buildings and pulled them down, wormhole by wormhole. He tried to be logical and think of the pros and cons of finishing with her, but all he could think about was his hard-on.

Karen banged through the door without chapping. Her breasts seemed to have grown bigger since he had last seen her, warring jellos under her white blouse, as she waddled over and looked down at him.

'Williams wants to see you.' Her voice carried an inflection of irritation, and she avoided meeting his eyes.

He lifted one knee over the other, hiding his crotch.

'Hurry up, then.' She flicked sweat from her forehead before toddling towards the door.

He waited for the door to close before springing out of bed, pulling on denims, rearranging his lime-green T-shirt in a fashionable, baggy formation around his midriff, and giving a final sniff to his oxters. He yanked open the door.

He was uncertain if Janine was waiting outside his room for him, or just hanging about to annoy him, but when she leered with a kittenish smile, he grinned back.

'What did that cow want?' she asked.

'Dunno.' He shrugged. 'Williams wants to see me.'

'Jesus, ugly people, and ugly fat people in particular, bug me.' She motioned in a circular movement of her cigarette towards Karen, who was standing alongside the pool room waiting for him. 'You'd think she'd do something with herself, go on a diet or something, but you know what?' She took another look, her face hardening into disgust. 'If she did she wouldn't be working here.' Her eyes met his, challenging him to disagree. But he shrugged and laughed, a hollow sound. 'Consultants in the medical wards want a hard on, not a headache – that's why they get rid of those hardheads, those with thick necks, the butch and the bitches. They're perfect for psychy training. Check it out.'

'I will,' John said.

'Have fun,' said Janine.

Her gaze held his. Oceanic blue. He thought he saw the future in them. She could see things in him others missed. Then he felt dizzy. It was as if the ward was a shoebox tipped up sideways and emptied out, and they had been godforsaken. Shapes brightened and dissolved. A shadow flapped and waved its wings at him, there was a buzzing in his ears and snatches of a nursery rhyme played inside his head. He stumbled and she held onto his arm. For a moment she looked as if she understood and was going to tell him something.

'I'll not be long.' He broke away from her.

Karen held the consultant's door open. Williams rose and met him with a handshake, as if they had not met before. He stank of fags and wheezed like an accordion when he sat down again. He shuffled paper, creating a space on his desk and seemed nervous. 'Take a seat.'

John squeezed past and sat facing him. His heart was pounding and his hands waxy as lemons, but he wasn't sure why. He glanced up. Jocky was loitering at the door beside the fat SEN.

The consultant launched straight in. 'I have received a bit of sad news from home.'

A shroud touched Williams's arm; his mouth was working, but he vanished bit by bit into the darkness. As he talked the psychiatrist's body wavered at the edges. It was as if someone had taken John's life apart, polished bits of it, stacked it like Lego blocks one on top of the other, and said it was finished. John already knew what Williams was going to say and he was falling, tumbling into a void.

John was laid out like a fish supper, in the recovery position, on the floor beside the desk. The office chair yanked sideways to give him breathing space. Head pounding. Light darted from wall to wall. Williams's face hovered bright and close, burning with knowing, with Karen's and Jocky's bunching behind his. Confident faces full of fattening foods and untested eyes that had no experience of lurking terror.

'You fainted.' William's accent grated, but John was grateful for him not breathing smoky breath into his face and for ushering the others out of the room.

He was brusquer when he returned to stand guard over him. 'Can you sit up?'

'Yeh.' John eased himself up, conscious that his body had been taken by surprise; his arms and legs were flighty things. The psychiatrist tracked his movements. He scraped the chair across the floor for John to sit on. 'Da's deid?' he spluttered.

'Yes,' Williams replied. His diminutive size and straggle of facial hair reminded John of a child playing at doctors in a baggy white coat.

The psychiatrist's eyes narrowed and he reached for the cigarette packet on the desk. He took his time lighting up. 'You want one?

'Na.' John inwardly cursed. He could have taken one, stuck it behind his ear and kept it for Janine.

Williams took a long puff. 'I'm curious, who told you about your father's death?'

'You did.'

Mr Williams shook his head. 'No,' he said.

'It must have been Karen then.

A shake of his head.

'Jocky?

Williams poked around the inside of his ear as he mulled this over. 'No, I don't think he'd been made aware of your father's sad demise.'

'Dunno then.' It was John's turn to shrug. 'You know whit this place is like.'

Williams considered this. 'Indeed I do,' he said. 'Indeed I do.'

'You need to let me out now.'

The consultant studied John as if he was trying to solve an algebra problem.

'My mum'll need me.' John's voice had risen, but laden with that subservient tone Da always hated. He could almost hear him saying, *For fuck sake, be a man*. He swallowed tears and spoke more matter-of-factly. 'The girls'll need me.'

Williams pulled open the top drawer in his desk and flicked his ash into an ashtray. 'Yes, I appreciate that, but what worries me is the girls.'

'Whit dae yeh mean?'

'Well,' he took a final draw, stabbed the fag out in the ashtray and pushed the drawer shut, 'you have these fugue states when you're sleeping and they have become part of your more conscious experience.' He glanced over, checking John understood what he was talking about – and in a way he did. 'And you've got to remember you admitted to violent fantasies of rape and incest. It would be unprofessional, with the added stress of bereavement, to let you go home at this stage.'

'Fuck right off,' John spluttered, half rising out of his chair.

The tired sullen droop of Williams's eyelids and the sceptical curl of his mouth softened. 'I'll try to arrange an escort for the funeral,' he offered.

John bit his bottom lip to keep from sobbing, his head

wilting onto his chest. Williams stood up, the interview over. He stuck his hand out for John to shake.

'Fuck off,' he spat, brushing past him into the brighter lights of the hospital corridors.

Patients stole past him, smoke a ghostly presence in their wake. He spotted Jocky coming out of Janine's room. The care assistant swivelled his big neck and grinned as he passed him. John gazed at his feet and kept walking, standing outside his room, his face flaming with jealousy and rage that he had not challenged Jocky because he was too scared. He spun round and barged into Janine's room. She was sitting on top of her bed, bare feet curled beneath her like a cat's tail, reading *Jackie*.

'Whit did he want?'

She let the magazine drop onto the bed. 'He wanted to ravish me because I'm so gorgeous,' she said. She tipped her chin up, throwing her arms behind her head so that her wee tits stuck out like a Hollywood film star's.

'I'm sorry.' His head dropped to hide his tears.

She scrambled off the bed and reached for his hand, nursing it gently in her own, until he managed to look at her. He thought she was as incapable of crying as a house brick, but there were watery blue tears in her eyes.

'What's the matter?' she asked.

'My da's deid.'

He put his arms around her. She rested her head on his shoulders. Rain drifted like cobwebs outside and he realised he needed to stop playing at getting out of the ward and really escape. She sobbed silently then with great clean gulps of air; rivulets of mascara and foundation fractured her face. Her fingers latched more firmly onto his shoulder to keep her balance. Her sobbing slowed to a stain on his Adidas top, and her neck was a tender, broken stalk as their eyes met.

'Love you.' She chewed her bottom lip. 'Really love you.'

They stood apart, lost for a few seconds. He put his arm round her and leaned his head on her shoulder. He stroked her hair. For once she did not know what to do with her hands.

'I don't know if I even liked my da much,' he said.

She cried in the anxious, bitten-off way of someone crying with no one to listen. Their faces collided like a pile-up on the M8. Crooked tongues finding space, becoming everything unsaid. Warmth flooded through him and he realised he had been shivering. The locked sadness – the image of Da's face – was opened, allowed out. He sucked in the warmth of her breath, but they disengaged, their bodies floating away from each other. Their lips remained the only place they touched. She was crying his tears for him.

They stood facing each other, shaken. 'I'm sorry,' she sniffed, pawing at her tears with the back of her hand.

'Shit,' he said. 'No, I'm sorry. Giving you all my problems.'

Her eyes blazed and what she was going to say passed, unspoken, over her face. She nudged him back against the wall. Her busy tongue in his mouth. Her hands clasped the back of his neck. His hands slid down her back. He pressed in close, but never close enough. Her lips stung his mouth as he whispered, 'There's only us.'

She took his hand, guiding him towards her bed.

DAY 45

'For God sake keep an eye on her so she doesn't do something silly.' Auntie Caroline was scouring dishes in the kitchen sink and handing them to Auntie Teresa, the second-youngest sister, with the unfortunate twist to her left eye that never came nor went. The same Auntie Teresa of family lore who went away to be a nun, but did not like the idea of being married to God very much and married wee Charlie instead. They seemed destined for each other. He was said to be the only one blinder in the family than Teresa. She was patting the dishes dry with a dish towel she had cleaned the table with and meandered around Auntie Caroline to stack washed plates in the cupboards. With so many people in the house and the noise of the telly, which was on constantly to keep the kids entertained, Auntie Caroline had to strain to hear what she was saying about Mary.

'She's the saddest face I've ever seen.' Auntie Teresa swept a few digestive biscuit crumbs from the second-bottom shelf, before putting one cup inside another to save space. 'Like she's drowned and the outgoing tide has left its mark.'

Auntie Caroline kept washing and rinsing, holding a chipped plate mid-air, wondering what to do with it.

'You're right,' she said. 'She could do with some filling out.' There was something calm about her bulk and her ways, but it was not genetic; her other sisters were a bit jumpy.

Later, Mary lay in bed, her feet stung with the cold. She missed the warmth of Joey's feet, the weight of Joey's arm on her shoulder to slow her thoughts down. The urge to sit up, to get up, was crushing, but the futility of where to go, and what to do when she got there, left her flat. Dying yet unable to die. Living for the kids. People had been so kind. Their condolences putty without the window. She longed for people to get drunk, to hear laughter, stupid jokes, not, 'Sorry, sorry'. Sober normality was too much. She nodded off for a few seconds, wrangled with what Joey was saying and not remembering, because it made no sense. Her hand struggled for his in the bed beside her.

Milkmen passed the back window, softening the dark hours, sorting different doorsteps with clinking bottles; the pad of the boy's running feet in the dark. Seconds, minutes, hours slipped the garrotte of time without respite. Morning broke into the house, creeping through the windows. The echo of workers' feet hurry-scurrying on the streets was a relief because it meant she could finally give up wrestling sleep and roll out of bed.

For most of the day she sat on a hardback chair. Time slowed to sips of tea filling her mouth, to a length of tobacco, Embassy King Size. She avoided new arrivals, their puppy-dog eyes carrying sorrowful stares, their truncated conversations. Joey took up too much space in her mind to think of anything else. Their first kiss. The way her legs went all googly and she had laughed out loud.

'You alright?' Auntie Caroline asked.

Mary nodded – she was.

'You want tea?'

She shook her head – maybe later.

Mary mustered enough energy and tact, and sprung the occasional lopsided smile, to show she was glad her sisters had come in and taken over the ever-growing list of things that needed to be done. Auntie Caroline brought tears and manful hugs. Auntie Ruth brought her well-mannered ways, her well-cut dark skirts, matching jackets, and a business brain well-suited to arranging a funeral. The other sisters, Teresa, Catherine, Phyllis, Ann, Maureen, Jane, Agnes, Louise and Rose, brought their husbands and children. Living room, kitchen and the three bedrooms were like a public playground with a fog of smoke, sweaty bodies, and endless jawing. In the evening, whisky was reserved for the men and vodka or wine for the women. Tongues were sharpened and let loose. Ally and Jo were plied with oodles of Coke and fizzy lemonade. They longed for days when their daddy would tell them they had drunk too much and under no circumstances could they have another glass; days when they did not have to wait in a queue for the toilet and heed the blithe chatter of grown women moaning about bursting all over the place.

Manny, Ruth's husband, found Mary in her usual spot in the kitchen. 'That's the undertakers outside. They've brought your husband home, as you asked.' His beard was an untidy grey. He got so excited by the gravity of what he was saying that words came flecked with saliva. 'It's a closed coffin,' he added.

'No,' she said. 'I want to see him. I want to hold him for one last time. I want him to know I was there for him.'

'I don't know if they'll allow that.' He searched for his wife to help him out.

Mary's voice pinned him in place. 'You don't know. They let him get squashed like a bug under some big fucking beam. Nobody thought to look out for him, yet I'm to be protected from him. Get a fuckin' life, Manny. Get a life. I want to see my husband. I want to be with my husband. And I don't really care what you or anybody else thinks.'

'Sorry,' said Manny.

The undertaker hovering at the kitchen door cleared his throat, letting Manny squirm away to stand with his wife, who consoled him by patting him on the cuff of his sleeve.

'Where do you want the coffin?' The undertaker was younger than Mary, which threw her for a few seconds. But he was deferential, head bowed, holding a black top hat as if he had stepped into a Charles Dickens novel and she was Miss Havisham. Auntie Caroline stood lurking in the kitchen door, and behind her stood wee Charlie. The girls had been marched to their room.

Mary had not really thought about it. 'In the living

room, I suppose.' She had been thinking of Joey as alive, not a mere problem of space.

The undertaker turned to go. She had been sitting too long. Her knees almost went from under her when she stood up. The way he gawked round the living room: mantelpiece to telly, to the shabby couch at the door; she could see he had already triangulated how much space they would need to park their charge and leave, and figuring how much wee extras could be added to the final reckoning. She brushed past Auntie Caroline and tapped his elbow, startling him.

'I've changed my mind. I want you to put Joey in our bedroom.'

The young undertaker did not look at her but glanced at another man, dressed in the same garb, who stood viewing the living room and those in it with a proprietary eye from the hall. She took him to be the funeral director because the rainbow striations of his bulbous nose and the fine-lined cracks in the raspberry of his cheeks gave him the appearance of seniority. He wet his lips as if unused to speaking. His voice was a low, flat grumble. 'That would be fine.' He turned to go, leading the solemnities. Coins jangled in the younger undertaker's trouser pocket as he hurried to catch up, making him seem more human.

Mary keeked through the venetian blinds to oversee them bringing Joey home. A black hearse from the Co-op was parked tight against the pavement, the hood angled down towards the phone box. The funeral director sprung the tailgate and it hung in the air, the dark wood of the coffin exposed, but instead of sliding it out, the younger undertaker's head disappeared and he pulled out two wooden trestles. The older man stood guard at the hearse as the young undertaker followed the path and doubled back towards the house. Mary looked round, Auntie Caroline was loitering at her back with that pained and patient expression everyone had been adopting with her.

'I've checked, I don't know if there'll be enough room in your bedroom for a coffin.' This was Auntie Caroline's way of saying it would be a bad idea.

'We'll make room,' Mary said. 'Even if I have to take the double bed out.'

Auntie Caroline nodded and patted her on the arm. 'We'll make do.'

'But where will you sleep?' Auntie Teresa said. She was sitting on the couch, her eldest boy, as bored-looking as a Pekingese dog, using her leg as a bolster to lean on. Charlie squatted on the arm of the couch, his wife's hand on his knee, puffing Senior Service.

'I'll sleep in my room,' said Mary.

'With the coffin?' asked Auntie Teresa.

'No. Not with the coffin. In my bed,' said Mary.

'Teresa!' Auntie Caroline said, cutting in.

'No, it's OK,' Mary said. 'I'm sick of being mollycoddled.' She faced down her sisters' concerned eyes.

'Won't you be scared?' Charlie cupped his lit fag, hiding it between a nicotined thumb and the fan of his forefingers as he spoke.

'Why would I be scared? We loved each other.' A sob

escaped her throat, making Charlie sniff and look away. 'He didn't hurt me when he was living. Why would he hurt me when he's dead?'

A movement from outside caught Mary's attention and made her inattentive to what was being said. Hugging her arms to her chest, her eyes rested for a moment on a snowdrop, which speared out of the ground underneath the privet hedge, its foliage shiny and new, sheltered from drifting wind and rain. The undertakers lifted the coffin and, with a slap on the frontrunner's shoulder, were bringing him home. She darted towards the living room door, almost kicking over a mug half-filled with tea by the side of an armchair, and took a custodian position.

The younger undertaker carried the head of the coffin, high-stepping over the front step and into the house. It was more of a palaver reversing into the toilet with the coffin balanced on his shoulder and swinging back out into the living room, before the senior undertaker could make the right-hand turn in the hall. They had to make the same manoeuvre backing into John's room. When they got the coffin into the master bedroom, the funeral director asked for a few moments to get things organised and clicked the bedroom door shut.

Mary waited outside the door for them to come out. They dipped their heads as they passed her in the hall, the briefest acknowledgement. Auntie Caroline stood behind her sister's back, her presence offering support, but Mary held up her hand, a sign that she wanted to be alone with Joey. She shut the bedroom door firmly behind her.

The coffin was set down across two trestles and squeezed in between the wardrobe and the backboard of their bed. The lid was propped against the chest of drawers, reflected in the swing of the mirror, creating a shadow and cutting the light from the window in half. Joey brought with him the smell of lilies mixed with the scent of a dentist's chair. But the undertakers had brought a stranger.

'What have they done to you Joey, my Joey?' she asked.

His head was the shape and colour of a dark mushroom and someone had lacquered and parted his hair in a middle-shed. His lips were pallid thin lines. His flesh melted away, his cheekbones more pronounced and higher than his forehead. The broken skull was working its way to the surface.

She held her hand over her mouth. 'Oh, Joey, Joey, what am I goin' dae without you?'

DAY 46

Mary sat in her usual spot in the kitchen, watching lunch, or whatever it was, being prepared. It might even have been dinner.

'You've got to eat.' Auntie Caroline plonked a mug of tea and a sandwich on the table in front of her, white bread cut into triangles, delicately balanced on a china saucer engraved with a hummingbird.

'I'm no' hungry.' Mary mouthed a sip of the tea to placate Auntie Caroline and slid the plate a few inches away from her.

Auntie Caroline made a huffing noise and sat down opposite her sister. She reached for Mary's packet of fags, nicked one, and lifted her lighter. The sandwich sat untouched between them.

'The girls want to see their dad.' Auntie Caroline studied the cooker in front of her as she spoke. 'Jo thinks she's old enough.'

'Over my dead body.' Mary tried to explain, 'She's got her whole life to be old enough.'

'That's what I told her.' Auntie Caroline clawed the overflowing ashtray towards herself and knocked fag ash into its tarry base. 'But she still wants to.'

'What she wants and what she gets are two different things.'

'Maybe. Maybe.' Auntie Caroline juggled with words to fix on the right tone. 'We should put the lid back onto the coffin so they can't sneak in and get a look. I've already caught them at it a few times. Warned them, and their cousins. Kids will be kids.'

Mary's eyes glittered like dull knives as she glared at some fixed space in front of her. 'I've already told you, not until the boy gets to see his Da for the last time.'

'And I've already told you, they won't let John out. Ruth's been on the phone countless number of times, and you know what she's like. But they just won't listen to rhyme nor reason.'

'We'll go and get him.' Mary's voice rose in agitation. 'We'll get a taxi. Me, you and—' she gulped down the word '—Joey.'

'It's not a matter of transport. Rose and Mary Jane have got a car. They won't let him out. They said he's not well.'

'Shite.' The vehemence in Mary's voice was a warning to tread carefully. 'There's nothing wrong with him.'

'Aye, I know. He's a good boy, but he has been seeing things. Doing things. And the doctor did say he would be able to come to the funeral.'

'That's very noble of him. The wee Hitler. Who does he think he is? I don't want him at the funeral. I want him here beside me, beside his da, now.'

'We'll see what we can do.' Auntie Caroline stubbed her fag out and stood up. 'We've asked the priest to come up later to say the rosary for the repose of Joseph's soul.'

Mary chortled smoke through her nose, coughing. 'Oh, I'm sure Joey would love that. I'm sure he'll be for-ever grateful.'

'Mary, mind yourself.' Caroline wandered through to the living room to check on the kids. One of the older boys had his head stuck in the curtains, standing guard, waiting to alert them to the arrival of the men of the cloth.

Canon Martin in his black suit and long gabardine coat shuffled so slowly up Dickens Avenue it was like watching a rock move. A younger priest with a sprig of dark curls, Father Malloy, accompanied his confessor.

A kitchen chair had been brought into the bedroom for Mary to sit on. The two priests brushed their way past mourners standing in the hallway and spilling into the living room. A space had been reserved for them beside the immediate family in the bedroom. As the clergy loomed closer, the noose of people tightening around the coffin loosened to make room.

Canon Martin knelt using the side of the bed as a prie-dieu to lean on. Father Malloy shadowed him. The older man's gnarled hands were ungainly as they held the rosary beads. He tapped the crucifix against his forehead before beginning, calling the house to order with his opening prayer. Conversations ceased. 'In the name of the Father, and of the Son, and of the Holy Ghost, Amen.' He made the sign of the cross. Eyes were guided upward towards Daft Rab's house and the heaven beyond that. The keening see-saw sound of the rosary was intoned by the Canon, following its circular paths, and in the journey round the beads his voice grew younger and firmer.

Father Malloy helped the old man get to his feet when the fifth decade of the Rosary was finished. 'I'll be alright,' he wheezed, holding more firmly onto the curate's arm.

'Best be off.' Father Malloy's youth, earthy voice and beaming smile filled the awkwardness between the ordained and the laity. He addressed his remark towards

Mary, but she ignored him, sitting on the chair like a broken marionette, with her pale hands in front of her.

Mourners drifted away and laughter came from the living room. Kids' feet thumped down the hall and squeals could be heard on the grass outside. A child was chastised, 'You better behave yourself. I'm tellin' you. This is your last chance.' The two priests headed towards the front door, addressed by jubilant voices now that they were leaving.

The house emptied slowly. Mary kept her vigil on the hard seat beside the coffin. She barely registered the ebbing daylight and the growing darkness in the room. Thoughts chased round her head like charged particles in an endless circuit of newfound knowledge – there was no forever after, just endless regrets.

She welcomed being alone and the wind washing through gaps in shut windows. The yellow glow from the light bulb in the hall dappled her feet. The crumpled sheets, the carpet, the chest of drawers with its ill-matched two shades of lacquer, the wardrobe with all his clothes standing to attention, every little thing reminded her of Joey, except the thing that was lying in the coffin.

Auntie Caroline pushed open the door. 'Were you talking to someone?' She looked suspiciously round the room and back at her sister who said nothing and remained stationary. 'The girls want you to say goodnight to them.'

Mary got to her feet, her bum numb, and legs drunk with sitting. She drifted after Auntie Caroline through to the girls' room. Sheets and blankets were tucked up over

Ally and Jo's chins and they lay straight out and still as the spines of a book. She tiptoed along the passage between their beds. Kneeling, she flung her arm over the mound that was Jo, drinking in her warmth and the sweet but slightly musty smell of bedding. Pulling her eldest daughter roughly into her chest, she kissed her forehead. Jo stared up at her, long-faced. Then she tugged the sheets from her mum's hands and turned her back. Mary hovered over her, anxious to explain, but said nothing. Her youngest daughter reacted differently. She clung to Mary's neck, would not let go and stifled a sob. Mary covered her face with kisses.

'Love you, Mum,' Ally said.

'Love you too, darlin''. She patted Jo under the sheets to include her in their exchange. 'But can you maybe do me a wee favour, darlin'?'

'Yes, Mummy.' Ally's head darted up out of the sheets and she grabbed onto her cardigan.

'Can I speak to Lily please?'

'Don't, Mummy! Don't!' Ally batted Mary's fingers away as she grabbed at her arm. 'You're hurtin' me.' Her eyes were splotched with tears.

'For God's sake.' Auntie Caroline shook her head, advanced toward Mary and pulled her away from her daughter by the elbow.

Jo sat up in bed. 'Mum,' she shrieked, tears running down her face.

Mary looked slowly from one to the other before her eyes settled back on Ally. She tried to explain, in a voice rickety with longing. 'Tell Lily I just want to speak to Joey. Just for a minute. Just for a minute.'

DAY 47

After lunch John squeezed in beside Janine, in what had become acknowledged among other patients as a doubler – the old married couples' seats facing the corridor. His hand encircled her wrist, his thumb wedged inside the band of her baggy red sweatshirt embellished with the legend 'Shout', a word she thought made her seem vaguely feminist. It was not often anyone came to her for advice.

'You need to help me get oot of here, for good this time. Whit am I goin' to dae?' John asked.

The clinking of bottles made John glance round to check nobody was listening. SEN McMurty, the grumpy granny, positioned the edge of the trolley against the far pillar. Jocky played nurse and acted as her legs, doling out the meds. Most of the patients were stuck to the padded chairs, arranged in a rectangle, facing the telly, watching an Open University programme about differential equations. Others sat at the stacked tables used during visiting hours, their worldly possessions safe beside them in thin plastic bags. Fast Eddy's eyes hoovered for douts on the glassy mopped floor, but with no luck. The cleaners left behind the sharp bouquet of disinfectant and the camouflage of cleanliness.

Janine took a drag on her cigarette as she considered

her answer. 'The best thing you can do is play them at their own game, suck up to them and act normal.' Her shoulder dropped and her head fell sideways, a comfortable fit against his shoulder.

'But I am normal.' John sat up straighter in his chair, and looked around, as though challenging anybody to deny he wasn't.

'I know that, sweetie, but there's normal and there's normal.'

'Whit do you mean?'

She patted him on the back of his hand. 'Well, when I first came in here I was like you on a short-term detention order. But that was only because I wouldn't cooperate with social workers or psychiatrists ... or anybody much.' Her mouth tightened into a thin, lipstick-red line. 'The court sent me here for background reports.'

'Whit did you dae?' he asked.

She laughed. 'Everything.'

'No? Really?'

'Yeh, really. I had my ain wee house when I was fourteen, back and front door, spit of garden at the front. I was meant to have care workers living with me, but I just told them to fuck off.'

'And did they?'

'Well, more or less. They gave me lots of what they called "free time". But that's the last thing I wanted. I never felt safe in the house, was always standing beside the front door waiting to get out, roaming the streets and getting into trouble. I was one of the youngest inmates ever remanded to Cornton Vale.' She stuck her chest out and preened. 'They used to call me Jackanory in there because of the stories I'd tell them. But they were all true.'

'That's terrible,' said John.

She shook her head. 'No, it wasn't. I used to go into Off Sales and walk out with a crate of beer or a bottle of vodka. They used to watch for me coming, stop me from going in. "No' tonight Jinty", they'd say, or "You're barred Judy". I got a bit of a reputation. They called me "Janine, the psycho-queen" and phoned about to warn other Off Sales I was on the prowl. I loved it, but nobody would put up with me long unless I'd something to give them. So I started stealing out of ordinary shops. I'd go in and pick up a telly and stagger out of the showroom with it. The sheriff looked at my sheet and said I was a danger to society. He said I was looking at time. But I told him to fuck off. The thing was, the only place I felt really safe was behind closed doors in prison. I never felt safe in a wee house on my own. But they kept putting me away, until I was sent here for a report.' She sniggered. 'They adored me so much in this ward, they couldn't bear to part with me.'

He grinned back at her. Jocky handed him his meds, two white tablets and a pinkish one and he slipped them into his shirt pocket. Janine stuck out her hand and a prism of different pills of different sizes and shapes fell into her palm. She swept them with a dramatic flourish into her gob. She delicately sipped water, made a face, and returned the plastic cup to Jocky. The care assistant jabbed the cup in front of John's nose, as if asking him to smell it.

'No thanks.' John waved him away.

'You'll need this for your tablets.' Jocky's voice was insistent.

'I don't need anything cause there's fuck all the matter with me. Now fuck off and go and dae something useful with yourself, like getting a life.'

The grumpy granny padded up cat-like and stood at Jocky's shoulder. 'Is there a problem here?' she asked.

'He won't take his tablets.' Jocky slouched stiffly, not sure what to do with the half-filled cup of water in his hand.

'I've already taken them.' John's cheeks flashed pink and his eyes bent away from SEN McMurty's tired gaze.

Jocky spoke in a smug tone. 'They're in his top pocket.'

'Ya, fuckin' grass.' The chair creaked as John stood up and faced Jocky, breathing heavily.

'Calm down, boys.' SEN McMurty's voice registered a notch above apathetic.

'He's just a waste of space,' Jocky sneered. 'Look at him. Don't worry, he's all talk nae action.'

Janine's nails seemed to come out of nowhere, ripping across Jocky's cheeks. He jolted backwards as John's forehead melted the bridge of his nose. The plastic cup fell on the floor and he slipped trying to get away from them. His arms and hands stuck out blindly like antennae as he tried to hold off kicks and punches. It seemed like hours, rather than minutes, before a bell rang. Janine had a moulded orange chair poised above her head and Jocky squealed in anticipation of being hit, but John plucked it from her hands, like a wayward kite, as staff from the office and the ward next door flooded into the day room.

John was heaved across the room by a burly nurse and his cheek squashed under a chair as a pile of bodies fell on him. He tried to look up, to locate Janine, but his fingers were bent back and someone hissed in his ear.

'You want us to break them? Do you?'

He stopped struggling and felt a needle pierce through his denims. He could just make out Janine's platform shoes, circled by shiny black work shoes, before everything went grey.

DAY 48

Janine took a seat beside John's bed waiting for him to come round. Then she slipped in cheek by jowl with him. When he failed to respond to her teasing fingers, she skipped away to do her hair and face in her own room. But he was dimly aware of her, his brain a smaze in which Lily shouted a warning, 'Tomorrow, tomorrow,' muffled by the raspy rattling of his own breathing; Janine's heels going away from him; the door whooshing open and thudding shut. The faintest echo of Lily's voice resonated afterwards, as if coming up from a drain, and the smell of cigars.

'Janine.' He called her name, calling her back, but his tongue was a shoehorn. He sat up slowly. A fantail pigeon cooed on the sill, rain slanting down and high winds ruffling its feathers. He focussed on one thing at a time. His thoughts felt as though they had cardboard backs that needed to be punched and processed into the right pinholes. The pain sneaked up on him. Legs stiff. An ebbing throb in his back. He shifted in the bed, his torso blue with bruises. He caressed the bridge of his nose with his fingertips. Somebody had dunted it, but it was fine. He examined the sheets for blood, and grew furious without knowing the reason. The back of his neck was burning and itched before he remembered with a start.

He tried to swing his feet out of bed, but they were the wrong feet on the wrong legs, the feet of an old man. He stumbled and went down in stages onto the floor, his head buzzing. All he could think about was how parched he was. He crawled, clinging onto a chair near the window to help him stand. He lurched towards the door. Wearing only Y-fronts, his gangly body a slow-moving spectacle, John was conscious of the shadowy presence of other patients, but felt no embarrassment. He focussed on getting to the toilets.

The stalls stank, as they usually did, of someone else's shit. His main concern was the sinks and the cold water tap nearest the door. He stuck his gob under it and drank lukewarm water as if he was kissing the tap, breathing through his nose.

Janine genuflected in front of the small cracked mirror. She used it to paint on her eyebrows, made them soar like eagle wings, and did something with her hair, setting it rigid with half a can of hairspray, a mould round her face. Jackie, the care assistant, knocked on her door and eased it open. She was a top-heavy girl who seemed happy in herself, and was always smiling. In hushed tones, she informed Janine that Mr Williams wanted to see her. Janine raised an eyebrow. Then she stooped to apply her coral lipstick and patted powder around her face to take the shine off. This was the consultant psychiatrist's usual reaction when something kicked off. He didn't specify a time – he moved in mysterious ways – but he had already sent her a message that he would send for her. The implication was she would do as she was told. Janine decided to explore other options. She followed behind Jackie, catching up with her in the corridor, where Jackie grilled her for big, fat, spicy details about her love life, which she delighted in fabricating. When Jackie broke away to give Fast Eddie a light for a limp fag, Janine strutted towards the consultant's door and rapped on it.

Williams clung to the door handle, his face giving no indication that he was expecting her. She swished past him, her dress a sticky-out, sixties number, with a clasp belt as wide as his forearms. Seamed nylons and heels made her four inches taller than him. Her perfume was as subtle as a dirty, honking laugh and filled his office with her presence. She kicked off her shoes and sat on Williams's chair, spinning round and rubbing her red painted toenails against his desk. He closed the door quietly and stood watching her like a bemused adult with a kid on a roundabout in the public park. Clearing his throat, he spoke hesitantly, in his best Oxford accent, 'I was just thinking about you.'

'I was thinking about you too, Tommy.' Her eyes remained pinned to his face, but she stood up and flounced to the grey moulded chair nearby.

He slipped into the swivel chair, facing her. She leaned forward so their hair was almost touching. So close he could see a patch of freckles round her eyes and dods of mascara, like the residue from the legs of a dung beetle, on her eyelashes.

'Cat got your tongue?' she asked.

'No.' He licked his lips and rubbed his jaw. 'I was just thinking that it's maybe time that you moved on.' She said nothing as he continued speaking in a level voice. 'This ward is perhaps not the most conducive environment for your progress, and I think it's maybe time for you to spend more time at home.' He shrugged, a suggestion of languor in his slow movements. 'Perhaps with some input from the community outreach team I'm thinking of putting together.'

'Really?' She patted the teeny pockets of her cardigan, which were not designed for carrying things but to set off the Crayola-coloured material and the V-shape of the low-cut dress beneath it. 'Have you got a light, Tommy?'

He pulled open his desk drawer, and placed his lighter on the desk.

'Have you got a cigarette for a lady to go with that fancy lighter?'

She laughed and he smiled. He rooted in the drawer and pushed a cellophane-wrapped packet of Regal towards her. He watched her opening them. Her long fingers glided over his hand as he held up the flame for her to get a light. They faced each other over the glow of a cigarette.

'What about John?' She kept her tone frothy and light.

He cultivated a deadpan look and tone. 'Oh, you know I don't discuss other patients.'

'What if I told you I was pregnant?' Through the film of smoke, his eyes coloured to chocolate pennies. 'What if I told you it was yours?'

He coughed, beating his hand against his chest. 'That's not possible.'

'Why, Tommy? Why?' She moued her lipsticked mouth, tilting her chin at him. 'Cause I'm too old for you now, Tommy? Cause you prefer sixteen, or was I fifteen then, when I had to have that abortion?'

He barely breathed, then hissed, 'Don't try and blackmail me.'

'Oh, that sounds like a threat Tommy. You've got me into such a state.' She stamped her feet in a drum-roll on the floor. 'You must long for the old days when your sort could put their little toothpicks inside people like me and then scoop out part of my brains, or fry them on some machine like a hamburger. Just remember this, Tommy boy, I've got friends in very low places and if I walk, I talk.'

'I don't think so Janine.' The ghost of a smile played on his lips.

'You might brazen it out.' She patted his knee. 'I wouldn't put it past you. You and your two-point-four kids, but it will always be there in the background. You'll never get another promotion, or head some charade of a community team to tell us all how well we're all doing, with you doing most well of all. You'll never move on. You'll be stuck here with me. Only I won't be here.' She leaned forward and whispered in his ear. 'I'll be outside blabbing to my social worker. Crying in cop shops about the port-wine stain on your upper thigh. Talking to reporters from the *Daily Record* and the *Sun*. All those fancy snaps you took with your fancy camera when your wife was away at her mum's, and we had the big old place all to ourselves – it makes me go all weepy and womanly.'

Someone chapped on his door. He swivelled round and shouted in an angry voice, 'In a minute. Just give me a minute.'

'Oh, dear,' said Janine, when he turned back to face her, dabbing at the corner of her eyes with a blue silk hanky. 'We're both so upset. And for your information – it's probably better to know these things than not to know these things – Jocky tried to rape me in my room.' She shrugged, 'And if he's been trying it on with me, there's a fair chance he's been sticking his little weeny in someone else.'

She clapped her hands. 'We're like one big happy family in here. But you know what I think would be a really, really, really good idea? I think it would be great if you decided to let John out, say, for starters, a three-month probationary period. Think about it. All that input from social workers and psychiatric nurses out there. I'm sure he'll be fine.' She stood up and beamed a beatific smile at him. 'Don't you? A humanitarian gesture. I think it's his dad's funeral soon. A fine gesture from a fine man.' She smudged his forehead with a lipstick kiss on her way to the door.

DAY 49

Ally was playing up. She pushed her plate of cornflakes away without touching the spoon and her lip twisted like a squiggle. Mary tried tempting her with the offer of a nice bit of toast with orange marmalade. That usually got her hooked, but she sat on the armchair near the window, shoulders hunched, pouring herself into the spread of pictures of rock god David Cassidy featured in *Jackie* magazine, before carefully flicking over to the next page, then back again, as if she had missed something the first, second or third times, trying to work out why Jo fancied him and if she should too.

Mary scampered to the kitchen cupboard and tore open the packet of Orange Clubs she had bought because her brother was coming with his wife from Canada for the funeral. She swooped through the living room and, a few steps from Ally, chucked the chunky biscuit at the side of her head.

'There's breakfast. You think the world revolves around you.' She turned away, marching through to the kitchen for a quiet smoke, ignoring the shock in her daughter's face and the fall of tears. 'You're just spoiled.

Spoiled rotten. Sometimes I wish you'd never been born. If the homes weren't already full of bad girls, I'd take you there right now.'

But all Ally did was listen, curled up in a ball of snot, clutching the biscuit, listening.

When it was time for school her face was pink and puffy and the chocolate had melted through the wrapper. She had left the biscuit on the arm of the chair, a bright orange dash on the dusty, dull brown. She was quiet. The kind of quiet she had specialised in lately. Her body went rigid as her mum zipped her into the padded anorak. The familiar smells of fag ash and sweat worked loose the ball of her clenched white fists.

'Love you, Mum.' She flung her arms around her neck, feeling the familiar warmth as her mum hugged her back and kissed her on the cheek. 'I'll be good, just don't put me in the home.'

'We'll see.' Mary straightened up, towering over her with mock solemnity. 'Best be off to school now.' Her daughter yawned. Mary gave her shoulder a little push, watching her totter forward, pick up her school bag and sling it over her shoulder. She turned to see if her mum was still watching and, delighted to find that she was, gave her a thousand-watt smile. One last wave before opening the door and closing it behind her.

The radio had been left on in the kitchen, the saccharine voice of Tony Blackburn faded as Mary sloped up the hall to sit with Joey in the bedroom. The parish priest had said they were too busy to bury him. They would have to wait until Monday. She had grown used to other people making decisions for her and accepted it. Let her sister, Ruth, orchestrate the funeral and have it pushed back when she heard their brother Morris was flying all the way from Montreal. Her husband's poor mangled face looked up at her. 'What do you think, Joey?' she said, snorting through her nose.

Mary had decided the night before how she was going to pass the morning cutting out history. She scraped together their family photographs. The colour, the black-and-white and the sepia were sealed like spaghetti in a Scotty biscuit tin with an embossed picture of a white terrier with tartan cladding round the edges. A pair of silver shearing scissors glinted against the mirror and lay on top of the tin. She squeezed past the coffin and picked up the scissors and the tin. The photos tilted and slid, shuffling and running together.

Opening the tin, she picked and brought order to the smilers, then those that shied away from the camera. She lopped her head and body off any picture she was in. Then she cut Joey out too. Her children were left orphans in the frame, which she could not bear. After the first few cuts it was easier. An arm, a leg, a face, another arm, they all fell together, like ash into the coffin.

The front door clattered. She was heartsick of visitors, and wanted the problems they brought and everything to do with funerals and mourning over and done with. She reached into the pocket of her floral-patterned pinny and, sighing, lit a fag to give her strength as she went to answer the door.

A woman, shifting from one foot then the other, stood on the front step. A raddled fox-fur hat sloped over her forehead and down to her nose so she had to tilt her neck to make eye contact with Mary. A smudge of dull lipstick peeked out and curved into a line that might have been a smile. Her coat was the same furry material as the hat, but thicker, more substantial. She looked like a Yeti.

'I'm Maeve, I've heard so much about you.' Her accent was definitely north of Hollywood, and she shot out a black-leather-gloved hand. Mary loosely gripped three fingers and gave them a perfunctory shake. She looked over her shoulder for some clue as to who she was.

A taxi was parked on the road, the engine ticking, and a man backed slowly out of a side door carrying two suitcases the size of small pit-ponies. She recognised her brother. His hair was a monk's crown and he wore a long, tan leather coat which seemed feminine and far too young for him. The taxi rattled off the kerb and drove up the road. He caught her looking at him and held a hand up in a wave. 'Won't be a minute,' he shouted, in a trans-atlantic accent that would have failed to be authentic on any continent Mary knew. He picked up the suitcases, took a step, and put them down again. 'It's my arthritis,' he drawled.

Maeve stepped inside and stood behind Mary in the hall, peering over the top of her shoulder as Morris hirpled round the path, picking the bags up and putting them down again, looking up at the door, drowning in martyrdom, but keeping his head up. St Stephen's school bell peeled in the air, a clear sound signalling the fifteen minutes of morning playtime. Mary could take no more. Playtime would be finished by the time he had the bags in the house. She bounded down the stairs onto the path and lifted a suitcase. His face was a road map of threaded veins and watery red eyes. On his last legs, she thought, just as quickly correcting herself and believing the opposite; he would probably outlive the rest of the family. When he made no objection she lifted the other case as well.

'It's my arthritis.' His brave smile was on display with a full panoply of plastic teeth.

'What in the hell have you got in here?' She tried to sound unruffled as she lugged the bags into the house, but disapproval showed on her face.

'Just a few wee things.' His transatlantic accent disappeared as quickly as the petrol fumes of the cab. He caught up with her, gawped up and down the hall as if newly slaughtered moose heads and ancient family portraits were hung on display, not whitewashed wallpaper and a chipped, gold-plated model of Dürer's Praying Hands. 'It's a grand house you've got here.' He sighed and, like a man changing hats, adopted a more sober tone. 'It was so hard to hear about poor Joseph.'

He patted Mary on the arm, in consolation or commiseration she was not quite sure. She imagined word of Joey's death blowing over the Atlantic, drifting over Africa, settling like dust in North America and Canada. The house smelled of the outside from his long coat, fresh as a squall of rain and she felt guilty, because his fingers were bent back and stuck together like sardines.

'Small,' Maeve remarked, to nobody in particular. She unbuttoned her coat with one hand and grasped her hat in the other. Her bobbed hair was like a blue-black hair-net draped over a full-moon face.

'Can I take your coats?' Mary remembered her manners and stuck her arm out.

She guessed Maeve had dressed for comfort on the flight over. A white swirl-about blouse of lace curtain material that covered her cleavage appeared along with navy blue elasticated slacks, distended by a pygmy hippo's buttocks. The coat she dropped into her waiting hands was warm to the touch, like road kill.

'Where were you thinking about staying?' Mary asked, making conversation as Morris huffed and puffed out of his coat. He wore a grey pinstripe suit, frayed at the cuffs, but still above reproach.

'We've not really thought about it yet, May.' His watery eyes looked towards Maeve. 'We just came straightaway when we heard.'

The memory of being called May by him when she was wee brought a lump to her throat. She opened the cupboard door next to the bathroom, using the frame as a hanger for both coats. 'I suppose you could stay in The Boulevard. It's not far. A couple of quid a night.'

Morris spluttered, 'We're not made of money.'

Maeve cut in, her accent see-sawing through what he said and smoothing things out. 'We've not changed our money yet, we've only got Canadian dollars.'

Mary dipped into her pocket for her fags and lighter. Took her time to light up. 'How did you pay for the taxi then?'

'Oh, that,' Morris clawed at the back of his neck, flakes of skin falling like bits inside a snow globe. 'I gave him ten dollars. That's a lot of money, you know.' His chest swelled as he waited for her to challenge him, then he scratched at his chin and seemed to deflate, adopting an ingratiating tone. 'We came straight here. We've not had time to stop off for the necessities yet.' He eyed the cigarette stuck to her lower lip.

'Sorry. Sorry.' Mary flapped as she pulled out her packet of twenty Regal, handing them to him with her lighter. 'Do you want one, Maeve?' She waved the cigarette she was smoking about, to show what she meant.

'I don't really smoke,' she said, but when Morris handed her a cigarette out of the packet she bent forward so quickly to receive it her top set of falsers fell out. She popped them back in as if it had happened to someone else and she had simply caught them. Mary had visions of Johnny Morris in *Animal Magic* talking to a camel, and the camel chewing out an answer. Maeve breathed out smoke and smiled unconvincingly.

Mary took them into the kitchen to make tea. Their bags were left at the front door. Everything was fine or hunky-dory in Montreal, or wherever it was they were from. Mary did not have to say much more, just nod and pass over the packet of cigarettes she had stashed in a kitchen drawer for emergencies. They kept gabbing, conversation strung between them like a kite. The feeling of being alone was washed away, consumed by company that never shut up talking about themselves.

She tried to get away. One or both of them dominated the spaces in front or behind her, backed her against the wall, jammed her thin body against the window and the sink. She fiddled with the lace curtains in the bathroom to let in more light, even though they were fine. Folded the towels again and again. She washed the coal tar soap after she used it and washed it again because it was too soapy. She smoothed out brown paper bags in the kitchen to reuse later and smiled, glassy-eyed, at Maeve as she did it. The washing machine was dragged out and clattered and spun; the perfume of beeswax insulated her from an overdose of conversation in the living room; the nasal-damaging, bottle-brush of Co-op bleach kept her head down the toilet pan; the neck of dishrags were wrung in savage swishes and chamois cloth squealed on anything vaguely wooden. Work rippled out from Mary. But the sound of flapping feet behind her chased Mary round the kitchen, living room and bedrooms.

She stuck on a headscarf and a camel coat and went outside to the front green, holding the neck of the coat shut against the driving wind and rain. She picked the snowdrop from under the hedge and brought it inside to stick in a milk bottle. Mary thought about swapping places with Joey in the coffin to get some peace, but when she glanced out of their bedroom window at the back green for something else to do, she noticed how dark it was getting. Bolting through to the living room, where the couple had taken up residence with the two bars of the fire and the afternoon telly on, she peered at the Westclox on the mantelpiece.

'Is that the time?' Mary asked.

'Aye,' said Morris in a cheery tone.

Maeve checked her watch. 'Well, we're five or six hours behind in Montreal so I'd guess that's roundabout right. You lost something?'

'Ally didn't come in for her lunch.'

'Oh, you know kids.' Morris shook his head and squeezed his lips together in a way that suggested if anybody knew kids, he did.

'Jeez,' said Maeve, 'when I went to school we had to walk five miles there and five miles back. If we were lucky we had a piece of day-old pie.'

The sound of the front door opening and shutting gave Morris a chance to practise his I-told-you-so look.

Auntie Caroline came into the living room and shook water off her plastic rain hat. Her gaze shifted from Morris, to Maeve, to Mary. Mary's features sloped into an unsung wail. 'What's the matter?' Auntie Caroline asked.

'Ally's not come in for lunch.' A whimper escaped from Mary and she found herself enfolded in her eldest sister's arms. 'She always comes home for lunch. Always.'

'I think—' said Morris, but he got no further.

Auntie Caroline glared at him, spat out what she thought. 'You're not entitled to an opinion. You're entitled to shut up.' She gave Maeve a warning look and shushed Mary until she had gathered herself. 'Did you have an argument with the wee wan this morning?'

'Not really,' said Mary, 'well, nothing that would have made her stay away.'

'And has she missed coming home for lunch before?'

Mary angled her head to think about it. 'Once or twice, when she gets caught up with things.' She smiled and moved towards the window, peering out as rain dimpled the pavements. 'You know what they're like at that age.'

Auntie Caroline gawked at the clock. 'Another hour before the schools are out. Best wait and see, eh? Best wait and see.'

Mary's eyes were a new world of sadness. Without blinking she studied the whorls of the carpet, the whirls of orange and red, as though she could read her own face in them.

'I'll get you some Andrew's Liver Salts,' said Auntie Caroline, 'that'll do you the world of good,' but she remained gridlocked. The telly brought the drama and noise of other lives into the living room.

'I'll make dinner,' said Mary.

'No. No. I'll get it. You're too—' Auntie Caroline searched Morris's and Maeve's faces for help with the right word.

Mary brushed past her, barely registering her presence or what she had said. 'I'll make chips. That's Ally's favourite. She loves chips.' She coughed, searching her pockets for her fags, slippers dragging like tombstones into the kitchen.

She peeled spuds like a machine, peelings corkscrewing into the sink, as she gazed out of the window, searching for some sign of Ally. Outside, it grew darker, turning windows into imperfect mirrors. Her own eyes and wan face stared back at her, condensation running like tears down the pane. Reaching blindly under the small sink for the chip pan, she grunted with effort; it was a heavy pot with a heavy lid, kept on top of an old *Daily Record* to keep the shelf under the U-bend from becoming sticky. She swung it up and over in a half-circle to the cooker. It was half-filled with animal fat, a solid of white lard dotted with the dandruff of brown crispy fries which floated to the surface when she turned on the ring. Droplets hung in the air, its perfume clinging to her drab clothes. She waited until the fat was hot enough to blush her cheeks before dunking in the sliced and diced corpses of potatoes. The air in the kitchen was heavy with the smell of cooking.

The front door cracked open, thudding shut again.

'Mum!' Jo shouted.

For a moment Mary held onto hope, then, recognising Jo's voice, her face sank and fell, her lips stuck together in a flat line of forced cheerfulness.

Jo banged into the living room, a breeze of adolescent indifference. She traded a prim smile with Auntie Caroline, standing with her back to the fire. Jo scrutinised the two adults sitting in the best seats and they looked back at her. Pencil-thin straps from the mock-leather school satchel slipped from her shoulder, leaving empty homework books at the door, and she traipsed through to the kitchen.

'What's the matter?' Jo asked her mum.

Mary shoogled the chips inside the metal basket. 'Nothing's the matter, hen.' She reached for the fag on the windowsill, sucking in smoke, the glowing tip burning down. 'It's just your wee sister isn't in from school yet.'

Jo brought her breathing under control; her tone was upbeat when she spoke. 'She could be anywhere, at Ann's or Pauline's. There's hundreds of places she could be.'

'Aye, hen, you're probably right.' Mary lifted the basket of chips out of the fryer, letting the emulsified fat drop back into the pot. 'You want chips for your dinner?'

'What are we having with it?' Jo asked.

The question caught Mary unaware. She stiffened with the basket of chips in her hand, her face flushed, the whites of her eyes congealed like a duck egg and her irises flickering. 'It's just, she never came in for her lunch.'

Auntie Caroline stole into the kitchen, squeezing past Jo, taking the pannier out of Mary's hands, moving the chip pan to another ring, turning the cooker off and balancing the cooling chips on top of the upturned pot lid. 'I think it's time we phoned the police.'

There was a breathy silence. 'No. That'll be too much bother.' Mary took a last drag from the fag. 'Jo will go out and find her. Won't you?' She waved her hand towards her eldest lass.

'Oh, Mum,' was all Jo could manage. Tears spilled down her daughter's cheeks and a white clenched fist was pressed against her lips. 'What about all those other wee girls?'

'I'm going to get Morris to phone the police.' Auntie Caroline stood straight as a totem pole, and stomped into the living room.

Morris looked up at Auntie Caroline. He had heard what was said but made no move to get up from his seat. 'Is it no' a bit early for that kind of fuss? I'm sure she'll turn up.' He glanced over at Maeve.

'You goin' to phone them or no'?' Auntie Caroline loomed above him.

'It's funny, but we left a few things unfinished in Montreal.' Maeve picked and plucked at her pearl-drop earring.

Auntie Caroline turned to face her. 'For God's sake. What's that got to do with anything?'

'Och, I'm sure the wee lassie will turn up,' Morris groaned, using the cushioned armrest of the chair to lever himself up. He stood beside his big sister, a crumpled paper bag version of her. 'We'd rather not involve the police.' Jo slouched against the door jamb, listening. He shrugged, repeating himself, wiping drool from the corner of his mouth.

'I'll phone,' said Jo.

'You do that, hen.' Auntie Caroline nodded at her as a sign of encouragement. 'You know what to say and what to do? Just dial 999 and tell them you want the police. Tell them your sister's missing. Tell them to come as soon as possible.' She glowered, head turning one way then the other, as she searched for her bag and purse she had left lying on the couch. 'You'll need a two pence for the phone. Where's my bag?'

'You don't need money for 999 calls.' Jo shot out the living room and the front door clicked open and banged shut behind her.

Maeve exchanged a glance with Morris and shimmied up out of the chair, toasting her hands on the two-bar electric fire. 'It's so cold here. We'll just be going, better book ourselves into a hotel with a nice hot tub.'

'We'll just get our bags and be ofty-pofty.' Morris patted his sister on the arm. 'We've got problems with our passports. You know what they're like. You won't mention to the police we've been here?'

She scraped his swollen fingers from her arm. 'Scram.'

Maeve smiled at Auntie Caroline in passing, ignoring her withering look, as if she had been offered the keys to the house as keepsakes. Morris paused at the kitchen door, peered in at Mary and offered her some advice. 'Sometimes you have such a run of bad luck, hen, you think that nothing good will happen again, but you know it does. It does.'

She made no movement to show that she had heard, muttering to herself, 'I've killed them. Killed them. If I hadn't cut their photos up. I've killed them. Killed them.'

DAY 50

Janine breezed into John's room, her sheer nightie wrapped round her body like a spider's web with breasts.

It remained dark outside Although she had not slept, she was wired with nocturnal energy and had to tell him the good news. Standing ghoulishly beside his bed, she chuckled at the fuzz of his hair and his agreeable face. She leaned over and nipped his nostrils shut with her thumb and forefinger to stop him snoring. He made rude choking noises from the back of his throat before he opened his eyes.

'Whit?' His jaw tightened and his head burrowed into the pillow to get away from her nipping fingers.

'You'll never guess what I've just heard?' She pulled the blankets back and slipped into bed beside him. He grunted and turned his back on her, his bum poking against her shaved legs, but her tone remained light. 'They've moved Jocky. He's working in Morrison Ward now.'

'So whit.' He tried to snatch the blankets, but she was alert, keeping them tight to the bed as a tympani.

'It means that you attacking him has all blown over.' She tickled his bum. He wriggled away and gave her more room in the bed.

'Whit are you witterin' on about?' He struggled to wipe sleep from his face. There had been something in his dream about falling. Falling and Lily shouting from far away, but the memory was swamped by thoughts of Janine. He took a deep breath, lifted his head and slowly turned to look at her smiling, cocksure face. He breathed her in and reached across to pull her closer. His pecker was one jump ahead, more forgiving of her chafing presence, and already hard.

Janine giggled and batted his thrusting forays away, she mumbled about needing some downtime and shrieked about her insides being as watery as a First World War trench. But he was so insistent. So masterful, and when he got on top of her, in such rollicking rude health. She really couldn't hold back his advances.

'That was nice.' She smacked her lips together after sex, and slipped out of his bed as easily as he had slipped inside her. She knew he was ogling her arse as she padded towards the door. Her hand was on the aluminium handle before she turned to check – he was. 'You'll get some good news today about going home.'

'How'd you know?'

Her head dotted forward and she playfully tapped the side of her nose. 'Cause I'm a witch.' Then she was gone, flinging the door open and disappearing through it with a cartoon laugh.

A headache hovered above his temple but Janine had left him with a big daft grin on his face. He swung his legs out of bed, needing to pee. Shuffling feet and the faraway clinking of the drug trolley, combined with the sound of running water and the clanking of pipes vibrating through the walls, reminded him how late it was getting. He dashed into the hall hoping the lavvy pans would not yet be stinking, full of unflushed shite, and the gents full of mad people who, first thing in the morning, looked worse than he felt.

After a breakfast of cornflakes and milky tea, he swallowed his meds with a sip of water and, like the other patients, did not ask awkward questions about how many tablets he was asked to take, or what those extra two pinkish ones were for. He left fussing to people whose bodies did not ache and took his frustrations out in the pool room next door.

He cued the white ball up and down the green baize, popping red balls off at different angles into the pockets. Periodically, he lifted his head and glanced through the window and along the corridor, waiting for Janine to come out of her room. But she failed to appear. Jackie came instead. She knocked lightly on the window. He watched her shy smile, as if about to share a secret, as she jounced towards the door and pushed it open. She stood on the threshold, bent forward, as if undecided whether to come inside.

'Mr Williams wants to see you.'

'Now?'

'I'd guess.' She nodded, turning sideways, unsure if she should say more.

John lined up a red and smashed it into the bottom bag near the door. The recoil of the balls striking made Jackie jump back a little. He left the cue on the table and the game unfinished. 'Sorry to keep you waiting.' He watched a shy smile warm her face and flashed a wolfish grin at her. Everybody liked Jackie, even Janine, it was one of the rules in the ward, like the telly always being on. He tagged on behind her sashaying, blue-Wranglered bum and discovered she had nice chunky legs and a clean, girly smell. She lightly rapped her knuckles on the door.

'Whit's he want to see me for?' he asked.

She shrugged her shoulders and gave him a prim smile, leaving him to find out for himself.

'Come in,' grunted Williams.

He watched her walk away and when he stepped inside, he found he too was infected with her smiling malady.

Mr Williams reached across and picked up a steaming mug. He swilled the contents around, warming his hands, before supping a mouthful and clunking it back down again. Nodding and sighing through his nose as if he had come to a decision, he sat up straighter, before speaking. 'I've decided to let you go home on compassionate grounds.' He watched the smile on John's face catch fire, and he put his hand up to dampen the flame. 'But there are some things you need to know before you can go.' He paused before continuing. 'The police are investigating the disappearance of your sister Alison.'

'Whit do you mean? What about her?' John's eyes were suddenly hooded and a tug of war played on his lips. 'I don't understand.' Near to tears, his head rattled from side to side.

'Your sister didn't come home from school yesterday. They've reason to believe there's been foul play.'

John waited for the laugh, the joke, 'foul play' was something out of *Dixon of Dock Green*, not something that happened in real life. Mr Williams's fingers intertwined, hiding his mouth. His grim look and the briefest of nods confirmed that what he had said was true.

He stumbled out of Williams's office as if he wore horse-blinkers and failed to acknowledge anybody in the corridors. Pushing open his room door, he staggered inside and stood at the window, looking out onto the mismatched bricks of other buildings, and allowed the tears to come, streaking his face. A sucking, groaning noise filled the room. He remembered Ally as a little-bitty thing he could fling over his shoulder to burp and carry like a shawl. He remembered tickling her plump little body on the moth-eaten rug in front of the fire-place.

The realisation came slowly that he had already con-signed her to the past and he did not want to think of her in the present, in the hands of some pervert and wondering what he might be doing to her. He unclenched his fists. Da'll kill him. The thought came unbidden, a jagged thing. He was the man of the family now.

Part of the dream he experienced the night before, Lily's voice, and a sense of falling, had been a warning, a jigsaw piece that did not fit, but now slotted into place. To find Ally, he would have to try and find Lily, but he did not know how to do that. He had already tried and failed. The room was claustrophobic. An old pair of faded Levis, threadbare at the knees, lay on the floor, and an Adidas top was scrunched up on the chair near the window. A black bin liner for his dirty washing lay unused under his bed. He dragged it out and tipped whatever was nearest into the bag – washed or dirty, jumbling clothes together inside its plastic membrane. The round toes of his Adidas Samba sannies poked into the plastic bag at his feet. He gazed round the room wondering what else he would need. He needed nothing that locks, medication and a routine that dulled mind and body could provide.

John charged towards the door and flung it open. Then he shrank back into the room, knelt and opened the bag to haul out his Wrangler jacket, pulling dirty socks out of its pockets like squiggling worm bait. With his arms through the sleeves and the familiar denim uniform on his back he felt halfway home.

He dropped into Janine's room, hoping to tap the train fare off her. Her make-up was piled to overflowing on the bedside cabinet and the room smelled like a burnt-out boudoir but, as usual, she was not in the place he expected her to be. A quick circuit of the ward offered no clues. She came and went as she pleased. He pushed his hands deeper into his jacket pocket. The smell of food wafting from the kitchen made his mouth water, and he felt suddenly ravenous, but food could wait.

Rapping on the window of the office, the features of a waxen face peered through at him, then another puppet face and another behind that. Nurse McMurty edged the door open, her hip jutting one way, shoulder bulging another and head jabbing out like a chicken. She waited for him to speak.

'I'm gettin' out today,' he said.

Her head turned and he heard a woman's voice from behind her saying, 'I don't know anything about that.'

'Give me a minute,' Nurse McMurty said, the door clicking shut in his face, but he could follow her movements clearly through the glass panels. Sitting in front of her was one of the white-coated doctors that came in periodically for psychy training. He picked up the receiver, dialled and spoke to someone on the phone. Nurse McMurty opened the door wider, but stood square, attempting to block his view of the office. 'That's right,' she said. 'You've got home leave.' She would not meet his eyes.

'Can you tell me where Janine is, please?' he asked.

'Is she no' on the ward?'

'Nah.'

She turned her shoulders and head, looking behind her for help. Nobody said anything. She faced him, sniffed and licked at the fuzz on her top lip. 'That's confidential,' she nodded. 'You'll need to sign a few things before you leave,' she added.

He leaned forward. 'No, I don't. You've been told. Just let me out. And hurry up about it.'

The ward keys jangled on the chain she carried as she shuffled towards the door. She seemed to take the whole of creation to find the right key. He had one last look along the corridor for Janine. Nothing. The SEN's parting words were a whispered warning. 'I'll see you when you get back.'

'Fuck off,' John said.

John bounced down the front steps of the ward. Purple and buttercup-yellow crocuses sprung out of the soil and grass. Soggy bushes and the burning sunshine colour of witch bane bent against a faraway wall. He pulled his collar up like Elvis and began walking, the rain sweeping in and a squall of hailstones soaking through denim before he had even reached Crow Road. But he kept plodding on, kicking through litter, passing walls and the sides of shops styled with Fuck this and Fuck you red-lettered graffiti. Thoughts of his da and thoughts of Ally kept him trooping, mile after mile of roads in Scotstoun and pavements in Yoker.

Out of practice walking any distance, his denims chafed his legs and his sannies made sucking sounds. He traipsed up the hill at Dickens Avenue, past the phone box, almost home. That was sunshine enough. He gawked in the living-room window, looking for signs of life, like a day tripper passing through Calderpark Zoo. There was nothing to see, only the dimmed-down venetian blinds. He trekked around the familiar path and wondered if anybody would be in. He was lucky. The door was unlocked, and he squelched up the hall and into the living room. Auntie Caroline was yakking to her friend Gloria. Their conversation abruptly stopped. He felt counterfeit, the wrong person in the wrong house.

'Where's Mum?' he asked.

'You're soaking,' said Auntie Caroline. 'You better get yourself changed.' He nodded. 'Your mum's having a wee rest. With the police coming and going at all hours, she's been up most of the night.'

But before she had finished speaking Mary's bedroom door squeaked open and she stumbled down the hall. She was wearing a newish and heavy dun-coloured nightgown. Her hair was unrecognisable, frizzed up in the shape of a flying-saucer, but she was thin as a whip of celery and her eyes sunk like bilge into the hollow caves of her face. Her complexion, once a ruddy pink, looked transparent and contrasted with the veins in her neck, which bulged out like pale-blue pipes. Mary hurried the last few steps between them and wrapped her arms around him. She plumped her head on his shoulder, taking no notice of his sodden state. He breathed in the familiar smell of fags and roll-on deodorant as he hugged her back, lifting her off her feet.

'My big boy is home.' She sniffled and cried, asking no questions.

He cried too. They locked against each other until she pulled away and apologised. 'Sorry for being so daft.' She looked up at him. 'You'll be wanting a cup of tea.'

'I'll get that.' Auntie Caroline, a reassuring presence, lurched away to the kitchen.

Mary pulled at the sleeve of his jacket. 'You're wringing wet. You'll get your death of cold. You better get changed.'

'Aye,' he whispered. 'Any word about little Ally?'

Her head dropped like a raggedy doll and her hands searched the side pockets for her fags, which was answer enough.

'Where's our Jo?' he asked.

The feel and rattle of a box of matches calmed Mary. She had a fag in her mouth and lit it before she replied. 'I sent her down to Linnvale to stay with your Auntie Teresa. It's safer down there – away from me.'

'Right,' he said, not quite knowing what to say. 'I'll go and get changed.'

The familiar cut-out pictures of Celtic players, arms folded, not a care in the world, stared down at him from the walls in his room. His breath fogged in front of his nose and he shivered; his feet were sore and the coldest part of him. He ransacked the top shelf of the cupboard near his bed for a change of clothes and left a sodden mass of dirty washing piled higgledy-piggledy on top of the bed. Searching through the bottom drawer of the dresser for clean white pants and thick football socks, his thoughts skated over having a bath. The boiler would take hours to heat. Besides, they had guests and that added to the hassle. He pulled his Y-fronts over the slap of his penis. Lopsided, he stumped backwards and slumped onto his bed. The white socks he picked out matched the shrivelled, waterlogged skin of his feet. Flinging on the clean clothes he felt warmer, a new man. He hurried to the living room and the balmy heat of the two-bar electric fire.

Gloria drew her feet in close to give him space to warm his hands. In the kitchen he could hear the low murmur of his mum and Auntie Caroline talking. The smell of fag smoke drifted into the room. Gloria filled the awkward silence. 'You've had quite a time of it, eh?'

'Aye.'

'You been in to see your da yet?' She paused, her eyes twinkling with a kind of knowing. 'He's awful good,' she added, her head bobbing, pink earlobes wagging underneath her short hair in agreement. She took a deep breath. 'He's at rest.'

Auntie Caroline came through from the kitchen, which saved him from telling Gloria what he really thought. She carried a glazed mug of tea in her hand, careful to keep it from slopping. John retreated from the fireplace to the couch and the mug was pushed into his waiting hands.

'I'm glad to see yous two gettin' on so well.' Auntie Caroline looked from one to the other.

'You want more tea?' she asked Gloria.

Gloria shook her head, blew out her cheeks and made a puffing noise. 'If I drink any more tea I'll burst.'

John supped at his tea, his lips making smacking noises. His head felt fuzzy and the light needled his eyes. The mug he gripped shook and tilted. Auntie Caroline made a grab for it, taking it from him.

'Easy, easy,' Auntie Caroline talked him down as if he was a bucking horse.

'He's having an episode.' Childish glee stretched Gloria's mouth, animating her face, and she shuffled her bum forward to the edge of her chair. 'Is there something we need to know?' she enunciated in the elocutionary voice of a stage-performer, leaning on the armrest for support. Her mouth hung open as she waited on a reply.

John heard faraway voices whispering, like wind blowing through the leaves of the trees in Rouken Glen Park. He was aware of the stomp of feet and his mum charging through from the kitchen. She flung herself at him, knocking his shoulder against the wall, clinging onto him, wailing, 'Don't die, son. For God's sake, don't die on me!'

The disconnected feeling passed as quickly as it came. He straightened up and gently disentangled himself from his mum's clutching fingers. With the show over, Gloria looked at the clock on the mantelpiece, and remarked, 'Is it thon time already?'

Auntie Caroline took Mary by the elbow and helped her to stand. 'Maybe it would be a good idea if you had another wee lie down?' she suggested, escorting her towards the living room door. 'You're awful tired looking.'

Mary let herself be guided. She looked over at John. 'You be OK, son?'

John's face flushed, embarrassed, he tried to make a joke out of what had happened to him. 'Aye, Mum. Don't worry about me. Rest up, since you're pregnant.'

The slow shuffle of feet stopped. His mum turned towards him, her voice like a damp facecloth. 'Aye, son. How'd you know?' She held her two hands flat against her stomach. 'Wee Joey's in there, waiting to be reborn and come oot. C'mon, son. It's time.' Mary nipped forward, taking advantage of the stunned silence, and found her fingers weaving into John's hand, pulling him up and out of the chair he was sitting in. Her hand paddled flat against his back. She guided him through the hall, took him through to the back bedroom and gave him a minute alone with his dad.

He stood at the foot of the coffin with his head bowed and fingers shaped in prayer. He peered in and bit down on his lips to cover the sense of disappointment and the unsettling urge to laugh. His da looked like Captain Scarlet from *Thunderbirds*. His gaze drifted up to the ceiling and his stomach and shoulders began heaving; he tucked his chin into his arm to try and prevent his mum from seeing him gurgling with laughter. But he kept expecting to see strings lift Da up in the coffin, and him hanging there flubby-dubbying and saying: 'Thunderbirds are Go!' He lost it, laughing until he had to hold onto the trestle of the coffin.

Mary stood in the door with Auntie Caroline behind her. They had come to see what all the fuss was about. 'It's not funny,' Auntie Caroline said, when she finally caught his eye.

'Aye, I know.' He straightened up and then bent over sniggering again. 'I'm just so upset.' He took a deep breath and practised holding his face straight. 'I need to go to the toilet.' He brushed past them with his hand gagging his mouth.

'That takes the biscuit.' Auntie Caroline guided Mary into the room, but for all her bluster, she smiled at John's antics. 'You go in and have a wee lie down. You'll feel better for it.'

Mary sat obediently on the edge of the bed. Auntie Caroline stretched down and coaxed the slippers from her feet.

'That little spell in hospital will have done him the world of good,' Auntie Caroline said. 'Helped sort him out. Them doctors know what they're doin'. And the girls were certainly sleeping better and not up and down like yo-yos at all hours.'

'You think so?' Mary lay down on the bed and shut her eyes, too tired to argue.

'I know so.' Auntie Caroline bustled down the hall. Through the reinforced glass of the front door, the silhouette of a dark uniform stood stark against the light outside. The police, she supposed, would be wanting to speak to Mary again and interview her about what exactly had happened. She fiddled with the lock before they knocked, finding it already open.

'Oh, Father! I'm sorry to keep you waiting so long.' She waved the young priest inside.

Father Malloy looked down at his broad, black shiny shoes, searching for a doormat to wipe the street off. Seeing none, he stepped daintily into the hall, a tab of white collar flashing and his outdoor cassock swishing behind him. 'I'm sorry to bother you, but I came as soon as I heard about poor little Alison.' His curly hair was sprung with rain and he sounded breathless. 'Canon Martin wanted to come himself, but he's just not up to it.'

'That's OK, Father, come in and get a nice cup of tea.'

The toilet flushed and the catch in the door clicked. John, sombre-faced, stepped away from the sour stench of the lavatory. The two men nodded politely at each other before going through to the living room. Auntie Caroline ambled into the kitchen to make everyone tea.

'I'm a well-known spiritualist and medium, you know.' Gloria took the initiative and jumped up from her chair.

She gave Father Malloy a firm handshake, her eyes refusing to bend away from his face.

'Well, we're in the same bone trade.' The priest's deep voice sounded incongruous in the small room, as if it should inhabit cavernous churches and cathedrals. He tried to catch John's eye, but he had settled in the chair near the window and was gazing at the blank telly screen, where the priest saw in dull outline a reflection of the blackness of his coat.

Gloria warmed her feet by the fire. 'That's funny,' she said, a delayed reaction to the joke, and squeezed out a grin like toothpaste.

Auntie Caroline brought in a tray. A pot of tea was hidden under a knitted two-tone cosy, alongside sugar, milk, and a packet of ginger snaps. She settled the tray on the side table. 'I'll just get the cups and you can help yourself.' Despite what she had said, she could not resist serving the priest his tea. John and Gloria made do with what was left.

'So what exactly happened to Alison?' Father Malloy stirred his tea and munched on a ginger snap.

Auntie Caroline sat beside him on the couch, a cup and saucer perched daintily on her mannish thighs, and answered him with whispery regret. 'She went to school and she never returned. That's all the police have been able to tell us. They interviewed everybody up and down the street. All her teachers. But nobody's seen hide nor hair of her after she left here.'

'But somebody must have seen something,' the priest said. 'Heard something.'

John spluttered, putting his mug down on the table.

'It's like all those other little girls.' Gloria didn't miss a beat, sipping her tea and dunking a snap. 'All them that went to local schools. And all them that went missing in the same way. They say the schools are jinxed.'

'Whit other little girls?' John's voice dangled in the air, stiletto-sharp.

'You must have seen in all the papers? There was a big kerfuffle. How the police have been on the same cases for years and made a pig's ear out of them.'

'John's been in hospital,' Auntie Caroline pointed out.

'That's right. The hospital.' Gloria flicked crumbs from the corner of her mouth. 'That doesn't matter a jot. That one's got the second sight and he's a dreamwalker. Our family's had one in every second generation. He's got the astral connection. I bet he's better than a bloodhound when he gets a sniff.'

'Guff,' snorted John, cutting her short. 'I've never heard so much guff in my life.'

Auntie Caroline leaned across to Father Malloy. 'I'm sorry, Father. You shouldn't really be hearing this. She just gets carried away sometimes.'

'Actually,' Father Malloy's cup clinked against his saucer as he spoke, 'I shouldn't really be saying this, but it's not entirely counter to the Church's teachings. God is light and exists outside time. There is no past or future, there is only an eternal now. But the negation of light, an act of evil as a physical manifestation, must have a dark energy, leave a marker in time, and travel out from a fixed point. Think of the Crucifixion. Some people we call saints are attuned to this light, but they can also see the shadows of darkness in themselves and others.' He looked from one face to the other and laughed. 'Does anybody know what I'm talking about?'

Auntie Caroline's shoulders dropped and she scrutinised the inside of her cup.

'Haven't a scooby,' said John.

'That's just what I was saying,' Gloria nodded vigorously. 'When somebody dies in a ghastly manner and their body isn't laid properly to rest, neither is their soul. They find gaps in others' lives to become manifest.'

John spluttered into his tea, 'For God sake. Ally isn't dead.' He looked up to find them staring at him.

Mary could have wept with tiredness; her brain on full-spin cycle. She wished she knew where Ally was, but she did know the police were hindering rather than helping. They had badgered her about John. If he had not been locked up in hospital, well, she did not like to think about what they would have done. There was no point in thinking about that either. She patted her stomach, although there was nothing to feel yet, the knowledge of his seed there, his life, was enough. Part of her envied Joey lying at rest in his coffin. Then she felt a terrible gut pain and sat up so suddenly she felt dizzy.

Mary drifted out from the bed to the hall and into the toilet, a fag wired to her bottom lip. She heard them chatting in the living room, and somebody chuckling, but when she nudged open the living room door conversation stopped. A pall of cigarette smoke hung under the discoloured white polystyrene tiles that crisscrossed the ceiling. But the priest, she forgot his name, surprised her. He was chain-smoking Capstan Full Strength, one ready to dot his conversation and another burning down in the ashtray at his feet. An educated man, she thought he would have smoked a more refined kind of cigarette, something like Regal, that her sister was smoking, or even those noxious Mayfair Menthol Superking things that Gloria favoured. John, his eyes watering, was the only non-smoker. They looked up at her as if they were playing a game of statues.

'Has there been any word?' Mary asked. She knew there had not been, or she would have heard the comings and goings, but had to ask.

'Nothing.' Auntie Caroline shook her head.

'Is Jo alright?'

Auntie Caroline answered automatically. 'She's fine.'

'How'd you know?'

Auntie Caroline pouted. She glanced across at Gloria and looked to Father Malloy for help, but neither took her on. 'She's with Teresa. She's safe. She'd have phoned if anything had happened.' Coughing, she banged on her chest.

'Fat lot of good that would do. We havenae got a phone and even if we did—'

'What Caroline is trying to say is she's being well taken care of.' Father Malloy's well-modulated voice and his manner made it seem true.

Mary eyed him suspiciously, wafts of smoke drifting

round a straggle of hair over her left eye. 'You trying to say I didn't take good care of my daughter Alison?'

'Mum, she's fine!' John's outburst softened her eyes and face.

'She's in God's hands,' added the priest.

That got her dander up again. 'Well, if there is a God, He's not making much of a job out of it either.'

Auntie Caroline covered her mouth as she cried out, 'Mary!'

Father Malloy blew smoke through his nose. 'I'm sure God understands. His love excludes no one.' Acrylic swished as he crossed his legs.

'I don't want understanding. I just want my wee lassie back and to be left in peace.' Mary's voice rose an octave. 'Is that too much to ask?'

'No. No.' The priest flapped his hand in a placatory gesture, then stabbed his fag out. 'Perhaps this is the right time to say a little prayer and ask for God's help.'

'Perhaps it isnae.' Mary turned and scuttled into the kitchen, closing the door behind her.

Auntie Caroline knelt at the side of the couch, her eyes closed and fingers clasped together, hands set in prayer.

'O Heavenly Father,' Father Malloy bowed his head and shut his eyes, hoping for inspiration. John loped after his mum. Gloria looked on with mild interest and glanced at the clock, hoping she would be home in time for *Coronation Street*. 'Help this poor family in their time of need. Bring back to them, in body and soul, the daughter they have lost. And may their poor father find peace in your heavenly embrace.' He opened his eyes and smiled shyly in a way that made him seem younger. 'Amen.'

'Amen.' Auntie Caroline bowed her head and her eyes sprung open.

Father Malloy left a few minutes later, promising Auntie Caroline he would see her on Tuesday morning at Joseph's funeral. He whispered, 'Tell Mrs Connelly I'm away,' as if it was a secret.

After he had gone, Gloria also stood up to leave. 'My Simon is useless, he hasn't had his dinner yet,' she explained, smacking her lips together.

'We'll probably get something in,' said Auntie Caroline, which meant chips from the chippy, but she thought that sounded vulgar. They stood stiffly on the rug facing each other. 'I'll get your coat.' But before she went, she asked, 'What did you mean by that thing about dream-walking?'

Gloria's head seemed to shrink into her shoulders, a slider turtle retreating into its shell. She was in defensive mode. 'It just means that instead of dreams ruling him, he can rule his dream. He can go anywhere, anyplace, heaven or hell, enter the door of another's dream and leave it just as easily. It's a very ancient form of clairvoyance. Lucid dreaming has been with us since the dawn of time.'

Auntie Caroline interrupted her with a question. 'Can you do it?'

Gloria's head popped up a smidgen in response to the challenge. 'Sometimes, if I'm not too tired.'

'Well, how do you know John can?'

'That's an easy one,' laughed Gloria, brushing past her, already halfway to the door. 'Because I'm psychic.'

Auntie Caroline stood, temporarily discombobulated, and her voice acquired a wheedling tone. 'But what about John? Is he psychic too?'

Gloria smirked and huffed through her nose at the suggestion. 'This whole family's like a psychic warehouse that's been set on fire. And John, he's the most psychic person I've ever met. He can make the dead walk and talk.' She shook her head at Auntie Caroline's naivety and finished her explanation with a flourish. 'He's more psychic than Houdini.'

Auntie Caroline screened her mouth with her hand to hide her grin and to stop her teeth from popping out if she laughed.

John went to bed early, leaving Mum and Auntie Caroline smoking, drinking tea and yakking in the kitchen. He remained restless, but after *Star Trek* there was nothing worth watching on the telly. Yawning, resting with his back hard against the headboard, he felt he should be suffering outside, scouring the streets, beating sticks against bushes and dragging streams for Ally. In his own fickle way, he had tried.

He had volunteered to go down to the chippy to get a couple of fish suppers, and two pickles for everyone, apart from Mum who disliked pickles and claimed she had lost her appetite. He took the usual route, made a break from the road to the shortcut, but first he dodged behind the huts at the phone box. The orange halo of street lighting extended little beyond the pitch of the roofs. The shape of bushes at the bottom of the steep hill appeared as flattened ink blobs. He took a step forward and almost slipped.

Back on track he slowed as he got to the junction of Shakespeare and Well Street. For a second his stomach shrank and his Adam's apple bounced up and down like a tennis ball deucing the net at Wimbledon, because he saw a girl wearing a school uniform. But she was older, much taller than either Ally or Lily, and it was the wrong colour of garb. She walked arm in arm with an older woman wearing a turquoise headscarf, slogging up the hill, amidst a steady stream of supplicants leaving half-past-six Mass.

The Ready Friar chippy on Dumbarton Road had customers doubling up round the counter and out the door. The longer he stood, bathed in the bouquet of frying food and lashings of vinegar, the hungrier he got. Although his package was double-wrapped in newspaper, he found his fingers worming in and sneaking out a few chips.

Outside the chippy, he walked slap into a boy's chest. The boy was about a head taller than John and, although they had been in the same class at school, twice as thick. It was proof positive that he had learned something in remedial maths: two negatives didn't make a positive – they made Tam Scanlan.

'Geez a chip,' cried Scanlan, trying to snatch one from the poke.

John pushed him away. 'Fuck off, Scanlan.'

'I'd heard your da died and they'd flung you in the loony bin.'

'You heard right.'

'Whit did they let you oot for?'

'They didnae.'

An older man in a checked jacket weaved in between them. Scanlan stepped to the edge of the pavement. 'Whit dae yeh mean?'

John took a step closer to him, his eyes unblinking, rooted to his wan face. 'Ah escaped.' His left eye began to flutter and tremble and lips bent into a rictus tremor.

'Good yin.' Scanlan slapped him on the shoulder. 'You always were a weirdo.'

The sound echoed in John's ears as Scanlan's steps receded. He hurried up the road and straight into the warmth of the kitchen. His mum ate a chip or two. Auntie Caroline gave it a decent try, but John ate until he would not have dreamed of eating another fry. Then he did. Vinegar soaked through the bunched up newspaper, the warm smell hanging in the air, and stained the varnished table.

'You've not lost your appetite anyway.' His mum lit one fag from another and blew smoke into the gap between them. Her feet shifted beneath the chair. 'I didnae like the thought of you in there, but with so much happening here . . .'

'It's alright, Mum.'

'At least you'd a wee friend.' She turned her head towards Auntie Caroline seated in the corner chair behind the door. 'He'd a girlfriend you know. A right wee madam.' Her hand wafted in front of her face, to flick the thought, or the smoke away. 'Janet or something. At least that's all over and done with.'

'Plenty more fish in the sea,' Auntie Caroline offered.

'It's no' like that.' John leaned and picked up another crinkly chip, sniffing it before putting it in his gob.

'I only want you to be happy, son.' His mum crossed her legs, knocking fag ash into the ashtray on the table, then stubbed her cigarette out as the conversation drifted. She scrambled up to go to the toilet.

'The girl give you the bullet?' Auntie Caroline had on her serious you-can-talk-to-me face.

John laughed. 'Aye, you could say that.' He spun on his heels, ready to mosey into the living room, but Auntie Caroline's voice dropped and she hunched forward in the chair.

'You know my friend Gloria.' It wasn't a question. 'She says you're a very special boy.'

He narrowed his eyes, his interest revived. 'Whit dae you mean?'

'She says you can see ghosts.'

He tutted, feeling a bit stupid, but it was out before he could stop himself.

'And she says you can go places in your dreams.'

'Whit places?'

'Anywhere.'

'Like where?'

Auntie Caroline peered at him as if he was stupid. 'For God sake, just try it. Where do you want to go?'

Mary came back flushed and reached for her fags. John and Auntie Caroline exchanged glances before he tacked off to his room.

Dreaming was not easy, especially when he could not fall asleep for thinking about it. He gave up and conked out. He heard an incantation, *Frère Jacques, Frère Jacques,* over and over, that took hold of him. Then what felt like a gust of wind passed through him and he was outside. The stars were above him. In a twinkle he was above the stars and could hear the great rumbling as time turned into space. He could hear their celestial song to each other. Nothing in his life prepared him for such atonal beauty. Then he was back in the ward in Janine's room. She stood at the window, her head angled sideways as she looked up and over the roofs at the stars. He was behind her and she turned, as if aware of his presence, but she remained blind to him. Attached to her chest was a thin cord made out of stardust. It travelled a short distance. In the corner of the room was a presence, in the guise of a man, hooked onto Janine. The colour and texture of uncooked liver – it leaped at him. He wouldn't have recognised him, but for the cigar.

DAY 53

Detective Close drove to the house in an unmarked police car, a lime-coloured Cortina. His shiny black shoes clicked on the path and he stood straight-backed composing a can-do expression on his face before he chapped the door. Brylcreemed hair, slick as a cat in the rain, sat on his shoulders, above regulation length and just the way he liked it. The collar on his mohair coat was up, double-breasted, lapels standing out like knives. The chunky Windsor knot in his drab blue tie slid down his neck and the top button of his white shirt was undone, hinting at a maverick streak.

Mary had barely slept, would have given bone-tired a bad name, and rolled out of bed mealy-mouthed at the disturbance. She recognised the cluster beats on the front-door chapper that followed a familiar rhythm: police, police, police. At the bend of the hall, Auntie Caroline stepped out of the girls' room and got in her way as she went to answer the door. Her elder sister, without her falsers, covered her mouth as she spoke. 'Who's that at this time?' She yanked tight the cord on her quilted nylon nightgown. Mary snorted, and continued down the hall, shaking her head at her sister's wilful inability to fathom the calling-card thump of the constabulary. She turned the Yale and pulled the door open.

'Mrs Connelly?' Detective Close edged his way into the hall without being asked. 'I've got some news,' his voice was chipper, but was met with corner-to-corner silence, both women looking at him as if he had shit on the bottom of his shoes.

Mary sucked through her teeth, looked him up and down, and sighed. 'You best come in then. I'll make us a cup of tea.' She shuffled up the hall, the police officer and Auntie Caroline following behind her. The boy's door snaked open and John peeked his head out before snapping it shut again.

With the kettle on the back ring and a fag in her mouth, Mary felt like her old self. 'Whit's this big news then?' She knew it was important not to plead, not to cry; she had done all these things and they had been no help. Pity was a guttural clearing of the throat, a foreign sound that police officers tended to practise around her. He stood at the kitchen door looking in at them, waiting for the right moment.

'You better sit down.' He strode into the kitchen, ducking under the arm of a jumper drifting like seaweed from the clothes-pulley above his head, dragged a chair from underneath the flaps of the kitchen table and spun it around to face Mary.

Auntie Caroline lifted the kettle from the back ring, slopped warm water into the teapot, swirled it around and flung the contents into the sink. Mary sat down as her sister busied herself searching for the caddy and, measuring a heaped spoonful of tea for each of them and one for the pot.

Detective Close dipped his hand into the side pocket of his coat. With finger and thumb he fished out a Moleskin notebook with a red pencil wedged into the binding that smelled faintly of Old Spice. He flicked it open, slapped through the pages, and licked his lips. The rattle of cups made him lose his place. He looked across at Caroline. 'Milk, four sugars,' he remarked. Flattening out the page he was looking for, he said, 'It's all a bit hush-hush,' he said, 'but we've found Alison's anorak—'

'My God! My God!' Mary rocked backwards and forwards on her chair, holding her elbows tight to her chest. She whispered, 'Is she alive?'

Caroline slapped a mug of tea down in front of her, forced her to meet her gaze. 'Drink it. For the shock.' She had put a good dash of brandy in it, a treacle-like substance hidden out of harm's way behind the soup pot in the bottom cupboard.

One of Mary's hands covered the other in her lap, trying to soothe it enough to lift the tea. Auntie Caroline's cool hand found the back of her neck and held her head steady. She let her sip tea, bird-like, the rim of the mug pressed against her pale lips. She blinked with her eyes, her arms and legs trembling, to show that she had had enough.

'We've no' found a body.' Detective Close chewed on his lower lip.

Auntie Caroline glared at him so hard he studied his notebook and began again. 'We've not yet found Alison, just her anorak.' Only then did he receive his prize of tea. She pushed the sugar bowl towards him.

'Where was it?' Auntie Caroline patted her sister on the shoulder.

'It was in the cloakroom at her school.' He seemed pleased with that, as if he had discovered it himself. He spooned sugar into his cup.

'Who found it?' Auntie Caroline asked.

'One of the teachers.' He slurped tea one-handed, his fingers flipping pages filled with spidery pencil notes. 'A

Miss Hone. All the children had gone home and she'd seen it sitting there on its peg.'

Mary stirred herself, sat up a little straighter, colour flooding back into her face. 'When was that?'

He scratched at his chin. 'A few days ago.'

'And you didn't think to tell me until now?' Mary's eyes glistened.

He gulped down some tea. 'We had to establish it was her jacket. Forensics.' He left that bit open, nodded sympathetically. Science was always a trump card to play in any case.

'It's got her name on it.' Mary spat out. 'Alison Connelly, I sewed the name tag on myself. You dragged the canal. Dogs everywhere. Sniffing up and down closes, sniffing peoples' arses. God sake, you never thought to check the school she went to?'

'What does it tell us now?' Auntie Caroline asked in a more placatory tone, placing her hand on Mary's shoulder.

'It tells us that that morning,' he weighed his words more carefully, his eyes shifting from one face to another, 'she went to school as usual and somebody took her from St. Stephen's.'

'But is she alive?' Mary asked.

He remained silent.

John waited until he heard the sound of the car choking and flooding into life before he ventured into the hall. He wanted to tell someone, anybody, about his dream. But when he saw Mum slumped like a ragdoll in the chair beside the fireplace, it seemed childish. He slipped into the more natural, lived-in warmth of the kitchen. It smelt faintly of fried onions and fag smoke. The tranny on the windowsill was jammed onto jaunty fiddle music accompanied by what sounded like somebody duelling in high Appalachian squeals as they sawed their own legs off. Auntie Caroline made him a cup of tea and a bit of toast slathered in margarine with a tang of orange marmalade, the way he preferred. She told him about finding Alison's anorak before changing tack. 'Hurry up and finish that or you'll not be able to go to Holy Communion.'

His back molars stuck together on a burnt crust. Instead of saying he had not been to chapel since being sectioned in hospital, he spluttered, 'I'm not goin' to Mass. I've no' been for years.'

A shake of her head showed her disappointment, but she snapped back, 'Your mother's not well enough – and we need all the prayers we can get.' Her eyes caught his. 'Don't we?'

His head slumped. 'Aye,' he said, voice flaring, 'but whit about those millions of Jews. You no' think they were all praying their heids off during the war? And look where it got them.'

Auntie Caroline gave him one of her looks.

'I'm no' goin' to Communion,' he said.

'Suit yourself.' She picked up a dishcloth and turned her back to him, humming along with the more sedate Doris Day's 'Que Sera, Sera' on the radio as she dried the dishes and stacked them in the cupboard.

John consoled himself with the thought nobody went to nine o'clock Mass but decrepit oldies. Outside the house, he hunched his shoulders and set the pace, not waiting for Auntie Caroline who toddled along behind him. As they got closer to the Kerr's hedge he slowed, lingering, and slapped his hands over his mouth to warm them with his breath. 'This was where I first spotted Lily.' His chin moved a fraction and he talked out of the side of his mouth.

They stood close together in reverent silence. His aunt's long winter coat protected her from the cold rain. The venetian blinds in the Kerr house were dubbed down, locked tight. In the distance, straight-lined rooftops shimmied through clouds, a rainbow and sunbeam strayed, finger-painting the flat-roofed council houses with an unearthly glow. A biting wind pushed them inch by inch closer together. A woman with a buggy trundled past them, the child under a protective bauble of plastic sheeting, shimmying in her bucket seat as far forward as buckles would allow, peering out at them with honest curiosity, turning her head as she passed, straining the straps, ready to jump out in her red wellies and claim the world.

'We'll be late,' Auntie Caroline reminded him, nudging his elbow. They walked close together. 'Did she ever say anything?'

'Nothin' much.' Although there was no traffic, he let her loop her arm through his as they crossed Duntocher Road. They were almost the same height. 'Just something about big people not being able to understand.' He slipped loose of her grip when they reached St Stephen's, turning sideways on the congested pavement, allowing a middle-aged couple to nip past them. A few reluctant churchgoers wearing Sunday best set themselves against the brick wall outside the grounds to sneak a final fag before going inside. His gaze drifted towards the school a few hundred yards behind the church, where his sister's jacket had been found.

'Any idea what in the hell Lily meant?' he asked.

'I'd need to consult Gloria,' Auntie Caroline panted, slightly out of breath. 'But I'd guess that as we get older the world becomes a much smaller place. Our beliefs harden. Children see what they see and we batter them and tell them not to.' A stout, bearded man wearing a long plastic raincoat swished between them. The opening bars of the entrance hymn from the church organ spilled out, claiming them. Cigarettes were stubbed out and dropped. Smokers and non-smokers fell into single file, marching into the fenced-off hallowed grounds and the protective embrace of Sunday worship. The smell of beeswax polish and incense clung to the chapel. John dubbed his fingers in the font at the door, dabbed his forehead with holy water, and crossed himself: 'In the name of the Father, And of the Son, And of the Holy Ghost. Amen.'

Auntie Caroline set the lead. With a crooked smile she negotiated her way past two men, clean-shaven and lantern-jawed pass-keepers in Sunday suits, holding out shallow collection plates lined with green baize and filled with loose change. She bumped through the double doors into the nave of the church.

Celebrants rested hymn books on top of the pews in front of them. Some of the pages were wedged open and the more spirited church members sang loudly and shrilly. The less biddable mimed, hiding behind organ accompaniment and the church choir's rendition of 'Walk with Me, Oh My Lord'. Back seat renegades whispered to each other. Everyone but the smallest child knew the drill: eyes front, no smiling, talk like John Wayne out of the side of the mouth.

John followed his elderly aunt with growing dread. She skipped past the back seats, disdained empty seats beside the pillars that framed the roof sixty feet above them, and kept going until she found an empty slot in the front row. It was close to the side altar dedicated to the Virgin Mary. This was the place where all the holier-than-holies liked to congregate, basking in the holy glow of Canon Martin looking down on them from the pulpit.

John knew the drill. He knelt, sat, stood and sang with the best of them. He listened to Canon Martin hectoring them to pray more for little Ally, to do more to bring her safely home, and put more money in the plate lest the church would fall round about them like soggy paper. John thought the likelihood slim. He grew bored and looked about. St Stephen's was a modern red-brick building. Clear glass framed the choir stall above the entrance and flooded the seats below. Stained glass told pictorial stories older than words for children sitting nearby to decipher.

John let his mind drift during the long sermon after the Gospel. God was keeping an eye on them. That was usually how it went. Canon Martin's story was no different. Distilling their dirty thoughts and deeds into something by the power of something called Grace. Presenting them with a new, sin-proof suit to wear and walk around in a shiny new self, cloaked in Hope.

Nodding off, John's ears filled with a buzzing sound. He recalled the Old Testament reading, which Canon Martin had quickly skated over. Jacob in his tent by a river, wrestling with an angel, day after day. An angel that was flesh and blood and not straw and wings and feathers plucked from a children's Christmas play. Jacob's mortal body sweating and fighting, grunting, pushing hard against a body shaped by joy, struggling against the void of nothingness, finding eternity's weight in a hip, and its weak spot in an ankle, and putting the angel on its back and holding it down, making it submit. He waited until Holy Communion and sneaked out the side door. He remained in the dark about how to find Lily, but he knew he had to try. That was the only way he would find Ally.

DAY 55

Mary and Jo stood to the side of the hearse's tailgate, exhaust fumes, fag smoke and aftershave wafting in front and behind them combining into a toxic mix. The nervous jingling of pocket change was like horses' reins, a reminder of fellow mourners held in check, waiting for Joey's last journey. Mary grasped Jo's hand tightly. A peaching of lipstick on her daughter's mouth, her plucked eyebrows and a fingertip of eye shadow reminded her how grown up she was getting. Everyone searched the back of wardrobes for funeral attire, except for her brother Morris and his floozy, who did not turn up.

Mary opted for Joey to be buried, not cremated, or rather her sister Ruth played referee and settled on that choice. Mary briefly shut her eyes, determined not to cry again, her shoulders rising and falling, throat choking into her chest. After the inevitable delay, the arrival of Joey's coffin had made the funeral real enough; he was shouldered out the door and into the hearse by John, wee Charlie, Lonnie and Joey's cousin. Bird's foot trefoil and speedwell poked up through the gaps in the slabs their feet shuffled over, new life seeking the sun. Watching Joey paraded around the back of a hearse by two guys in silk top hats and frock coats was a jump back into a different century and slightly surreal. No fuss, Joey would have appreciated that, Mary thought, but perhaps not the flowers – floral pillows and sprays on top of the casket, along with plastic wreaths with messages poking out of polystyrene that he would never read. Like him, they were all for nature's bin. She kept losing track of things. But she needed the show of mourning to be over and done with so they could renew their search for Ally.

Canon Martin conducted the funeral mass in St Stephen's at his own slow, steady pace. Mary, flanked by Jo and John, insisted on leaving a space at the end of the pew for Ally. Mary's sisters, their partners and children took the pews behind them. Relations, friends, work-mates and people who knew Joey, and even parishioners who did not know him, filled the other seats. People sprawled out from the pews and stood black against the white walls of the chapel.

John did not want to turn round and stare, but one of his fellow mourners had a rich baritone voice that soared above their heads and out-choired the choir. His rendition of the twenty-third Psalm made John's head dip and he cried into the lapels of his borrowed jacket. He stood within touching distance of the coffin, choking on incense. The clanking of the thurible called to mind a childhood memory, the straining sound of the chains on the Erskine ferry on the Clyde crossing before the river coursed on to the yard where his da had worked. The old priest pontificated, said all the usual things about Jesus and God's will. Before the consecration of the coffin, he asked that a special prayer be said for Alison, but it was the same old dogma heard week in, week out; year in, year out. His wheezing monotone voice and empty words sickened John. It felt as if Ally had been stuffed inside the coffin along with his da and he had nailed down the lid with banalities. John wanted to stand up, to scream and shout in protest; instead he bit his bottom lip, bowed his head and studied his hands.

A signal from the undertakers, who had ghosted up

the aisle, and John and the other pallbearers lifted the coffin and took the weight on muscles not used to the strain, but by some miracle the body was light as a child's. John kept his head down, his face blurry with tears. He carried grief down the aisle and the coffin outside into the waiting hearse.

He sat in the back of the hired car with his mum, facing a tearful Jo and Auntie Caroline. His auntie patted him on the knee. 'You did well, son.' They sank into a chauffeured silence, rain washing against the window, and studied people going in and out of shops, getting on with their lives.

Wind funnelled down from the Old Kilpatrick Hills and Dalmuir Crematorium, and the boneyard was a cold spot made colder. Joey's grave had been dug, the kickboards a walkway on the grass, and the gravediggers, in fawn overcoats and work boots, stood a few feet away from their work. Mourners arrived in fits and starts. Cars were parked all along the path and on the muddy grass against the wall at the top of the graveyard, which separated the crop of the dead from the harvest of farmer's fields on the other side. No room for manoeuvre, graves were pencilled in straight lines. Borders between old plots and new were marked by marble headstones, sunken stone, and a scattering of angels, weary with moss. Canon Martin came in his own car, a jalopy with only two doors. He was helped out of the passenger seat and along to the graveside by a balding, middle-aged, altar boy.

With the noise of the wind, and traffic from the

nearby dual carriageway, for most of those gathered it was a mime show – a game of watching the old priest turning pages of the missal and matching it with the mutter of moving lips. Soon it was time to drop Joey's coffin into the cut trench. The undertaker handed John one of the cords for this duty. He distributed the other cords to men Joey had worked with in the yards, big, broad men bursting out of their suits, not scared to get their clean shoes dirty on the runnel of dirt at their feet. They took the job seriously. The man across from John, the biggest of them all, with a quiff and sideburns, gave him the nod when the time came to lower the coffin. They dropped the cords in and bowed their heads a fraction to each other at a job well done.

'I was very sorry to hear about your da.' The man with the quiff shook John's hand. 'He was a good man.' He squeezed his fingers in a handshake. Hazel-brown eyes locked on his, steady as his gravelly voice. 'And I was sorry to hear about your wee sister too. Bastards.' He spat into the grave and introduced himself, 'Bobby Rodgers. If there is anything I can do let me know.'

'Cheers.' John sounded unsure. Not because of anything that had been said, but he was sure he had spotted Janine's braided hair swinging back and forth across her back as she walked away from the graveside.

He trotted through the crowd. People he knew vaguely bit their lips and nodded at him, and mourners he was distantly related to offered condolences and tried to catch him in conversation. He left them behind and caught up with Janine. She stood with her head bowed and hands tucked into the pockets of a smart navy jacket with flashy silver buttons in front of a mildewed wooden marker, which John realised was a tombstone. The council workers had left a skip on the path, creating a chicane. He slapped her on the back as if they had been playing a game of tig. She flinched when he touched her arm.

'You came.' He leaned across and pecked her on the cheek, making an awkward grab for her hand.

'Had to. Sign of respect.' She pushed his outstretched fingers away. A green Hillman nosed out of the path, almost skimming them so they tucked their bums in and stepped closer to the grave. The car rattled on the shoulder of the exit and chugged onto the dual carriageway with a string of other cars backed-up behind it.

'That's funny,' said John. 'The Poole family. They've got the same second name as you. Whit's the chances of that, eh?' He drew his finger casually down the list of names interred in the plot. His eyes oscillating back and forth, finger tapping, and drawn to the final name, one he had become familiar with, Lily, *Gone But Not Forgotten.* 'And that girl Lily died the same day as our Ally was born. I'm ninety-nine per cent sure, but I'd need to ask my mum. Jesus, the chances of that are about a million to one.' He turned to check where the hired car was. Many of the cars waiting in line had taken a detour, and a different route, along another row of graves. Janine gave him a searching look, but said nothing.

'Wait there and I'll give you a lift.' His voice rose and he smiled encouragement. Her face was shiny clean by

Janine's standards. No make-up. 'You're coming to the do, aren't you?'

'No.'

'Don't be daft. You need to come.'

He watched cars speeding past them, gaps opening up between them, until, last of all, the priest's jalopy crawled out through the iron gates. He told her his secret, 'I saw you the other night, standing at the window, looking out at the stars.'

'Did you?' she said. 'I'm thrilled to smithereens.' She walked away from him, her heels clicking on the tarmac.

'Hing on.' He easily caught up with her. She slapped his hand away. The limousine slowed and stopped beside him. The passenger door opened and his mum stared out at him. She patted the empty seat beside her and he found himself filling it.

'Jump in,' he shouted at Janine.

She shook her head and kept clumping along, without turning back or looking at him.

Mary followed her son's gaze as the car passed her. 'That's a strange girl that.'

'She looks trouble,' said Auntie Caroline.

The do after the funeral was held in St Stephen's Church Hall. White-linen-covered tables were set out around the perimeter of the wooden floor that John had played football on when he was younger. The glitter of the silver ball above the mourners' heads was on standstill, waiting for Friday night disco lights to revive it. Women from the chapel committee had done them proud, ferrying back and forth with industrial-sized tea and coffee pots, plying the tables with sandwiches and sausage rolls, smoothing things out with remarks concerning what kind of fillings were best. They even provided plates of cakes and chocolate biscuits for the kids. Men's ties loosened and then were shoved in their pockets, belts slackened. A nip of whisky. That was their lot. They stayed on after the sandwiches, talking about football. Women's shoes were kicked off tortured feet, buttons popped, and they had a confab about their kids. A vodka with coke or lemonade. Enough to wet their whistles and help them on their way.

Mary did the rounds, thanking everybody for coming. Jo, at her elbow, listening in, being told what a big girl she was getting, managed a nervous smile.

'It's a terrible shame,' was the common refrain.

Whether they were talking about his da or his sister, John was unsure, but he said nothing. He was with his aunties and their kids, stuck in a seat near the toilets, a can of orange juice in front of him. While he was making chit-chat with his Auntie Caroline, he glanced over at the stage and the emergency exit, to his da's mates at the makeshift bar – a plywood hut in the corner of the hall. They supped cans of Pale Ale, but that was better than nothing. They leaned, lounged, hunched, smoked and drank with raucous laughter and looked as if they were plotting for the world to end.

Bobby Rodgers broke away from the group and cut across the Guild's dance floor to where John was sitting.

'A few of us are goin' to the pub for a few jars. We'd like you to come wae us.'

Auntie Caroline shook her head across the table, warning him that he should be sensible. Bobby smiled and kidded on that he had not seen it.

'Ah cannae,' John said.

'Too good for us?' he chuckled.

'No, it's no' that. I've got to keep an eye on my ma,' John groaned. 'And I'm pratted.'

'You don't need money,' he snorted. His big hand patted Auntie Caroline on the arm, tagging her. She looked up at him. 'I think this good lady will keep an eye on your wee ma.' He winked, made it seem so reasonable, that she nodded. John's chair scraped on the floor in his haste to get up and follow his new mate.

Bobby was first through the door of the Club Bar, his hand on John's shoulder and a crowd of men behind them. The barmaid, a thin woman with a beehive hairdo, watched them spilling in and grinned with tobacco-stained teeth.

'A pint of your best slops, Agnes, for this young man. And unlucky for some, thirteen half-and-halves for the rest of us.' Bobby swept his hand out, an introduction to the other men crowding the bar.

'Hing on. Is he eighteen?' She leaned her head to get a better look at John. 'He doesnae look eighteen.'

Bobby pulled out a tenner, put it on the bar and tapped his forefinger against it. 'That'll get that. And there's plenty more where that came from.' He turned and studied John's face, who, in the throng, was pushed up against him. 'That boy's not eighteen. He's twenty-one and he's an American and not used to our crude ways.'

The barmaid poured half pints of McEwans from the taps underneath the bar. She pirouetted, her arm outstretched as she held a short's glass up to an upturned bottle of Bells in the gantry. 'You twenty-one, son?'

Bobby nudged him.

'Aye,' John said.

'You don't sound American.' She held the glass up to fill it again.

'But does he sound twenty-one?' a balding man with a flushed face piped in from the back of the crowd, and folk standing nearby started laughing.

The crew of mourners good-naturedly took over the pub, piling into the corner tables at the long curve of the mock-leather seats, the wall of opaque windows above their heads. Status Quo hits played on the jukebox near the toilets. John was told so many stories about Joey that he swelled up like a bullfrog. It made him think for a minute his da was just outside, waiting to fall in and join the company. He was fed salted crisps and watered-down whisky, which was good for you. When he had to use the loo, he realised he was wobbly on his feet, flushed pink, with puffed-out cheeks, but they seemed to take it in turn to line up and slap him on the back to show how impressed with him they were. He was just like Joey. He was a chip off the old block.

He found himself wittering on to Bobby about the

dreams he had, trying to explain their significance. Janine was a succubus that was draining him, or he was an incubus draining her. He fell into a conversation with somebody else and failed to remember who was who, or what he was talking about.

Bobby shook his head and gave him some fatherly advice. 'That kind of stuff's for old women with hair nets and tarot cards. Only daft women get involved in that kind of shite. Your da wouldnae have liked it.'

John got the message and was bundled into a taxi home.

After that, the glop of sick, hemp and the feel of his living room carpet under his cheek were too real to be imagined.

DAY 56

John thought a hangover was something old fogeys suffered from, but the next morning his neck felt chiselled out of Bridge of Don granite and his head was leaden. He wanted to die, or at least lie in bed with his mum mopping his forehead and holding a bowl out for him to be sick into.

Instead, she smacked him hard on the back of the head. 'Ya dirty bugger. Look at the mess you've made.' Her concern was for the carpet, not him.

He lifted his head to mutter. 'Someone must have spiked my drink.'

She clattered him again, harder this time. 'They didn't

spike it enough. Get into your bed and out of my sight before I really start on you. As if I've no' got enough to contend with.'

He crawled slug-like across the living room. Negotiating the door, he monkeyed a few notches up the evolutionary tree into something bipedal. He flailed like a blind man, shoulders banging against the walls, and stumbled into the sanctuary of the toilet where he crouched and grasped the womb of Shanks' toilet pan for support. Throwing up green bile his stomach worked the miracle of turning lavvy water wine-red. His belly spasmed, but brought only gut pain.

By mid-afternoon he felt able to sip water and watch telly. His mum gave him withering looks and did everything but poke him with a stick. She had arranged for Jo to stay with Auntie Teresa for another week; whether that was because of his antics he was unsure. Auntie Caroline tutted, but appeared mildly sympathetic. He was glad that her daft friend Gloria hovered in attendance because it meant he had no need to feign an interest in their conversation. A brackish tendril explored the back of his throat and he rushed once more to the toilet.

When he returned, plonking himself back in the same seat, he watched his mum stumble over the join of the carpet between kitchen and living room. Her wrists were white, fragile as lollipop sticks, and her hand trembled as she passed him a glass of water and an Askitt. He recognised it as a truce, tipping his head back and letting the contents powder the pink of his mouth. She stood by his chair until he had finished swallowing tepid water before turning and taking the glass back into the kitchen.

He dozed to the theme music of *Blue Peter.* His fingers shaped and curved into talons. Hand-clutching marked the beginning of a loosening of his body. A moment of extreme clarity and then falling. He dreamed something was above him and he panicked as asphyxiation threshed his body. He tried kicking up and out. But each breath was more hurried, shallower than the last. Life tapered. He was looking through a keyhole. A drumming sound he thought of as rain, but his bones recognised as the weight of soil. His right leg shook. A cut-throat blade of fear cut across him. He clawed his way up and out of hellish reveries, gasping for breath.

'You've had one of your visions again.' Gloria, self-satisfied, nodded at Auntie Caroline to confirm the truth of what she said.

'What did you see, son?' Auntie Caroline asked.

Mary sat on the couch beside her, blinking with tiredness, yawning and half-listening.

'I don't know,' John said. The frantic energy his trance had given him leached away and his body went slack. He tilted his head, fingers dragging through his hair and scalp for evidence of the pockmarks of divots, which he was sure had struck him.

'Mocking laughter. I heard mocking laughter and saw men in police uniforms.' He turned and looked over at his mum to gauge her reaction. She watched him, her pupils like watery moons he was falling into. He wanted to tell her the truth that he could no longer be sure that the laughter was not his own, but a sensation of exaltation flashed through his body as he realised that she already knew. She had always known. There could be no longer be any secrets between them and there never was.

'You need to really listen. Open yourself up to the breath of your fellow man. The breath of life. Those that have gone before.' Gloria flushed with satisfaction. 'The future casts a long shadow into the past.'

Mary brushed imaginary crumbs from her legs before standing. 'Well, some people have got work to do.'

'You don't want to find Alison?' Gloria asked.

Auntie Caroline leaned forward, eclipsing Mary, but her younger sister held her off with a sharp look, and was quick to reply.

'Don't get sarky with me, madam. Anymore of your codswallop and I'll be putting you out the door, personally. I've asked God for help. I've asked Him till my knees buckled and my fingers fused. You know what I think?' She looked at her son and shrugged. 'I think God's out there and we're in here. I think we're cursed. That's what I think.' Her voice grew calmer before sputtering and rising again. 'But I'll tell you this, lady, if there was a chance of finding my Alison I'd follow the devil straight to hell to do it. I'd give my immortal soul just to speak to her one more time, to hold her one more time, to find her safe.'

'I'm sorry. I didn't mean it that way.' Gloria's face flushed a mottled pink and she sounded contrite.

Mary ignored her and shuffled into the kitchen. The

sound of the taps running could be heard, and behind Gloria's shoulder the hum of the boiler kicked into life.

Auntie Caroline's voice was hard and her manner no longer polite. 'I think it's about time you left.'

Gloria shrank into herself. 'OK.' She tried a half smile, but it puttered out. Gathering up her cigarettes and the handbag at her feet, she swayed as she stood up. Auntie Caroline, waited to escort her out.

Gloria turned back and apologised again. 'I shouldn't have said that, son. But you've got the gift.' She sniffled and dabbed at her eyes. 'If you need my help, you know where to find me.'

'Don't worry about it.' John felt sorry for her, but also uneasy. He tried not to show it, but with all her meddling, his brain had unrighted itself and left a submarine-size hole in the way he felt. But there was a bright side to it, Gloria getting flung out allowed him to sneak past his mum and auntie and spend time alone in his room. He carried a comic book in his hand, but with no thought of reading it, more an alibi he could wave should anyone ask what he was doing. He edged toward the window and his legs went numb from standing motionless. He felt on the wrong side of the glass, as if something alien, something Gloria might have recognised, was inside him, and pushing the furniture about to make space for something life-changing. The reek of putrid flesh made him gag, but a split-second later the night segued into something more recognisable and manageable. His mum's room was a dark grotto full of the familiar childhood smells of fags and unwashed sheets. Without knowing how he had got there, John found he had picked off the floor a metallic dot. Hardly there. But when he looked more closely it was a fragment of a black-and-white photo of his mum smiling at him and clinging to the picture of a world already gone.

DAY 57

John went to bed after his mum, limbs heavy with fatigue, but he had trouble sleeping. He eyed with distaste the Christmas-tree brightness of the yellow light shade above his head and the heavy brocade of winter curtains hanging like gaudy flags from the curtain rail. Despite eating nothing more exotic than spuds and beans with brown HP sauce, an aftertaste of bitter herbs clogged his mouth. Clammy skin, oily with sweat, and his heart playing a banjo tune made his eyelids pop open. He sat up sharpish and listened, not sure what for. His thoughts drifted to Janine and he had a wank. His denims were sitting frozen in the chair by the window, waiting for a body, a hanky in the back pocket. Seed dripping from his fingers and palm made him act decisively. He darted to the toilet in his Y-fronts, cleaned himself up, and had a quick pee. Yawning, clock-watching, time suspended, he ambled back towards his bedroom, but hesitated and stuttered. He found himself standing outside his mum's room, his breath punched out in front of him.

It seemed stupid, a stunt from *Monty Python*, but he

put his ear to the door. Then drawing away, he rapped politely with his knuckles. No one answered. He knocked again. Through the wall of his sisters' room he heard bedsprings groan, weight being shifted. A few moments later a click, a parabola of light, and Auntie Caroline stood framed in the doorway. She tugged her nightgown over any hint of breasts. Her presence gave him permission to press his hand against the door panel. He heard the ball-catch release and hinges squeal as he pushed the door.

'Mum.' He spoke into the darkness of the room, his voice unsure

There was no answer. He stood suspended in two worlds, no longer certain if he was in the right house, or if he was dreaming and would wake up in his hospital bed, wondering what all the fuss was about.

'Mum.' He spoke a little louder, urgency in his voice. A musty smell mixed with cigar smoke made his body tense even more.

The shuffle of slippers and a deep-rooted sigh. Auntie Caroline stood next to him, steadying him. He felt rather than saw her arm snake past his chest. Time slowed. The light clicked on and he was running. His Auntie Caroline cried out, but he could no longer decipher words; he scrambled to make connections between sentences, but it was as if she had started speaking Igbo.

He found himself outside, halfway down the street and unaware of his destination – the phone box. Slowly, he became conscious that his feet were sore, speckled by jaggy stones, his nose streamed and his skin shone with rain. He pulled open the heavy door. He was careful with his footing and leaned across to dial 999, the numbers ratcheting in a cone-shaped curve and whirring as the dial returned to the starting point.

Bubbling tears into the receiver, the calm pool of a woman's voice reassured him; he wheedled and prayed for them to come quickly, asked the telephone operator to make his mum better, to make things the way they used to be. With a click, the operator was gone.

Slogging up the hill and back to the house, he positioned himself on the doorstep, the front door wide open at his back, scanning the streets for blue flashing lights, listening for sirens. 'How long? How long? How long?' he muttered. His hair in the driving rain clung round his ears like a swimming cap as he blinked the water away and shivered. Somehow he became more and more sure they would not come and less and less sure he wanted them to.

Keening sirens cut through what remained of the night and he spotted the strobe light turning the corner of Byron Street. The ambulance crew came charging out of the doors of the parked ambulance like action heroes; one tall, the other fat, the tarpaulin stretcher they carried between them was a bridge between words and action. There was the bustle of men asking questions that whirled round in John's head like helicopter blades: Who was he and where was she? What had she taken? Where was the medicine cabinet? He failed to answer, a ghost in his own life.

He followed behind them through the house. Auntie

Caroline was a more substantial presence, guiding them in an unfamiliar, faltering tone, answered questions as best she could. One question, from the taller of the two ambulance men, threw her, 'How long has she been like this?'

'Her whole life.' John spoke with conviction trying to contain his growing sense of panic. 'She's been like that her whole life. She's my mum. You can save her, can't you?'

The bed sheets hauled to the bottom of the bed were redundant. His mum looked smaller, her nightie riding up her legs and her face a bluish colour as they checked for a pulse at her neck and wrist. 'It's no good,' said the fat medic to his companion. 'She's cold, been gone a good while.'

The stretcher was a companion beside her. Mary's body was eased across, rolled over the lip, parcelled up and disappeared out of the door. Then sirens and flashing lights; unholy silence and darkness.

DAY 60

The front door banged at an ungodly hour. No watch, no alarm clock, to tell him the time, John mashed gummy sleep from the corners of his eyes with his knuckles. Dropping off to sleep had not been easy. Too many thoughts warred in his head, too much reality leaving him stranded in a fecund field of what ifs?. What if he had been nicer to his mum, more patient, more kind, paid her more attention? What if he had known? What could he have done? He stumbled, cold-footed, down the hall and turned the Yale lock.

Policemen barged in. A platoon of night-crawling uniforms fanned out and took over the house. A swish of nylon clothing, a hand on his shoulder, swivelling his body in a loop, a bended knee pushed into the back of John's leg and his cheek squished and sliding down the wallpaper. 'Who else is in the house, with you?' screamed a voice in his ear. His locked arm jerked higher up his back, and tighter, to urge him towards speech.

'Nobody.'

No one waited for, or wanted, an explanation. Auntie Caroline had boxed her grief and gone home, could not stay a minute longer in that house. Jo was with his Auntie Teresa and it was unlikely she would return. A slackening in his arm, a loosening of his wrist and the shuffling of feet meant the policeman assigned to guard him was checking with the other cops. A smack in the back was more shocking than painful, it was aimed at the kidneys and meant to hurt, but the spittle dripping from his face from the cop guarding him hurt more. He was dragged out of the house like a paper bag, rain teeming down, wearing only his Y-fronts.

Flung into the back of a panda car, cuffed, he tucked his hands into his lap. His neck scrunched and the bones of his shoulders poked out, like a cricket ready to hop, as he made himself smaller in the back seat and tried to stop shivering.

The driver wore black leather gloves and his finger

tapped a light beat on the steering wheel. He turned to study John, the face beneath his cap shiny and close-shaved. His heavy lips a non-committal line, favouring neither smile nor frown. A movement outside alerted them to a fellow officer leaving the house. A constable was stationed at the front door on guard duty, hands behind his back, as if he would be there for the duration. The front door of the car clicked open and the senior officer folded himself into the passenger seat beside the driver, taking his braided cap off, flinging it against the windscreen, letting it settle on top of the dashboard. Hot air from the heaters wafted the damp smell of rain and Polo mints into the back of the car. Nobody spoke. The engine kicked over and they rolled smoothly down the hill, leaving behind the convoy of Black Marias and other police vehicles.

In the early hours of the morning the roads were free of other traffic. It took only ten minutes to get to Hall Street Station. Turning the car off-road and onto the cobbles of the side street, the driver negotiated the arched shadows of the rear entrance. The engine ticked over, the heating on. The senior officer let in a blast of cold air as he left the car, his long coat flapping and the back of his cap disappearing into the blackened stone of the building. The driver twisted his neck, chair creaking as he leaned back. 'Don't fucking move,' he warned. A shipyard hammer clanked a steady thud. On and on it went, marking time.

Two cops strolled across the quadrangle to collect their prisoner. They were insiders, wearing dark uniforms, but no hats against the rain. John shuffled his bum across the seat to get out. The car door opened. Blunt fingers reached inside for the prisoner and, although he offered no resistance, pulled him stumbling out of the car. The sturdier cop, standing behind his colleague, grabbed John's arm, tugging him in close to his hip, and mooring the prisoner between them. He ground the heel of his Doc Martens into John's bare foot. John squealed, a high, sharp sound that rang round the buildings.

He was dragged through long, damp stone corridors that sucked in light and heat, pulled to the booking desk and pressed up against the hatch.

'Jesus, is this what all the fuss was about?' The officer on the booking desk used a ruler to flip open a book on the counter which looked like a ledger. He looked across at John, his face blue and stubbly with new growth, flashing uneven teeth as he yawned. 'Let's get him fingerprinted and down to the cells.'

'I've been fingerprinted before,' John piped up, trying to be helpful.

A heel crashed down on his toes again. 'Speak when you're spoken to – Nonce.'

The sergeant's voice, bored as a parent at a children's jamboree, warned his colleague, 'That's enough, Linton.'

DAY 63

Clock time abolished. They left him to stew in a damp underground cell. Shiny white brick swimming from floor to ceiling. The caged light above his head created permanent twilight. A thin foam mattress and a scratchy blanket were his only possessions. He read the inscriptions on the walls and door of who was there, who was going to fuck who and fuck you, who was a grass, and Celtic and Rangers forever, until he knew what they said without having to raise his head from the mattress. He knew the drill. There was a thin ledge just off the floor that he and the mattress fitted onto.

The day went on without him. He heard the hatches opening in other cells, the shuffle of feet, shouts of 'Turnkey. Fucking turnkey,' followed by the rattle of a flat hand on the thick metallic plate, but not once on his door. Nobody came to give him a cup of tea, or lunch, or even dinner, but he was too scared to make a fuss. He grew used to cold, shivering spasms, the musty stench of his body, tears, and the dryness of mouth that felt as if he had cotton wool lodged in his throat. The only pastime was sleep, but that was as out of reach as Paris, the warm voices of his mum or dad, or the safety of home.

The rattle of a key in his cell door roused him. He heard a throaty laugh and a joke between gaolers, made funnier because they were shouting from one end of the corridor to the other. Tightly clutching the blanket, pulling it around his shoulders, making a suit of his discomfort, he recognised in himself the creeping aura of dread preceding his fits. The turnkey stood staring in at him, the door open as if in some kind of invitation.

'Let's be having you.' He took a step into the cell, the thick solidity of his body blocking the light behind him.

John remembered his name, Linton, because of the way he had mauled his feet. Scrambling to stand, he stood with his back against the wall and the sheet draped in front of him. But the guard showed only a dead-eyed interest, flicking his head to indicate that he was to follow him out of the cell.

Another turnkey, wiry with dank hair, was waiting outside the cell to act as an auxiliary escort. They marched John to the interview room where two suits were waiting. One lounged against the wall, smoking and watching John's arrival with a bored expression. He was prematurely bald, the white dome of his crown shining and the sides of his hair shorn dark into his scalp. The window high above his head was hooked open, bringing a tang of the river and the noise of cars and buses. Because of the brighter light and the open window, John initially felt the room to be bigger than his cell, but with the clutter of table and chairs it also seemed tacky, huddled together and smaller.

'What happened to his clothes?' the detective sitting at the table asked Linton in a blokey tone. His hair and suit were the same slate-grey colour and his eyes a watery pale green, wrinkling into a kind of wry amuse-ment, though everything else about him was ordered. He sat with his outdoor coat square on the back of the chair, feet under the table, notepad, pen, jug of water and two plastic cups lined up, tools of his trade, on his side of the table.

'That's what he was wearing when we arrested him, sir.' Linton snapped to attention.

'Or not wearing.' The balding detective laughed, shrugging off any impropriety, and took a seat behind and to the side of his colleague.

Linton huckled John round the table and into the seat facing them and went to stand guard by the door. The other turnkey marched off.

The man sitting across from John introduced himself. 'I'm Detective Chief Inspector Allan, and this is Detective Morley.' He nodded towards the man sitting with a pencil and notepad on his knee behind him and half turned to give John his full attention, 'You know why you're here?'

'I'm no' sure,' John admitted. He had thought of little else, but could not come up with an answer. His musings after his mum's death looped round his head. He imagined the ward had got in touch with the police, or the police had to get in touch with the ward and he would have to go back. But as far as he knew his mum had taken an overdose of prescribed medication and there was nothing he, or anyone, could have done.

'What have you done with your sister, Alison?' Detective Morley leaned forward to hiss at him. 'Where have you stashed her?'

John studied one police officer, then the other. 'I don't know whit you're talkin' about.' His voice grew angry. 'I was in hospital when she was taken.'

'No, you werenae, sonny.' Detective Morley, his pencil a prop which he waved like a weapon, did more talking than note-taking. 'We've been there and checked. They said you treated the place like a hotel and swanned in and out whenever you felt like it. They can't account for all your movements on that day.'

'For God's sake. I ran away once. Went back the next day.'

'So you do admit you absconded?' Chief Inspector Allan spoke with a forced familiarity, as if smoothing over a little difficulty between relatives.

'Aye, but that's different.'

'How is it different?' Chief Inspector Allan asked.

John brooded, weary for an answer. 'Nurses saw me comin' in and oot,' was all he could offer.

Detective Morley chuckled. 'What about all those other times when they never saw you coming in and out?'

'I don't know whit you're talkin' about. We were locked up twenty-four hours a day.'

Chief Inspector Allan spoke through tight lips. 'Easy enough to get out. And back in if you've a mind to.'

'That one time. And I went through the front door.'

He heard Chief Inspector Allan's shoe knocking against the desk. The investigator hesitated before he spoke. 'But you can see our problem?'

'There's more than one way to skin a cat,' Detective Morley added. 'We checked the window in your room. Unlatched. Ground floor. Easy enough to slope in and out without anyone being any the wiser.'

'And the psychiatrist, a Mr Williams, I believe,' the senior officer revelled in the pronunciation, 'said you'd a history of violence. You seriously assaulted a member of

staff. He was going to move you to a more secure unit.'
He let this sink in, gauging John's reactions.

'That's just pish,' spluttered John. He clutched his
hands and could not think of anything to counter with.
'Whit did he let me oot for then?'

'Quite understandable, compassionate grounds,' said
Chief Inspector Allan.

'That was a mistake,' Detective Morley cut in. 'People
like you have as much compassion as—' He rapped his
heel against the tiled floor, a crack that echoed round
the room. 'What have you done with your sister?'

'And all those other little girls you abducted?' Chief
Inspector Allan asked with a drier voice, his eyes drilling
into John's, until the boy looked away confused. He
poured water into one of the plastic cups, handed it to
John, and spoke in a paternal tone, 'It's your mother's
funeral soon. We could easily arrange for you to be back
on the same ward. Arrange an officer to escort you to
her funeral. Then back to the cosy little ward routine.
I'm sure you'll soon be out, but only if you admit to the
abduction of your sister and these other girls.'

John choked up with crying, rocking back and forth
in his chair, his downcast eyes focussed on the space
underneath the desk. 'But I didnae dae it.'

Chief Inspector Allan leaned across, close enough for
John to smell his Brut aftershave. 'That's not what your
mother said. She left a note. Mentioned you in it.'

Detective Morley spoke over the top of his colleague,
enjoyed telling him, 'That's why she killed herself.

Couldnae live with the knowledge of what her son had done.'

John wriggled in his seat, wanting to stand up and flee, but Linton and Morley's hostile gaze and Allan's more sanguine look, kept him pinned to the seat of the chair. He wiped his nose with the back of his hand. 'I loved my mum more than anything. She wouldnae say that.'

'But she did.' Chief Inspector Allan picked up his notepad. Underneath it was a scrap of paper, which he kept half covered with the fleshy part of his hand, as if reluctant to show its full content. He recognised his mum's handwritten scrawl in soft pencil.

> *To who it may concern Joey found out about me*
> *and came back to tell me little Ally went to hell*
> *and I wiz to ask John where to find her body*
> *and the other wee wans killed to god*

The uncrossed ts and stunted lettering broke him, and he bent over the table and sobbed. 'But I didnae do it,' he said.

He felt Detective Morley at his back, leaning over him, spluttering with flecks of saliva, 'You fucking well did,' drilling the message into the back of his head. Chief Inspector Allan gazed over, then looked away, engrossed in the study of the few notes on his desk.

Detective Morley crouched down at the side of John's chair. He slanted his left hand over his mouth, whispering, 'You've got another sister haven't you?'

John angled his head, his eyes darting sideways, and found himself also whispering, 'Yeh.'

'Jose-phine, isn't it?' Detective Morley broke his sister's name in two like a stick.

'That's right.' John's lowered his voice even further, the words tight and pinched as he held his breath.

'We'll need to drag your sister in, you know. Common decency suggests we leave no stone unturned. Bring her in for questioning. Sit her in the very chair you're sitting in. Aiding and abetting.' Detective Morley's laugh turned into a sneer. 'I'll guess she'll get time. It's up to you.'

John's legs buckled when he stood up. Linton moved towards him, but Chief Inspector Allan held a hand up and he backed off, once again standing sentry at the door. John stumbled towards the window, looking out. His narrow shoulders twitching as he cried.

'You admit to abducting your sister, Alison Connelly, on the morning of 21st February, 1973?' asked Chief Inspector Allan.

'I must have,' John said, wiping away tears.

Detective Morley punched the air as if he had scored a winning Cup Final goal. 'Yes.'

Chief Inspector Allan took his time reading out a list of girls' names, with the addendum of days and dates. At each one he paused to look up at John and let him answer, reminding him that a nod was not enough, he would have to answer for the record. When they finished, he slapped him on the shoulder. 'You did well.' But his self-satisfied smile was for himself and the other policemen.

'Good work.' Chief Inspector Allan reached into the back pocket of his coat and pulled out a five-pack of Panatela and took his time lighting up, smoke fanning out in front of his face. He rolled a slim cigar across the table towards John and watched the confusion on his face. Detective Morley snatched it away. Shoulders heaving, tie askew, the detective crowed in delight as he blew out cheap cigar smoke. Chief Inspector Allan's chair scraped across the floor. He passed the cigar packet to Linton, knocking formality on its head, and insisted he light up and join his senior officers in their moment of triumph.

EPILOGUE

Fastmoves, the estate agent, had planted a wooden flag in the front garden. A sign of progress. Jo had the money, the get-up-and-go, and she had bought their council house. They had agreed John would have to find somewhere else to live. Well, she had agreed. It needed far too much work before she could rent it to people like herself, working professionals. The fixtures and fittings were shambolic, still the same telly in the living room, screen like a fishbowl. Tan couch and chairs. Plastic tat Jo had called them, forgetting the reverence they were held in when she was young.

Da had barely allowed Jo, Ally or John to sit in them. Mum had glowed and kept the plastic covers on for a week, nearly two. They were supposed to hover above the seats like some kind of *Star Trek* teleport seeking solidity, but not too much at once.

And don't get Jo started on what needed to be done to the kitchen. It needed a bomb in it, she had said. It just wouldn't do. She crossed her arms over her breasts for a tour of their childhood bedrooms and heirlooms. The old wardrobes filled with photographs and clothes nobody would ever wear. It just wouldn't do. The windows and doors needed replacing. It was hellish. She wondered aloud how anyone could survive like that for nigh on twenty years.

John was not surprised to hear someone chapping at the front door. He took his time getting up from the armchair and traipsing down the hall to answer it.

He hadn't bothered overmuch with snazzing up, just pulled on an old brown cardigan, denims, and left his toes poking out of Jesus sandals, figuring whoever it was hadn't come to view him, but the rooms and their fixtures and fittings. But he wasn't sure. Over the years the press had turned up in droves. Camped themselves outside on the anniversaries when the girls first went missing, pointing cameras through the windows, so he was reduced to hiding in the darkness of his own home. Graffiti appeared like ectoplasm on the external walls and doors, telling him what he was and what was to become of him. He couldn't really blame them.

The police, after a formal review of their conduct by an outside force, had let it be known that although there wasn't enough evidence to prosecute, they weren't looking at any other suspects. He knew what that meant. It was written on his body. When he had been on remand in Barlinnie, the other cons had called it a waste of good sugar whilst a pot of boiling water was poured over his head, the sweet stuff acting as an adhesive. Slashed and burned with cigarettes. Sucker-punched and kicked. Fair game for anybody with a grudge and a reputation. He had been an easy target until he started to stand up for himself. All he wanted was to be left alone.

'Can I help you, pal?' John's tone of voice had grown harsh over the years. But the youthful features of the boy standing at the door threw him a bit. He had grown wary of folk trying to make friends with him, trying to drill him for information, but he looked gormless enough not to be a rabid homebuyer on the make. John speculated it was some new tactic Mormon missionaries were using, one that included not dressing in Marks and Spencer suits and shiny shoes, not turning up like identikit two-by-two clones, but going undercover in brown leather jackets and denim faded at the knees.

'Mum said there was only one person dafter in the world than her and that was you.' His light blue eyes crinkled, moist and good-natured, sharing a joke in which they both arrived at the punchline together. 'I'm Jack.' He stuck his hand out for him to shake, nails pearl-white as a baby's.

John stood motionless. He watched Jack's hand wavering and slipping down, slapping against his leg, and his adolescent grin sanded down to a straight line. 'I think you've got the wrang house, pal.'

'No,' Jack shifted from foot to foot, unsure, but stuck at his task with a stolid stubbornness. 'I recognise you from news clips from the *Daily Record* Mum showed me. She said you lived here. She said you two were really close once and you'd be able to help.'

'I don't think so, pal,' John lowered his voice. He took a step backwards, away from the neediness lurking in the younger man's eyes, and shoved the door shut, putting the sneck on the Yale and turning the key in the mortise. The boy's head drooped, reminding him of the tramped-down bluebells punctuating the side beds beneath the window, and for a few seconds he felt sorry for him. He was half way up the hall before he realised his mistake. Fingers and thumbs playing funny buggers on the locks slowed him down. Then he was outside, his sandals slipping off his feet as he ran down the hill. Out of breath, he caught up with the boy at the huts. 'Whit's your mum's name?'

'Janine Poole.'

A grin zipped across Jack's face, a near permanent feature, so unlike his mother, but the lips and eyes were certainly Janine's. The hair and the way he stood, however, reminded the older man of his younger self. 'You better come up to the house, then, for a cup of tea.' He traipsed up the hill ahead of Jack, listening to the footfall behind him, forcing himself not to look round, not to quickly check who was following him and if he had a weapon.

In the kitchen, John flicked the kettle on. He had forgotten the language of small talk. Jack sat in the corner chair at the table, the smug imperviousness of youth, waiting for him to say something. He ran two mugs, both chipped at the rim, underneath the taps at the sink, and found the tea bags. 'Whit dae you take in your tea?' Then he bridged his awkwardness with the bluster of another innocuous question. 'How's your mum keeping, anyway?'

Jack showed his good breeding. 'Just milk, please.' And dipping into that smile again. 'Grand. She's grand. She's an accountant. Doing really well.'

'An accountant!' John tried to keep the surprise out of his voice, the shock off his face. Behind him the kettle hissed, allowing him to turn away and flick the switch off, swill the cups out into the sink and make tea.

'Well, she's always been good with numbers and spreadsheets and working things out.' Jack's smile disappeared and he spoke in a doleful way that indicated that those were the areas where he was not gifted.

John tamped down a smirk and passed Jack his mug of tea. He sipped at his own, glancing through the steam, keeping his voice neutral. 'Whit about your da?'

'Oh, he's an accountant too.' His untutored smile and his earnest face made it easy to believe that the world was chock full of accountants and it was a sign of rebellion not being one.

'Any brothers or sisters?'

'No.'

'Just you, then?'

'Aye, Mum had trouble with her pipes and things.' Jack made it sound like a blocked connection to a spin dryer. His cheeks pinked and he looked away.

John gnawed at the jagged red skin round his thumbnail. 'And whit does your mum think I can help you with?'

Jack would not meet John's level gaze. Instead they scanned the woven straw placemats on the table. 'At first I'd nightmares, stupid dreams. I'm getting ready for school. It's always snowing outside. I keep slipping. I'm petrified, but I don't know why. A policeman comes to help me and he's joined by a school janitor. I don't know how I know that because they're wearing masks but I do. I run and run and run. They aren't really human. They're wolves. You know what I mean?' He looked up to gauge John's reaction before continuing. 'They easily catch me. And they put me in a dark room. That's part of the game. Then they can take their masks off. And I scream and scream and scream. But they love that. It only makes them hungrier and me more frightened. In a way, it's hard for adults, for bigger people, to understand. And I close my eyes and hear a daft tune: *Jack, Jack, where are you, where are you?* I don't know if it means anything,' he said, his voice dropping. 'I see what is happening and I'm there, but I'm also not a part of it. I can escape, and then I waken up safely in bed.'

'Drink your tea,' John urged. The cup lay in front of him untouched. 'So, in a nutshell, you have a bad dream and then you waken up?'

Jack curled his fingers round the mug and sipped. 'I've had the same dream for as long as I can remember.'

John coughed, slapped his chest, and cleared his throat. 'So, you've had the same bad dream?' He slurped at his tea, chewed it to help him think and made an 'ahh' sound when he swallowed. 'Did your mum ever talk about me?' He hurried on, 'You've seen bits and pieces in the papers. Whit I mean is, did your mum,' he swallowed, finding it difficult to say her name, 'did Janine put you up to this?'

'Aye, she did.' Jack brushed awkwardness aside with a dismissive flick of his wrist and he became more resolute, leaning forward and speaking firmly. 'But it was the little girl Ally. She said she loved you. I was to come to you because you'd understand. You promised you would find her.'

The front door chapped, saving John from maudlin tears. 'I better goin' and get that.' He stood up, slapping Jack's shoulder on the way out. 'I'll no' be a minute. Make yourself at home.'

Jack looked about him. The kitchen walls and ceiling retained the imprint of fag smoke and the linoleum floor was torn and worn with pitted holes. It smelt familiar as an old oil rag, and the worn diamond was a pattern that prodded memory. He stood up and shut his eyes. He felt sure he'd be able to find his way in and out the living room and three bedrooms. He felt as if he'd been in the house before, and he was comfortable with that. It felt like a home from home. The front door banging shut made him sit down again and sip his tea, his face screwing up because it had become cold.

'Sorry about that.' John slapped his hands together and laughed. 'Someone tryin' to buy my house dirt cheap.' He had a renewed energy after telling the profiteer where to get off. 'Where were we?' He refilled the kettle.

'I was telling you—'

'I know,' John cut in, coughing, holding a hand over his mouth. 'Whit dae you want me to dae?'

'I don't know,' Jack's voice was strained. 'I was hoping you'd be able to tell me.'

'Well, to be honest, I've no' got a clue.' John's lips parted in a slow smile. 'Let's have some fresh tea and we'll work something out.'

'You still see ghosts?' Jack said, feeling more at ease.

'Nah, the living haunt me in the way the dead cannae. That's enough for me.' John took the mugs over to the sink. He swilled them under the taps in a cursory way, splashing water on his hands, looking out at the bright spring weather and the brush of trees framed against the rain-soaked Old Kilpatrick hills. 'You search for something your whole life and you find it's behind you. Already passed. It's a hungry kind of knowing that burns your flesh from the inside. That's probably why all those saints have got a big burning bush round their heid and that startled look on their face, like they've seen too much. Or maybe,' he added, fussing around, fiddling with the tea things – dash of milk, spoon and sugar – 'they just need a good shite and it's just a bad portrait with an artist having too many flecks of gold paint left over.'

Jack giggled. Another mug of tea was pushed in front of him. He warmed the palms of his hands and fingers on the cup. He studied the older man's face and felt he had to explain. 'I'm sorry, I'm not a Catholic. I'm not much of a Christian either.' He brooded whilst sipping tea, concluding, 'I'm more an agnostic.'

'Ah, well, believe me, if you're no' a Catholic, then you're a Proddy. That's the way the world works. Agnostic means Proddy, unless you're a Catholic agnostic, which means you're simply misguided.'

'I'm neither Catholic nor Proddy.'

'Well, in my da's day there was a simple solution to

that.' John took a gulp of tea. 'Whit team do you support?'

'I don't support any team.' Jack glanced at the damp patch under the armpits on the older man's shirt, then at the sink, his nostrils flaring from a sour smell. 'I'm not much interested in football.'

'Nah, you're no' allowed to say that.' John joshed the boy. It had been a while since he'd laughed. 'That's like saying you support Partick Thistle. Which team would you support if you had to support a team that was not Partick Thistle?'

'I prefer rugby, to be honest. I played in the first team for the school.'

'Ah, well,' he admitted, 'you got me there. You might as well have told me you were Jewish. But then I'd need to ask: "A Catholic Jew or a Proddy Jew?"' Growing more serious, his tone flattened. 'Whit happened to you?'

'I don't know, I've always been kinda different,' said Jack. 'I thought it was normal to have an old woman sitting beside my bed every night, watching over me.'

'Whit was she like? Did she ever speak to you?'

'No she seemed content to just sit. She was old-fashioned, like something you'd see on the telly, reddish hair and a bluish dress made out of dowdy candlewick material. The smell of cigarettes always alerted me to her being there.' He leaned across the table as if to speak in confidence, 'I liked her. She made me feel safe.'

John's chair squeaked as he shifted sideways, dipped his hand into his back pocket and brought out his wallet.

He put it on the table, opened it, and held out a black-and-white picture of Joey and Mary for Jack to look at. 'Is that her? Is that the old woman?'

Jack pursed his mouth. 'Yeh.'

'Whit about the little girls then? The one you called Ally.' John asked, ducking his head slightly and lowering his tone.

Jack hesitated, his Adam's apple bobbling up and down. He slipped the photo back to John before he spoke. 'When I was wee I didn't bother. I'd my trusty teddy. Nothing scared me. Childish nightmares about spiders, or snakes, or falling, I faced up to them all. Then, later, the girls invaded my dreams. Took them over. Took me over. Broad hands pressed down, squeezing me. Faces looming out of nowhere, dark and sudden. As I said, they were part of my dreams. But they scared me. I wanted them to go away.' His head dropped and he looked down at his lap. 'I even prayed that God would take them away, that he would save me.'

'I did that too.'

'You did?' Jack perked up. 'And what happened?'

'Disaster after disaster.' John tried to keep it light and jocular. He didn't want to scare the boy. 'Mum said we were cursed.' He swirled his tea. Placing the mug carefully back on the table, he sighed. 'We probably were.'

'So praying wasn't much use?'

John tilted his head and puckered his lips as he considered. 'I'm no' sure. It doesnae dae any harm. Probably at some level it does some good. Essentially it's a question with nae answer. Like one of those childhood origami fortune-telling games. "I am here God", and you shuffle about the handwritten responses in your hands to get an answer to the question, "Where are you?"' He laughed. 'And the answer always comes out flush as the same one: "I am here, where are you?" If we're goin' to believe in a God it stands to reason that the least we can do is crown Him with thorns and crucify Him.' He scratched the back of his head. 'You cannae murder a dream, so I guess we're sorted?'

Jack sipped cold tea. 'We would be if they didn't start to bleed into my everyday life. I'd be going to school and, out of the corner of my eyes, I'd see a little girl in a school uniform trailing behind me. I knew it wasn't right. I recognised her from my dreams, but when I turned and went chasing after her, she'd disappear behind a parked car, or another person, or a bush. I'm not sure how she did it.' He took a deep breath. 'It was a relief I couldn't catch her, but afterwards my dreams were even more vivid and intense. I'd hear voices, names: Ally, Carol, Ann, Rachel, Sarah, and they'd whisper to me in my sleep. Tell me things I didn't want to know. I became them. I was tortured, raped and buried. It got so bad I was terrified to go to sleep. I'd try and stay up all night, but I'd fall asleep at my desk at school. I was a nervous wreck. But it didn't take my mum long to figure it out. She pads about at night and never sleeps either. So after a few nights she started drifting into my room and asking me questions. Gave me the third degree.' He grew more subdued. 'Dad said I should go and see a doctor, a psychologist or something. Mum said I should come and see you. And she always gets her own way.'

'Aye, I remember that well. Your mum always got her own way.' John covered his mouth with his hand as he yawned. He grunted and stood up, his fingers winding behind his neck and stretching his chest. 'Well, as the man said, I'm a stranger in a strange world and that's for sure. Music waits to be heard. Books wait to be read. And ghosts are wailing that they're not dead. There's no use endlessly yakking about it.' He enjoyed watching the growing disbelief in Jack's face. 'Let's go.'

Jack scrambled out of the seat. 'Where to?'

'You'll see.'

The boy shook his head and smirked at the Crombie coat John pulled out of the hall cupboard and put on. John used Jack as a balancing post as he slipped on a well-worn pair of gardening boots with bulbous steel toecaps. 'Right, that's us set,' John said. 'Let's no' dae anything sensible.'

Outside, rain droplets spangled the pavement with watery sequins. 'It's no' the weather we want, but it'll need to dae,' John said. His coat protected him from the worst of it. Jack's leather jacket hung heavier on his shoulders. They walked close together. John stood for a few seconds at the shortcut, the young man at his elbow. He let his eyes wander over the changes wrought over the years: a tarmac pathway where there used to be long grass, muck and clay; concrete stairs cutting into the hill leading down to Shakespeare Avenue, with a stepped wooden fence backing onto the houses below.

'This used to be all overgrown,' John explained.

John clattered down the stairs, Jack following behind him. The rain eased and the sun came out from behind some clouds. 'Shite. We didnae want that.' He gripped onto Jack's arm. Fir trees planted close together and trimmed horizontal at the top acted as a screen, preventing them from looking along the street below. 'This is where I first saw Lily,' his voice had an edge to it. 'The weather was terrible, deep snow. This is the kind of coat we wore in those days. A man's coat. Something you could sleep in if need be.' His voice became more subdued. 'I walk down this way every day now, on the off-chance I'll see her again. Nothing.' They kept walking, the double-storey houses, whitewashed boxes, reflecting light against grey sky. John squinted. 'Can you see anything?'

'Aye,' Jack said. He squealed like a much younger boy as John clutched and held onto his arm. 'I see the same little girl I've seen her countless number of times. Her name's Ally.'

'Where is she?'

'Over there.' Jack sauntered ahead, sure in his step.

'I cannae see her.' John sounded disappointed. He tugged at Jack's sleeve to slow him down. 'Whit does she look like?'

'School uniform, blondish hair.'

'Hing on.' John put his arm across the boy's chest, stopping him from going any further. 'You seen a picture of my missing wee sister?'

'No.' The boy was unflustered. Behind him a crow

took off from the flat rooftop and cleared its throat with cawing.

'Whit colour anorak is she wearing?'

Jack looked down the street and then back at John's face. 'She's wearing a bluish anorak and a school blazer is poking out beneath it.' He turned back towards John. 'That's not a trick question, is it?' He began to sing 'Brother John, Brother John, where are you? Where are you?' to the tune of *Frère Jacques*.

The recitation bushwhacked John. He crouched low, as if he was going to be sick, and locked his fingers round his knees to keep his balance. 'How do you know these things?'

'I just do. I can't really explain it. Part of her is part of me and she's part of you too.'

'Can you tell her I love her?'

'You can tell her yourself.' Jack beckoned with his head in the direction of a hedge. 'She's just over there. But you better hurry. Any time I get close—'

He broke away from John, dashing the last few yards, heavy, clattering steps as if scattering pigeons.

'Where is she now?' John scuttled to Jack's side, his eyes scanning the hedgerow.

'She's here,' Jack said. 'I've got her by the hand.'

John bent down and peered, but he couldn't see her. He reached out to the side of Jack, patted the air around the privet, but felt nothing. 'Ask her whit happened that day?'

'She's not daft. She can hear you, just as well as I can hear you and she said you look really old.'

John laughed. 'That sounds about right.'

Jack cocked his head, listened to what Ally said and repeated it. 'She said you've to take her hand and she'll show you what happened.'

'I would, but I cannae see her hand. I cannae see any part of her. I cannae feel any part of her. Ask her if Mum's alright?'

'Come round this side and take her hand and ask her yourself,' Jack swivelled sideways, his arm out like a flag pole and his hand cupping air.

John's stomach clenched, his throat choked and he bit back bile. He felt the stupidity of it all, his life a sham, full of don't knows and make believe. He chuckled, but without humour. Hands were funny bones, just as likely to slap you as to tickle, so many separate pieces, all different. He took a stab at it, fingers fluttering and feeling about for something. He felt faint and himself dissolving into air.

Ally was a revelation standing between them, limply holding Jack's hand and his. Bawling like a kid, his legs went soft and he pulled her close to him, lifting and squeezing her into his chest. He plastered her cheeks and face with sloppy, salty kisses.

She put up with it for a minute before her head reeled back from him and accused him, 'You left me alone with lots of bad men.'

St Stephen's school bell rang. John knew the implausibility of that. Bulldozing and the planned construction of new houses on the land had been stopped because of a squabble about asbestos. The shell of the main school building was all that was left. Yet the insistent ringing was as much an unmistakable part of his early childhood as Kellogg's cornflakes.

'Hurry, or I'll be late.' Ally squirmed out of John's hands and stood on the pavement between them, looking quizzically from one to another. She nipped in front of them, her feet skipping towards the sound of the bell. They caught up with her in the midst of a sudden blizzard.

The yells and yips of school children, penned behind the old-style iron railings, was a ragtime of playground noise. Ahead of them, John recognised the lollipop man in his waterproof suit. He stood in the middle of the road, the pole as immovable as his peaked hat, blocking a Hillman Minx, engine tickling the air, as kids ambled across the road. Ally's legs worked like a filly in a wide-open field; she sprinted past the tree and jumped off the safety of pavement and kerb and onto the road fifteen yards from the school crossing.

'Hi, hi,' The lollipop man shouted in his usual grumpy manner, but she waved good-naturedly at him, safely on the pavement. He didn't look across as they passed in front of him at the school gates.

In the playground John swerved round a tiny boy in short trousers and black shiny shoes, whooping as he jumped into a puddle, water splashing onto his boots. 'You better watch you don't get your feet wet, or you'll get a bad cold,' John warned.

'Sorry.' The tot looked up at him, a snail-trail of snot running sideways from his nose and finding a path to his mouth, before he turned and galloped away from them on an imaginary horse.

The janny meandered past, going in the same direction as them. Ally flew up the four stone steps and into the main building where the youngest pupils' blocks of classrooms were situated. She took the side door into the cloakroom. Further along the corridor a teacher's heels could be heard tapping, walking away from them. Duffle coats, blazers, balaclavas and anoraks hunched together on the hook of metal pegs and cut-down frames that kept them from trailing on the stone floor. The cast-iron radiators on the wall clicked out heat which spread its net among the homely smell of damp clothes. Ally tried to worm her way out of her anorak, but the zip stuck. She panicked and tried pulling it over her head. The second school bell rang longer, a more insistent tone signalling school proper had started and playtime ended. Before John or Jack could help, the janny stuck his head in the door. Behind him children were lining up in crocodiles outside. He watched her wrestling with the anorak and darted up beside her.

'Wait a wee sec.' The janny patted her head through the quilted material. She stopped struggling, the adult voice reassuring her. He tugged at the zip on the anorak, his hand hesitated before his fingers sneaked up under her dress.

'Hey,' shouted John, swinging for him, but his fist swept through the janny, punching air.

Jack lunged across to help and his arms swept through

the man. 'Am I dreaming?' he asked John, his voice soaring.

'Nah, it's a fuckin' nightmare and we're the ghosts hauntin' it.' John tried once more, clutching at the janny, but his hands grasped nothing but despair.

The janny pulled Ally's hood further up and over her head like a sack and guided her out into the main corridor. 'We'll need to get a pair of pliers for this,' he explained to the girl in a strained voice, his head flicking from side to side, checking out if there was anyone listening.

He bundled her past the glazed stare of the statue of the Virgin Mary and took the little-used door out into the playground. Keeping close to the wall underneath the windows of the gym, his hand dug into her shoulder, pushing her head down and her body close to him. He walked so fast she had to run beside him to keep up. Jack and John, unmanned, pushed on beside them.

The janny spoke out of the side of his mouth in a reassuring and cajoling tone. 'I think I've got a pair of pliers in the boiler room.' He nudged her down the first few steps, and his clattering feet followed behind her, the smile slipping from his face as he searched for his keys. He shoved her inside. She stumbled and fell on the spill of coal for the boilers. One last look behind him before he banged the door shut and unbuttoned the top button on his trousers slashing his zip down. 'Scream all you want. I've got a few friends that will be along later. We love that kinda thing. Nobody can hear us down here. Just us. It'll be a little home from home.'

John gulped tears of rage and frustration. Jack clamped his hands over his eyes and tucked his head against the older man's shoulder, using his body as a post to hold him upright, and to screen him from what was happening to Ally, but it couldn't prevent him hearing. When it was finished, the janny forced a feathered shuttle-cock into Ally's mouth, gagging her with a bandage and handcuffed her to the boiler.

John gently unpicked the boy's fingers which clung to his arm. He crouched down trying to comfort Ally. From the terror lurking in her eyes, he knew she was in hell.

'Stay with Ally,' John told Jack. 'Even though she can't see us, maybe she'll sense somebody is close by that loves her. That's all we can hope and pray.'

John stalked impotently behind the janny's back as he locked the boiler room door behind him.

The janny whistled as he climbed the stairs, emerging into a windblown playground. He bent over and caught an empty crisp packet, holding it out, showing it as an exhibit to the lollipop man.

'Mucky buggers,' the janny said. 'Doesn't matter how many times you tell them. Never put anything in the bins. Might as well talk to yourself.'

The lollipop man fell into step with the janny. 'You're right there. The problem is they're spoilt rotten. And they get everything done for them.' A perplexed look crossed his face as he turned towards John, but John's outstretched hand passed through both the Stop sign and his wet raincoat.

John tagged on behind them. The lollipop man parked his sign against the wall in the corridor leading to the janny's office. He peeled off his waterproof and hung it on a peg, and plonked his hat on the one next to it. The janny made a show of depositing the empty crisp packet in a plastic bin. Then he slunk away to stick the kettle on. A two-bar electric fire had been left on, making his office snug, but filled with a mismatched table and chairs.

'You want tea?' the janny asked the lollipop man.

'Nah, I'll get a full breakfast with my Maisie.' The lollipop man edged into the room. Sinking into the plush chair, he kicked off his wellies, his arthritic hands feeling around beneath the chair for shiny brown brogues. He looked directly at John, standing beside him. 'Thought I heard something there.'

The janny laughed. 'Place is falling down. Better watch that, Charlie, or you'll end up in the funny farm.'

Charlie sniffed, stuck his feet into his shoes. 'You're probably right. Just got a funny feeling. Something's not right. Got that in the war sometimes.' He lurched up out of his seat and walked through John.

The janny waited until he was sure that he had left before he sidled into the hall. A phone hung on the wall. He picked up the receiver and dialed. John stood behind him and heard the whirr and click of the phone being connected and begin to ring.

'Chief Inspector Allan,' the disembodied voice on the other end of the line said.

'It's me,' said the janny.

'I thought I asked you not to contact me here.'

'Just to let you know, we've caught a little lamb.'

'I told you to hang fire for a while.' Chief Inspector Allan spoke in a clipped and commanding tone.

The janny was unperturbed. 'Couldn't help myself, too good an opportunity to miss. And fresh little fleece as white as snow, as fresh as fresh can be.' He smacked his lips together. 'Tender. Just the way you like it.'

'I can't get off till six,' said Chief Inspector Allan.

'Well, you know how quickly lamb goes off.' The janny laughed down the line. 'And I've still got a few calls to make.'

'You'll wait, goddammit,' said Chief Inspector Allan.

'I might have a little nibble first.' The janny hung up on him. He rubbed his hands together.

The stench of cigar smoke alerted John to the old man's presence, before he saw the glow of the tip of his cigar, and the stained uniform of a butcher's bib. He had a cocksure look on his face, and was perched behind the desk in the janny's office. He gawped at John, openly dismissive, and basked in the hatred of one that finally knew him. 'Oh, what a piece of work is man,' he intoned. 'Man that is born of woman is of few days and full of trouble. He cometh forth like a flower and is cut down. He fleeth also as a shadow, and continueth not—'

The janny popped his head around the door. He grinned, quickly sliding his arse into a PVC seat across from the butcher, eyeing him like they were old friends.

'Where have you been?' the janny asked. 'I've been waiting ages for you.'

'Going to and fro on the earth.' He waved his cigar like an orchestra conductor, listening to music inside his head. 'Walking up and down in it. A wager lost and a wager won.'

They howled with laughter at a shared joke.

John felt a familiar buzzing in his ears and his head jerked away from them. He backed towards the door, bumping against the wall, and crouched down into a ball. He covered his ears with his hands, tried to speak, tried to shout, but was branded wordless by their indifference and their braying laughter. His voice unspooled into a drawn-out howl and something in him broke. The butcher's eyes flashing like dangling mirrors shrivelled his insides.

'Over here Sarge.' Constable Lennon leaned over John.

John was pursed-up, naked and shivering among broken bricks and rubble in St Stephen's old school gymnasium. His tangle of hair was matted with snow and his mouth open like a chick catching flakes as they drifted down. Indifferent to the greatcoat Constable Lennon had taken off and wrapped around his shoulders, John continued looking up and searching the cold night sky.

'We better call an ambulance,' said Constable Lennon. He leaned down, his breath a vapour cloud, as he shouted into John's face, 'Whit's your name, mate?' He shouted even louder, prodding John's waxen arm, as an aid to understanding. 'Have you got a name, mate?'

John remained mute in his indifference.

Sergeant Boyle had taken a longer and more circular route across the snowy landscape. He was blowing hard by the time he got to them. 'Get an arm,' he said, taking command. 'We'll need to lift him.'

'But I've called in an ambulance,' said Lennon.

'We've not got time for that. He'll freeze to death.' Boyle wrapped his arms around John's back, feeling under the greatcoat for a hand-hold under his oxter.

John's mouth closed and opened like a fish on a line. He jerked upwards trying to escape the officer's grasp, his nose hitting against Boyle's chin and splattering a vermilion splurge on his chest, which also dotted the snow. Boyle held on lock tight. John's body slumped, falling in a dead weight against the policeman's shoulder.

Boyle looked across at his colleague, then at the smudge and reddish sheen on the breast of his long coat and reacted angrily. 'I thought I told you to get him.'

'I didn't know he was going to do that.' Lennon tried to make amends by nipping across and helping Boyle. He swung his arm under John's other armpit.

The two burly men lifted John like an empty grain sack, his bare feet trailing pale blue as they carried him across the slushy wilderness of the playground.

'If we take him to casualty, we'll have to wait hours to get seen,' said Lennon. 'And our shift's nearly finished.'

'Well, that's no' my fault, is it?' said Boyle. 'They keep letting him out of Gartnavel and he's completely bonkers, paranoid schizophrenic. He lives it. The voices in his head are not his own. Hears and sees things and thinks they're real. Babbles a whole load of shite about the devil. Doesn't know if it's Sunday or Christmas, and can go and howl at the moon, for all I care. Community Care! Those bastards have got a lot to answer for.' He reached out and pulled open the door of the van.

'You know him?' asked Lennon.

'Aye,' said Boyle. 'You sit in the back with him, so he doesn't fall about and hurt himself.' He grinned at his younger colleague's pissed-off expression, and held his hand out for the keys. 'I kinda knew his old man, he had a butcher's shop, drank it all away. Shame what happened to the family. A house fire – started with a burning cigar down the side of the couch. A row of bodies. All wee girls. Not a mark on them; smoke in the lungs. His mother was a good wee woman, but she couldn't cope. Took an overdose. Who could blame her? Shit happens.'

Supporters

Unbound is a new kind of publishing house. Our books are funded directly by readers. This was a very popular idea during the late eighteenth and early nineteenth centuries. Now we have revived it for the internet age. It allows authors to write the books they really want to write and readers to support the writing they would most like to see published.

The names listed below are of readers who have pledged their support and made this book happen. If you'd like to join them, visit: www.unbound. co.uk.

ABCtales.com
Olusola Samuel Aina
David Alsmeyer
Yvonne Anderson
Linda Andrews
Clarissa Angus
Sandra Armor
Lane Ashfeldt
Laurie Avadis
Patricia Bailey
Fiona Bain
Jason Ballinger
Matthew Bannatyne
Caroline Bayliss
Ann Beaton
Carla Belkevitz
Blackjack-Davey
Alan Brazil
David Brown
Ed Bruce
Michelle Buckberry
Anthony Burlton
Alan Cameron
Karen Campbell
Jonathan Carr
Steven Clanachan

Dave Clark
Lawrence Collins
David Connelly
Joy Conway
Paul Conway
Tony Cook
Linda Wigzell Cress
Eric Cunningham
Tommy Cunningham
Stephen Daly
Barbara Jean Day
Daniel Derrett
Wendalynn Donnan
Katy Dougherty
Carol-Anne Downie
Jennie Ensor
Silver Ether
Mike Ewing
Ray Farley
Joseph Figueira
Elaine Finnegan
Warren Fisher
Margaret Fitzsimmons
Oliver Franks
Lawrence Friel
Jim Galbraith

Claire Gallagher
Joanna Garrett
Amanda Giles
Anne-Marie Gorman
Liza Graham
J. C. Greenway
Annest Gwilym
Laney Halley
Suzanne Hamblin
Christine Hamill
Sylvia Hehir
Sandy Herbert
David C Herr
E O Higgins
Linda Higgins
Brendan Hillhouse
Karen Hillhouse
Lisa Hinsley
Peter Hitchen
Teresa Honeywood
Linda Hood
Jane Hymen
Jean Jack
Marjorie Johns
Molly Kelly
Matthew Kiely

Dan Kieran
Mark Kilburn
Joe Lawrence
Tom Lawrence
Ewan Lawrie
W Tom Lawrie
Claudine Lazar,
Inigo Lazar-Gillard,
Orlando Lazar-Gillard
Pia Lenau
Nicholas Little
Catherine Long
Annette Lumsden
Colin Macdonald
Heather MacDonald-
Archer
Maria Malone
Heather Marchant
Denise Marr
Abbie Mason
Archie Mc Dougall
Cassie McCallin
Kevin Mccallum
Julie Mccann
Laura McCormack
Pat McDaid
Stephen Mcdonald
Richard McDonough
Carolyn McFadden
Mari McGahey
David Mcgeough
Andrew Mchendry
Andrea McHugh
Rhona McInnes
Sharon McIver
Anne Mckeown
Garry and Janice Mclaren
Mary Mclean
Francis McMonagle
Christine McVay
John Mitchinson
Diarmid Mogg
Lucille Moody

Denise Mullen
Rona Mullholland
Carlo Navato
Luke Neima
Rob Newlyn
Louise Nicoll
Chris Nicolson
Bryan O'donnell
Phyllis O'Donnell
Tania O'Donnell
Bryan ODonnell
Kevin ODonnell
Tracey Odonnell
Brian Oharegreen
Michael Paley
Samantha Parnell
Anne Paterson
Ian Paye
Chelsea Pearson
Heather Pearson
Andy Pegg
Richard Penny
Carol Peters
Jon Petrusev
Teresa Phelan
Jennifer Pickup
Catherine Poarch
Justin Pollard
Rebecca Poole
William Porter
Helen Reece
Andy Rhattigan
Helen Richardson
Carolyn Robb
Moya Rooke
Catherine Rossi
Alan Russell
Benjamin Russell
Mary Russell
Robert Russell
Robert Russell
Georgina S
Tim Saxton

Mark Say
Rachel Schaufeld
Michael Schmicker
Alan Searl
Sangeeta Shah
Sooz Simpson
Jennifer Skinner
Ben Smart
Rachael Smart
Alex Smith
Maria Smith
Maureen Smith
Brian Smyth
David Smyth
Josephine Smyth
Paul Smyth
Lua Speakman
Craig Tabor
Stephen Thom
Adam Thomas
Wayne Dilwyn Thomas
Derek Thorburn
Alex Tomlin
Richard Trama
Christine Tuohy
John Urquhart
Jo W
Gerard Ward
Ian Ward
Michael Ward
Alison Wassell
Catherine J Watt
Rob Welsh
Simon Whitworth
Melissa Wilshaw
Bryan Winn
Tommy Winn
Love Writing
Robert Wylie
Louise Young
Vanessa Zainzinger